"I want to get a job," she blurted out. She looked up at Craig. She knew he needed help, but it wouldn't be coming from her. "I'm sorry."

"Ah," he said, his voice mild. "Very sensible of you to find a way out of this."

"I'm not trying to avoid anything," Vivian protested. "I do think Mrs. Hunt shouldn't be given the children. I will tell the judge that if you want me to."

"I'm sure we will be fine," Craig answered, his voice sounding brittle.

He was lying and Vivian knew it. He was trying to spare her the knowledge of how bad things could be.

Then he turned his blue eyes on her, and they were so intense she had to look away.

"You don't want to be my mail-order bride?" he asked.

Vivian shook her head. "Oh, no. It's not just you. I only agreed to be a bride so I could get Becky out of my brother's house. I meant to go through with it, but on the train here I decided I couldn't..."

Janet Tronstad was raised on a small ranch in the middle of Montana. Even though she has spent much of her life in cities, she still calls Montana home and has set most of her forty books there. Her books have been printed in various countries and their sales have put her on the *New York Times*, *USA TODAY* and *Publishers Weekly* bestseller lists. Janet currently lives in central California.

Books by Janet Tronstad

Love Inspired Historical

Visit the Author Profile page
at LoveInspired.com for more titles.

Wyoming
Mail-Order Bride

JANET TRONSTAD

LOVE INSPIRED
INSPIRATIONAL ROMANCE

LOVE INSPIRED®
INSPIRATIONAL ROMANCE

ISBN-13: 978-1-335-49846-5

Wyoming Mail-Order Bride

Copyright © 2023 by Janet Tronstad

Please recycle this product is recyclable

Recycling programs for this product may not exist in your area.

For questions and comments about the quality of this book, please contact us at CustomerService@Harlequin.com.

Love Inspired
22 Adelaide St. West, 41st Floor
Toronto, Ontario M5H 4E3, Canada
www.LoveInspired.com

Printed in U.S.A.

Whoso findeth a wife findeth a good thing,
and obtaineth favour of the Lord.
—*Proverbs* 18:22

This book is dedicated, with thanks, to all of the Harlequin editors who have had a hand in bringing *Wyoming Mail-Order Bride* through the production process: first, the acquisition editor(s), the story editor, the content editor, the line editor, the copy editor and the proofreader(s). And a special thanks to the marketing department for the cover and the title. Of course, the sales team has a very important part in the success of the book, too. It truly does take a village!

Chapter One

Wyoming Territory—the summer of 1869

On a moonlit night in July, "Big Craig" Martin rode his weary horse over a rise in the prairie and paused, glancing down at the dark buildings nestled below. He was covered in dusty sweat and smelled worse than the bawling cattle he'd just herded across the old Crow Creek, but even with all of that, he felt better than he had in years.

The hard labor of summer left him exhausted, but it also wore down his grief until he finally saw the truth. He had loved his late wife, Delores, and had done all he could to please her. But it had never been enough. Never would have been, either. She'd died two years ago and he'd just started to breathe free again.

Craig reached into his shirt pocket and pulled out a lemon drop. He'd started carrying them as a treat for his children, but they soothed the dryness in his throat, and tonight, he allowed himself the comfort of one as he glanced up, watching a cloud move past the moon, causing the orb to give off more light.

Gazing down again, he told himself he did not need a wife. This homestead and his children were sufficient for any man. Then his eyes caught a shape moving farther out in the prairie.

Suddenly, his lips parted. He sat up straighter in his saddle.

"What's going on down there?" he muttered, completely alert now.

He leaned forward, staring until he was sure of what he saw. A man was riding away from Craig's homestead on a white stallion that looked mighty familiar. He knew who it was, and icy fear sliced through him. Why had the sheriff made a late-night visit to his place?

Craig urged his horse into a steady gallop, only vaguely aware of a flickering yellow brightness below. His chore lantern, which often sat on the ground beside his front door, had been lit and turned low. It gave off just enough light to signal that his younger brother, Finn, was sitting there waiting for him.

Something important had happened, and Craig wanted to know what it was. Craig skirted the sod house to get to the barn. Once inside, he rushed to dismount from his horse, strip off the saddle and lightly rub the animal down with an old wool shirt he kept for that purpose. Then he hustled over to where Finn sat.

"The children?" he asked before he got close. He

kept his voice low. His two little ones would be sleeping in the loft inside, and he didn't want to wake them.

"They're fine," Finn said as he looked up.

"Then what did Sheriff Brady want?" Craig asked as he pulled up a three-legged stool like the one his brother was using. "We're a far ride from Cheyenne."

Sitting down, Craig could see Finn's face had a strange stillness to it.

His brother held up a piece of paper. "The sheriff thought you should see this as soon as possible. I can't believe it. It's about Delores's mother."

"What? She didn't die, did she?" Craig asked as he took the paper. He hadn't known that his late wife had any living relatives until he received a letter this past March from her widowed mother. Craig had been still grieving and had written back, telling the woman all he knew—about Delores's fall from the horse that killed her, the beautiful daughter they'd had and even the fact that Delores had given birth to her first child, Robbie, while waiting in Cheyenne for the boy's father to come. The man had never arrived. Finally, she'd married Craig instead.

"No, Mrs. Hunt is not dead," Finn said with a bitter note to his voice. "I'm afraid it's worse than that, Big."

Craig wondered what could be worse than death as he lifted the lantern so he could read the words of the official-looking paper aloud.

"'Attorney-at-Law James A. Timmens filed case in Wyoming Territory court July 9, 1869. Request on behalf of Mrs. Margaret Hunt (New York City) to take full custody of two children born to deceased daughter, Delores Hunt. Her marriage to Craig Martin (born twenty-eight years ago in County Clare, Ireland) not legal. Plaintiff claims Craig Martin wrongfully acting as guardian to children Katherine (Katy) Hunt (born September 10, 1865, in Wyoming Territory) and Robert (Robbie) James Hunt (born May 30, 1864, in Wyoming Territory). Mrs. Hunt claims insufficient care of children by Mr. Martin due to lack of mother in home. Mrs. Hunt offers wealthy estate, private schools, nanny, tutor, French cuisine.'"

Craig finished reading and looked over at his brother. "Can she do this?" he asked incredulously. "Take my children away? A woman I've never met? And she wants to feed them French food? Katy won't even eat chicken unless it's a tough old rooster. The others are her pets. And Robbie's so serious—he doesn't need a tutor unless the man can teach him how to enjoy being a child."

Finn nodded, looking miserable. "The sheriff says there's an 1839 law, the Custody of Infants Act, that gives mothers more rights. It's English law, but their grandmother might be able to argue it here. It gives the mother preferred rights for children up to seven years old. You need to stop Mrs. Hunt, Big. That's why the sheriff came to suggest that you send for a mail-order bride. And do it soon. He says the judge will see a mother as important in his decision. Very important."

Craig cut off his brother's words with a glance. "You know I loved Delores, but we were miserable together. I don't want another wife. And what does

Mrs. Hunt mean that Delores and I weren't legally wed? We had the preacher say the words over us. Man and wife. He'll tell them so if anyone asks."

Reverend Thompson would remember because he had initially balked when they'd asked him to marry them, suggesting they wait and get to know each other better.

"Not all women are like Delores," Finn said. "The sheriff told me about a man west of here—a homesteader like us—who's getting a mail-order bride from an agency in Boston. Says he fell in love with her when he saw her photograph."

Craig snorted in disgust. Some men had no sense at all, he told himself.

But then his mind flashed back six years to an elegant lady he'd seen in New York City. She'd had a porcelain-white face. Long blond hair. Violet-blue eyes. He'd been employed as a longshoreman on the docks when he saw her that evening—July 13, 1863, the night the draft riots began. Craig had been searching for Finn when he saw that her house had been set on fire by rioters. She was running out of it when a fiery beam started to fall from the top of the structure. Craig raced to prevent it from hitting her, but he'd been too far away, and the flaming wood had scorched the left side of the woman's face and shoulder before he could toss it away. He never knew her name, but he'd remember her for the rest of his life.

So, yes, he could see how a man could get his mind fixed on a beautiful face in a photograph and think he was in love with a woman he didn't know.

Finn cleared his throat and brought Craig back to the present.

"I think the sheriff is right," Finn said. "If you get married, it might be enough to make the judge dismiss the request from Delores's mother right away. It doesn't need to be a mail-order bride if you know someone else."

"I don't," Craig said and then suddenly realized that he did know a woman who would marry him. "Well, except for Mrs. Drummond. I've been talking to her after church. Or, rather, she's been talking to me. About marriage. I never quite know what to say. But she's a godly woman. She knows what life is like here on the prairie. And she's past the age of expecting any romance. Told me so herself. She said we'd have separate bedrooms. She'd look good to a judge, too."

Craig looked over and saw that Finn seemed uncomfortable. "What's wrong now?"

"It's just that Mrs. Drummond is nothing like our *mam*." Finn's brogue was faint, but noticeable enough for Craig to know his brother was remembering their long-ago childhood in Ireland. "I'm not sure Robbie and Katy would like her for a mother. She seems more like an army sergeant. Besides—"

Both men heard a rustle and a gasp. They turned, and there in the doorway stood three-year-old Katy, her curly copper hair in disarray and her white nightgown pulled tight as she clutched a squirming gray cat in her arms. Craig kept expecting that wild tom to scratch her, but he never had in the three months he'd been with them.

Five-year-old Robbie stood behind his sister protectively. The children both had wide eyes as they looked at Craig. Katy also had a trembling lip.

"W-we don't l-like Mrs. Drummon'," Robbie said, his stammer always worse when he was agitated. "E-even Kitty don't like her. H-he hisses at her."

Craig wasn't going to be swayed by the cat's sour opinion of anyone. The old tom glared at him, too.

"Mrs. Drummon' don't like us, either," Katy added in her soft voice.

Now, Katy was someone he listened to. Craig felt his plans crumble, and he opened his arms. His children ran over and snuggled close to him.

"How can anyone not like you?" Craig asked them tenderly as he rubbed their backs. The feline got squeezed in the hug and jumped down to eye Craig indignantly before stalking off.

Craig shook his head at the cat. It had been dropped off at their homestead by a trapper who was moving back east and didn't think the animal would adapt to civilization. Craig would have politely refused the offer, but Katy had already gathered the hissing ball of fur up in her arms and declared he was her "Kitty." No one could persuade her that "Kitty" wasn't a fit name for a beat-up old tomcat with torn ears and a mangled right paw.

But for the moment, Craig was content, holding the children to him. And then he started to wonder. He'd been surprised at how attached Katy was to that animal. Maybe Delores's mother was right about the children needing a female in their lives, too. He and Finn did their best, but was it enough?

Robbie hadn't been the same since Delores died. She'd tried to take the boy with her when she ran away, but as Robbie confessed to Craig later, he couldn't leave one-year-old Katy alone in the house, especially because she was crying. Katy shed tears frequently enough back then, although never without reason, and she must have sensed something awful was happening that day. No one could console her like Robbie could. Later, the boy claimed his mother's accident would not have happened if he had gone with her like she'd wanted.

"I w-would have s-stopped the horse," Robbie had added defiantly. It was the first time the boy had stammered.

Craig had repeatedly warned Delores about the half-broke wild horse he was working with in the corral. He'd forbidden her to even go close to the stallion. Why she had decided—on a day that he was away branding—to leave their home was a mystery. He had never refused to take her to Cheyenne, not even when he was busy. But she had climbed on that brute bareback and galloped away. Robbie told him that much. It had been almost dark when Craig found Delores's body, lifeless and crumpled beside a boulder that she had apparently hit when she fell off that horse.

Craig had tried over the years to ease the boy's mind, but Robbie's stuttering didn't stop. And Craig noticed that Katy hadn't cried since that day, not even when she'd fallen and scraped her knee.

"According to the sheriff, that rancher and his bride-to-be are getting along fine," Finn said a little more cheerfully. "The man's going to send for her to come by railroad to Cheyenne this fall. Your new wife could come the same way, Big."

Craig hated to, but he had to consider the prospect.

"I wouldn't even know what to say to a woman like that," he finally said. "Or what questions to ask."

"We could ask the bride if she knows how to make those little Christmas cakes," Katy whispered. "The ones with molasses in them and sugar on top."

"And m-maybe ask if she l-likes dogs," Robbie added. "Mrs. D-Drummon' doesn't even l-like puppies. I heard h-her say so."

"That's true," Katy said. "She says she doesn't like anything that brings dirt into the house."

"I always g-get d-dirty," Robbie lamented. "Is she g-going to put me out in the barn l-like she said she would with the puppies?"

"The barn roof leaks," Katy said in concern. "And the wolves might get in."

"Nobody is going to put either of you out in the barn," Craig said, knowing he could not marry Mrs. Drummond if the children felt that way. "Besides, we're going to fix the roof and the wolves are far away." *At least, most of the time they are,* Craig added silently to himself.

Craig liked having his children close, and for a

time, everyone was quiet. And then the night was disturbed by the distant howl of a wolf.

"He's just calling his pack," Craig said quietly, hoping to reassure Katy, who had looked up anxiously. He could hear Kitty snarling, too, his back starting to arch and his lips curling back, ready to attack whoever or whatever was making his little friend worried.

"Is a pack like a wolf family?" Katy whispered as she reached down and casually stroked Kitty, who had already crawled back beside her. "Do they have a father?"

"I suppose it's a family," Craig said, noticing how tame the cat had become as it turned around and licked Katy's little fingers. "And they do have a male leader. Even a mother in a way."

"Are we s-still a family if w-we don't have a m-mother?" Robbie asked then.

"I love you," Craig said fiercely. "Your uncle Finn loves you." He looked down at the cat. "Even Kitty likes you."

The boy frowned at the cat dubiously, and Craig was glad for the distraction. He left the main question unanswered. Mainly because he wasn't sure himself. There had been something about having a woman in the house that made everything feel better even though Delores never seemed to care about any of them except Robbie.

They sat there together as Craig noticed the moon start to slide down in the sky. He figured the subject of him marrying was closed for now. Hopefully, the attorney would have some other suggestions.

"Maybe the bride could be a princess with yellow hair," Katy said wistfully. "The pretty hair."

"I'm sure some princesses have red hair, too," Craig said as he kissed the top of his daughter's head. Delores had never liked Katy's hair, saying it made her look common. But Craig thought it was beautiful. His *mam* had had red hair.

Katy shook her head vehemently. "No, Daddy, her hair has to be yellow. That's what Mama used to say. All the princesses have yellow hair."

Craig doubted Katy could remember her mother saying anything at the age she'd been. But Delores had been given a book of fairy tales as a child and had read from it to both children. Maybe Robbie remembered something and had mentioned it to Katy. It would be like Delores to pick a color of hair that Katy did not have. But that was long ago. He needed to think about today.

"If we do get someone, she won't be a princess." Craig still read stories from that book to Katy, but he did it so his daughter would remember she had a mother, not because he wanted Katy to worry about the color of her hair. "She'd be a sensible woman. Someone who likes the prairie. She might not even know how to make cakes." Or to read fairy tales, Craig suddenly realized.

Craig knew he had to marry if the attorney said that was his only hope of keeping his children. He couldn't help being nervous about it, though.

"I c-could teach the bride about horses," Robbie offered, his eyes downcast. "So she won't f-fall or anything."

"You're not at fault for anyone falling," Craig told him firmly.

Robbie didn't look up, but Katy pressed her head against Craig's neck. "I don't care about cakes or horses. I just want a mama."

Craig rocked his daughter for a few minutes and studied his son's face.

"Robbie?" he asked.

His son looked up at him, his eyes full of misery, and nodded.

"Then we're going to write and ask about a mail-order bride," Craig said, trying to put some enthusiasm into his voice.

"It won't be as hard as you think, Big," his brother said, although he didn't sound convinced of it, either. "The sheriff knows where to write."

Craig saw the relief in his son's eyes and knew he had to do it. He worried about how Robbie would handle it if he had to live with his high-society grandmother in a place like New York City. Both Craig and Finn had been young when they'd stepped off the ship there, having sailed from Ireland alone after their parents died. Craig, barely thirteen years old, had hired on for a man's wages as a longshoreman. Finn, at five years old, had scrambled for small delivery jobs.

Finn had called Craig "Big" during those days, since Craig was his big brother. But they soon realized some of the other boys thought the nickname came because Craig was almost as tall as a man and had large fists. That fact kept even the meanest boys away from Finn; they never knew when Big would show up.

Craig looked at his son with concern. The other children would likely tease Robbie about his stuttering. And Katy would not be able to take her kitty.

Delores had told them all wonderful stories of the childhood she'd spent in New York City, but Craig had watched her eyes when she did so. There were fancy dresses and parties, but there was a dark past there that she'd never mentioned. It made Craig uneasy for the sake of the children.

Lord, we need Your help and protection, he prayed. *I can't bear to think of my children leaving for some city. I'd do anything to stop that, even marry one of those brides. If it's Your plan, I'll do my best to love the one You send. All I ask is that she be a simple woman like my* mam. *No ruffles or big hats with feathers. Just someone who can help Robbie laugh and be a boy again. And if she could make Katy feel safe enough to cry, that would be good, too. Delores's mother will have to be satisfied with that. Please, Lord, don't let Mrs. Hunt take my family away.*

"The children and I could help write an ad to send," Finn offered then. "The agency is called Last Chance Brides."

"She'd have to be a churchgoing woman," Craig said in alarm at the name. "I insist on that."

"Of course," Finn agreed. "We'll put *churchgoing*

in the ad. And I think she'll write and tell us more about herself before it goes any further."

Craig suddenly felt the peace he'd had after praying slip away. The woman would be a stranger no matter what she wrote in a letter.

"The sheriff figured we have until Christmas—December 24—to get it done," Finn added. "He said the judge could delay things that long. If Mrs. Hunt doesn't put in an appearance in the Cheyenne courthouse by then, the judge will side with you, married or not. If she comes before—as she sounds set on doing—the judgment will likely go to her unless you've got a wife by that date. There is plenty of time to send for someone to marry you."

Craig wasn't so sure how it would happen, but he'd do anything to keep his children with him. And if no bride came, they would just have to convince the judge that they were doing fine without a woman in the house.

After all, the Bible was filled with the names of men who never married. If God did not send him a wife, that would mean he didn't need one.

Then he looked up at the moon and sighed. For the first time in his life, he thought about how nice it would be if—just this once—they could step into one of Katy's stories and have a real princess come to them. He smiled, thinking of the expressions his children would have on their faces. And then the truth hit him.

Why, he'd be terrified! A woman like that would be even more difficult to please than Delores had been. It was just as well that fairy tales didn't really happen—and certainly not to immigrant homestead families like his—no matter what fantasies a moon-lit night seemed to suggest.

Please, Father, he prayed silently in a sudden panic. *Send me a scrub woman. Or a maid. Some-one who will be content with what I have to offer.*

Tremont Street, Downtown Boston—December 1869

Vivian Eastman adjusted the partial veil over her face before stepping into the brick office building be-hind her sister-in-law, Edith Waverly Eastman. Viv-ian would have refused to come inside if she had had a choice. Edith had been insistent, though. And the weather outside was very cold, especially when Vivian's gloves were too worn and frayed to use and she had been ashamed to ask to borrow a pair from her sister-in-law.

So, when Edith started to climb the stairs, Viv-ian followed.

"May I help you?" The secretary inside the office looked up from her desk as Edith opened the door.

"You're the Last Chance Bridal Agency?" Edith asked even though they both had seen the name spelled out on the front of the door they had just walked through. Edith's voice was haughty as she added, "I'm Edith Waverly Eastman."

Vivian smiled. Edith always emphasized her maiden name because that was where her wealth came from. Vivian's poor brother added nothing to his wife's consequence, and Edith made sure he knew it.

The woman behind the desk nodded but didn't seem impressed. She must be new to Boston, Vivian thought, not to know the Waverly family. Or maybe she didn't read the *Boston Herald*. The Waverly family were in politics, too.

Edith did not let the lack of response stop her. "This is the agency for brides that are hard to place? I think that's what you say," Edith added with a touch of something in her voice that Vivian could not identify. Maybe it was smugness.

"Yes," the woman behind the desk acknowledged. "That's us. But we have no current openings for brides."

Edith pointed at Vivian. "Well, there must be something. She needs to marry. She's twenty-six years old and a real challenge. No one ever wants her."

"That's not true," Vivian protested, stung by the unfair statement. Edith's claws had come out. "I've had dozens of proposals of marriage. You know that." They'd been in the same elite social circles as young women growing up in New York City. Six years ago, men had flocked to Vivian. Edith had been so jealous she once refused to even stand beside Vivian at a party.

Edith lifted an eyebrow. "That was before the fire gave you those awful scars." She reached over and pushed Vivian's netting aside. "Look." She demanded the attention of the secretary. "She tries to hide them, but they are horrible." Vivian winced and then Edith turned to address her directly. "No one's proposing to you any longer, are they? And with your grandfather dead, what do you have now?"

"I would hope to have the loving protection of my older brother," Vivian snapped back, turning away so her netting would fall back into place. After her invalid grandfather died a few weeks ago and the bank foreclosed on his house, she and her young ward, Becky, had left New York and traveled to Boston to plead with her brother and his wife to take them in. Vivian hadn't expected Edith to welcome them warmly, but she hadn't expected this, either.

"I'm sorry," Edith said sweetly, the steel in her eyes making a mockery of those polite words. "We might be forced to let you live with us—decent society expects that, I suppose—but no one would fault us for turning away your Becky. She's a housemaid's— well, let's just say her birth is irregular since no one knows who her father is. Even the workhouse has some standards and won't take her unless I give them a sizable donation."

"What?" Vivian gasped, horrified. "Why would you even talk to them about Becky? She's only six years old. Her mother was practically part of our family. And she helped me carry Grandfather out of the house when it was set afire in that horrible riot. She died a few years later from an infection. This family owes her. I promised to care for her child and I mean to honor that. Becky stays with me. Why, she could die in that workhouse—or worse!"

Edith snorted in disgust and then looked at the

files scattered across the desk, pointing at a worn folder. She stepped closer and tapped it. "Why can't Vivian take that one? It says right here—*unable to find a bride*."

"We got that request back in the summer," the secretary said, sounding cautious. "No one wanted to fill the—ah—position, so we're closing it out."

"She'll take it," Edith said. "I knew there would be a place." She pulled out a piece of paper sticking up from the folder and gave it to Vivian. "Look. Here's the ad."

Vivian read it aloud. "'Mail-order bride wanted. Must be sturdy and kind to dogs. Needs to like Christmas cakes and little children. A princess would be nice. Must go to church. Good cook helpful. Reply to B. Craig Martin near the Crow Creek, Wyoming Territory. Train will come as far as Cheyenne.'"

Vivian looked down at the piece of paper and saw the date. "July? It's been a long time since he wrote this." Surely, this was not to be her future.

The woman nodded. "But we've had several letters from him since. We received one last month, in fact, that said if we couldn't find someone who could arrive by December 24, we should not send anyone. The crisis, he said, would be over by then. That's why we're closing it out."

"Vivian will go," Edith said decisively. "My husband and I will buy tickets for her and the girl and put them on the train tomorrow."

"But I haven't said I'd go," Vivian protested firmly.

"And what about this crisis of his? Why wouldn't anyone else go? I want to talk to my brother."

"Talking to him will do no good," Edith said. "He didn't object when I told him your ward had to be gone by Christmas. I wouldn't rest easy celebrating the Lord's holiday with someone like her in my house. Such a vulgar birth. Those things bring down a family's name. No, the girl will go to the workhouse if she's still here after tomorrow. I promise you that."

"Oh." The agency woman, seemingly taken back by that bitter announcement, turned and looked kindlier at Vivian. "No one wanted the position because Mr. Martin is a struggling homesteader. He can't offer much. But he's a good man. He gave us a recommendation from his pastor." The woman paused for a moment and then continued in a voice so low it could be a whisper. "Also, if you decide not to marry, our investigator said there are a fair number of jobs in Cheyenne. They are respectable jobs, too. I believe a single working woman who could cook or sew could easily provide for a child there."

Vivian swallowed. She could do both. But no one paid on the first day of work. She would not sacrifice her pride to save herself, but she'd do anything for Becky.

She turned to her sister-in-law. "I know there was money left from my grandfather's estate. He mentioned leaving me a number of dollars, since I nursed him for the past six years when he was bedridden. Maybe you could give me fifty dollars from his estate. I think he'd want that."

Vivian happened to know that was less than her sister-in-law allowed herself in pin money each quarter. But the request made Edith's face turn sour.

"Your grandfather scribbled something, but we could not read it," she answered stiffly. "The only clear instruction he gave my husband was to give you that old family Bible he kept. Worthless thing, if you ask me."

Edith continued, "Your grandfather said nothing about any money for you. He likely believed—as I do—that you should have found someone to marry years ago. You insisted on waiting for love, and look where it's gotten you. But don't worry." The malice in Edith's eyes was now clear. "You're always talking about your faith. Well, we'll let God take care of you and your precious little Becky."

Vivian gasped like her face had been slapped. She hadn't realized Edith hated her so much.

"God certainly will take better care of us than you or my brother would," she said defiantly. In her heart, she knew that was true, but her sister-in-law's words still stung.

Several moments passed. Edith pointed her nose up in the air, clearly waiting for some contrite words. Finally, it all began to feel childish to Vivian.

"We'll go," she said. That seemed all that was left to say. Of course, since there were jobs in Cheyenne, she'd be better off there than in Boston. And Becky would be safer away from that workhouse and Edith. It would have been helpful to have the money she'd requested, but God would take care of them.

The secretary nodded, looking troubled. "I'll send Mr. Martin a telegram telling him that you should arrive early on Thursday, December 23. The train will take a week or so if all goes well. That will get you there just in time."

The next morning, Vivian and Becky stepped onto the passenger train well in advance of when it was scheduled to pull out of the Boston depot. No one had wanted them to miss this train, even though Edith's cook was the only one to come outside to say goodbye. The woman, who never used any name but Mrs. Cook, had given Becky a tin with small bags of various spices, since the girl had spent many hours in the kitchen learning to prepare simple foods.

Then the woman furtively handed another larger bag to Becky while the butler turned his back to talk to someone inside. After that, Mrs. Cook hugged Becky and then walked back into the house. The butler closed the door after her, and there was nothing left for Vivian and Becky to do but to climb into the waiting carriage.

It was just as well no one else had come to see them off, Vivian told herself as she ushered Becky to their seat in the passenger car. What else had there been to say? She had held out hope her brother, Joseph, would come outside to say goodbye, but he hadn't. They had been close to each other as children, and she'd always thought he held her in some regard. Maybe she had imagined the feeling, though. Even given his indifference, she would write a short note to him in a few months so he would know she was well. She doubted she would hear back or ever see him again. She swallowed the lump in her throat at that thought. She wanted more family for her and Becky, but there was no one else but Joseph.

Vivian tried to keep herself cheerful for Becky's sake, chatting as she stored her valise at their feet. The bag held several wool scarves she had knit, a small velvet purse with the few coins she had left, the two-shot Deringer gun her grandfather had pressed upon her after those riots six years ago, and the old family Bible he had cherished and left to her. She had no use for the gun, but she might be able to sell it at some point. The Bible, on the other hand, she would never part with. It was tied shut and knotted with several thick red cords. The spine was slightly cracked and the pages worn.

Vivian had decided it was best to leave the fragile Bible securely bound until they reached their destination. Just having it with her was a great comfort. In some ways, that Bible stood in the place of the family she longed to have. All of the births and deaths of the past were noted. She had hope that she would eventually add new names to the list. She had her own small New Testament that she could read.

While Vivian was stowing her valise, Becky had opened the cloth bag she'd been handed from the cook.

"Raisin rolls!" Becky announced in delight. "At least a dozen of them! And lots of my favorite white cheese. Some hard-boiled eggs. Apples and oranges, too. Enough for both of us!"

"Perfect!" Vivian didn't have to feign enthusiasm for that. They hadn't been offered breakfast, and she had few coins to spare for food. "See how the Lord provides."

"The Lord—and Mrs. Cook," Becky added with a grin.

"Yes, people are good, too," Vivian agreed with a smile. Mrs. Cook had been one of Becky's few friends so far in life. Her grandfather's household had been small, and toward the end, there had been no regular servants. Except for getting a woman in weekly to do the laundry and scrub the floors, Vivian did the rest. She hoped that in their new life Becky would have more friends.

Neither Vivian nor Becky was accustomed to the smell of smoke or the cinders from the train's smokestack that blackened the air, finding their way inside through cracks in the passenger car. They coughed some as they settled into their double seat. Finally, the rhythm of the clicking wheels soothed them and the two of them relaxed. All of the other passengers looked preoccupied, so Vivian figured she and Becky would likely be left to themselves on the journey.

Finally, it was their last night traveling. Like usual, they curled up on their thinly cushioned seat. The conductor kept a small lantern burning that made shadows dance up and down as the car swayed. No one could see out the windows into the darkness beyond. Unable to sleep, Vivian put her palm against the glass in the window beside her. It was cold and damp. After that, she slept fitfully and woke with a sore throat. She told herself that the discomfort in her throat would pass as soon as she had a cup of hot tea.

The faint light of dawn slowly seeped inside, but the conductor didn't come down the aisle offering any beverage. Another hour and a half passed before Vivian heard the brakes pull the train to a stop. They must have arrived.

Vivian wrapped one of the knit scarves around Becky's neck before holding her hand as they stepped down onto the wooden platform in Cheyenne. Suddenly, wind ripped at Vivian's wide-brimmed hat, and she needed to use her other hand to anchor it to her head. She looped the handle of her valise around her arm and hurried Becky into the nearby building.

"Well," Vivian said, catching her breath once she'd ushered Becky inside and closed the door. A black cast-iron stove gave off heat in the middle of the room, but Vivian herded Becky toward a counter with a uniformed man behind it.

"Is there a way to get some hot tea?" she asked, her voice sounding raspy.

"Are you sick?" the man asked, leaning away from her. "Where are you headed? Could I get someone for you? Winter illness can be deadly around here."

"I'm here to see a rancher named B. Craig Martin, over by the Crow Creek," she managed to say, breathing deeply so her cough would stop and her voice sounded more normal. She needed to inform that man he could disregard the telegram he had received from the agency. "I'll be fine once I've had some tea."

"I know Big Craig," the man said, looking proud of himself. "Anyway, it's providential that you asked about the Martins, since Reverend Thompson and his wife were just saying they met someone who came in on the train. I'm guessing it is the party that sent a telegram earlier asking for transportation to the Martin homestead. My boss arranged it. The Thompsons live out that way, so they are taking the man with them. If you find the reverend—" The man stopped and waved his arm, calling out, "Reverend Thompson. Over here."

A portly man with a white beard came over to the counter. A thin, birdlike woman trailed along behind him.

Before Vivian could even think about it, she and Becky were propped up in the back of the wagon with blankets around their shoulders and their trunks at their feet. Mrs. Thompson sat on the other side of Becky. The reverend and another man sat up front on the seat, the collars up on their coats and their hats pushed down on their heads.

The reverend had his wagon rolling when Vivian saw the man from the depot come out and wave his arms at them. He yelled something that she couldn't hear.

"He wants us to stop," Vivian turned to say to the reverend's wife.

The older woman looked back and waved at the man. "He probably just wanted to remind us to check for the mail. But it has already been picked up."

The reverend had set his horses to a steady pace.

"I'm sorry we didn't have time to get you and the child a hot meal before we headed out," Mrs. Thompson said. "But my husband could see the clouds getting dark, and he doesn't want the snow to get worse before we reach the Martin place. No one wants to get caught in a blizzard between here and there."

Vivian figured the reverend was right. Snow covered the ground everywhere, but she could still see the shape of the town as they drove away. There were no long boardwalks on the streets here like they had back in the east. The buildings themselves were a mix of styles. Some were canvas tents, others flat-roofed wooden shops. One had a false front proclaiming it was the Rocky Mountain Star Printing House. Another, a large wood-frame building, called itself the Cheyenne Hotel. As the wagon passed by, she saw a saloon with a sign that said Breakfast Cook Wanted in the window.

"There must be lots of jobs here," Vivian whispered, half to herself.

"Oh, you'll be too far away at the Martin place to work here," the reverend's wife said, curiosity in her voice. "Besides, you'll have those two precious children to look after. I'm surprised Craig wasn't here to meet you."

"The train had to stop and clear snow off the track several times so we were two days late in arriving," Vivian muttered. She'd already had to show the reverend and his wife the ad. "The agency sent him a telegram about me coming, but he won't know I'm late."

She hadn't told the couple that she wasn't planning

on marrying Craig. She felt she should tell him before anyone else that she had decided on the train to seek a job instead of marriage. She knew she wanted the love of a family. A marriage of convenience didn't seem the way to obtain that. It would be best, she thought, if she held out for the true love of a husband. From that, they could grow a caring family.

Vivian didn't have a strong enough voice to talk longer, so she huddled down with Becky and focused on keeping the girl warm. Before long, Vivian felt her eyelids start to close. The high seat on the wagon made a windbreak, and Becky was already dozing. Vivian could catch snatches of the conversation between the two men sitting up at the front.

"How long have you been out of prison?" the reverend asked the other man. Vivian could tell the reverend didn't like what the other man was saying. Whatever it was, though, Vivian decided it had nothing to do with her.

She must have slept for some time, because when she woke, the netting that spread out from her black hat was wet from the falling snow. She glanced around and everything looked white. Her throat felt swollen and not just sore. Her eyes hurt just looking at all the glare of the snow.

"Are we lost?" she asked, her voice croaking, as she leaned up on her elbow to see better. The land was flat, although hills showed up in the distance.

"My husband knows where he's going," the reverend's wife said serenely. "Don't worry."

A half hour later, the horses pulled the wagon up

a hill, and they could see a faint trail of smoke coming from the shallow valley below. The wagon rattled down the hillside and headed straight for the largest squat-looking building Vivian had ever seen. A buggy was parked beside it.

"Sod house," the reverend's wife said as though answering a question. "It's common around here. Nebraska has more of those buildings, but we're not far from there in this corner of Wyoming."

The wagon made enough noise coming down the hillside that several faces pressed to the two paned windows before they came to a halt.

"Let's hurry inside," the reverend said. "No one wants to keep their door open for long in a blizzard like this."

Before Vivian knew it, the ex-prisoner was lifting her down from the back of the wagon. The door to the house opened, and Vivian was thrust inside faster than she had expected. The ex-prisoner stood her on her feet, and Vivian felt a little tipsy, either from the fever or from sitting in the back of the wagon for so long.

Vivian squinted. Everywhere she looked inside the place, there were dark shadows. The light from the fireplace did not go far, although there were two narrow doors, spaced apart, that must lead to other rooms of the house. She noticed the two men staring at her in what appeared to be shock. Behind them were an older woman and two little children. They all stood with their mouths agape. Vivian lifted her hand to be sure her netting was still in place. She didn't like strangers to see the scars on her face.

"Who are you?" the man in the front—the one with the broad shoulders, muscled legs and deep scowl on his bearded face—demanded to know.

By this time, everyone from the wagon was inside and the door to the outside had been quickly closed. Even with all of the others there, though, that man was definitely staring at her. Surely, he wasn't Mr. Martin. The agency woman had said he was nice.

"I'm here to see—" Vivian tried to speak normally and then the words stopped coming. Her throat was on fire and she felt light-headed. She started to sway.

"She's your mail-order bride, you fool," the ex-prisoner yelled, throwing the answer at the man while at the same time stepping close to Vivian and sweeping her back up in his arms. "Vivian Eastman is her name. She just happens to be ill."

Vivian might have been fainting, but she could still hear the grunt of astonishment coming from the slender man in the shadows before he stepped up and slapped the scowling man on the back.

The ex-prisoner laid her down on a long wooden bench in front of the rock fireplace. The bench was hard and there was only a washed-out quilt on the bottom, but it had a back she could lean against. The room had grown quiet, so Vivian thought she could let herself fall into the darkness. There'd be time enough to sort out who was who later.

But then she heard a joyful shriek.

"It's our princess," the girlish voice shouted, sounding very happy.

Vivian opened one eye slightly to see a child with rosy cheeks and copper-colored curly hair running toward her. She was barely more than a toddler and she vibrated with excitement, clutching what looked like a wild bobcat in her arms as she cried out, "And she smells like oranges!".

By then, the little girl had come close enough to Vivian to whisper in her ear. "We didn't have Christmas—not at all—Daddy burned the porridge so bad we couldn't eat it. And Mrs. Drummon' was supposed to bring us oranges, but she brought lemons. Phew, they were nothing like the drops my daddy gives us. They made me scrunch up my whole face. And there are no cakes or presents or anything."

The woeful story made the girl look sorrowful. Then she put her free hand on Vivian's knee and wailed loudly, "And now it's too late for Christmas."

"It's never too late for Christmas," Vivian managed to say as she cautiously eyed that beast the girl was cradling like it was an innocent baby. "There's always Epiphany."

The girl's eyes grew big. "Epi-what?"

"The twelfth night after Christmas," Vivian whispered.

"The night the wise men brought their presents to Jesus," the reverend added from where he stood, helping his wife remove her cloak. "A most commendable day in the celebration of our Lord's birth."

"There's presents?" The girl's voice rose in enthusiasm. "Is there cake, too?"

"Now, Katy," the man—the one with the scowl—spoke, and she somehow knew he had been hovering over her ever since the ex-prisoner had laid her down. Which was not very polite of the scowler, she told herself. He was probably the type of person who told everyone else what to do. And that was annoying.

"The woman needs to rest," the man's voice commanded, and she could see the dark shapes move back.

Vivian opened her mouth to say she was fine. No words came out, but, really, she was beginning to feel less fuzzy. She looked up and thought that the man leaning overhead looked familiar. It might have been the smoke from the fireplace swirling around his head as he peered down at her from his lofty height, but something about him reminded her of fire. She could almost feel the heat.

That was all she needed, she thought vaguely. A man who wouldn't listen to her when she said she was fine and managed to change her temperature anyway. Something seemed wrong with that and then she remembered she hadn't actually said the words about feeling fine. Ah, she sighed slowly. He still was presumptuous. And this time, the darkness did claim her.

Chapter Two

Craig stood there, staring down at the crumpled woman lying on the mahogany bench he'd made years ago. She seemed to be breathing regularly, but she appeared slight, huddled as she was against the back of the seat. He noted with dismay that the faint light from the fireplace showed where, a few years ago, he had carved a string of outlandish characters, taken from the line illustrations in that old storybook, along the bench's back and side.

The woman would think them all daft when she woke up.

He'd made the bench for Delores as an apology for some grievance long forgotten, but now it belonged to the children. It was their story bench. He usually kept that old rag quilt draped over the back to cover the carvings. But as the woman—Vivian, he reminded himself—lay there, she somehow seemed to fit right into that circus of frogs, vines and dancing children. It was probably that preposterous black hat, he decided.

He wished he could see her face. He thought he'd seen a spark of something in her eyes before they drifted closed. It had looked like she was going to smile, and he'd felt an answering tug in his heart.

Lord help me, he prayed as he shook his head at his nonsense. It was too dark to be sure what she'd done or thought about anything, and he hadn't really seen her eyes. He was not living in one of Katy's stories. That beginning of a smile might be nothing more than an involuntary twitch from the fever affecting her. She could even be hallucinating. It suddenly struck him that the fever could be more than it seemed and here he was, stuck in some daydream.

He reached out and gently pulled Katy away from the woman. The children had never been exposed to any deadly diseases, and he wanted to keep them safe from any harm.

"Maybe you and Robbie should go up to the loft and take a rest," Craig suggested to his daughter.

"But we're not tired," Katy protested and kept standing where she was. Then she glanced over at the woman again, and Craig could see the expectant look on her face. He could tell she wanted to go closer, but she was obeying the hand he had just placed on her shoulder.

Then Craig released his hold on Katy and stepped forward to put three fingers on the woman's forehead. Her fever wasn't as hot as he'd feared. She might be more tired than sick.

He stepped back quickly before Katy could get any closer.

"I didn't know a princess would need to take a nap in the day," Katy whispered up to him in awe as she held on to his leg. "Just like you make me do sometimes."

"What I want you to do today," Craig added.

Katy ignored him. Instead, she shifted Kitty into her other arm and slid a step forward so she could reach out to touch the woman's skirt. Craig had to acknowledge that the woman's clothes were likely irresistible to his daughter. He supposed there was little harm in her feeling the texture of the fabrics. They were more fashionable than any garments Katy had ever seen—and maybe ever would see if she stayed in this area all her life.

"Vivian Eastman." Craig muttered her full name just to remind himself that she had a name. It made her seem less like a princess.

The woman's hat had been battered about by the wind and snow, but it was made of sterner stuff than the usual cotton scarves or straw bonnets most family-minded women wore here in the territory. The hat's brim still had some strength to it and the whole thing was hanging together. No prairie woman had made that hat while sitting by her fireplace in the evening. No, it came from a first-rate millinery shop and, no doubt, cost a fair amount.

And, the woman's dress was a heavy ivory brocade with enough tucks and swirls to show it came from a professional dressmaker in New York City or maybe even Paris. The stylish black wool coat, belted around her narrow waist, had a whole row of shiny buttons that would not have been cheap.

"She's not a princess, but she must be a society lady," Craig knelt down and whispered to his daughter. He wouldn't have even known how expensive that heavy brocade fabric was if Delores had not purchased a bolt of that kind of material shortly after they were wed. The general store had put it on his bill, and when he'd asked for an accounting, he'd had to take the fabric back.

That bolt would have cost all of the money he'd saved for their winter supplies. Delores would have been well-dressed, but they would have starved. He'd bought her a dress length of pretty speckled blue calico instead, but she never did make anything from it. She said it depressed her to think that was how far she'd sunk. That material still sat in the bottom of his trunk along with several other lengths of linen and calico—none of them good enough in his late wife's opinion.

Katy moved back closer to the woman. He'd almost forgotten she was standing patiently off to the side.

"Is she waiting for a prince to kiss her?" Katy asked.

Craig heard a snort of disbelief. He wasn't sure, but he thought it was the strange man who'd carried the lady inside who was responsible.

Katy looked up at Craig in confusion. "Can't there be a prince to kiss her? It happens all the time in my stories."

"It's fine in stories," Craig assured her.

And then he heard a few loud footsteps behind him. He turned, not knowing who he'd find.

"I never heard such nonsense," Mrs. Drummond said, putting her hands on her ample hips and taking a few steps closer so she could peer over Craig's shoulder. "I can't believe you let your daughter spout such foolishness."

"She's just turned four years old," Craig protested. He believed in letting children dream and imagine stories. They'd grow old soon enough.

Mrs. Drummond ignored him as she continued, "That's no excuse. She needs to face life. That's no princess lying there. What she is, I don't know, but she's not a princess. And Christmas ends at Christmas. There are no exceptions. Things are what they are."

Katy gave a soft gasp of distress, and Robbie stepped over and reached for her hand.

"I beg your pardon," Vivian spoke from the bench. Her scratchy voice was barely audible, but the words were clear. Her face was still in shadows. The effort to talk must have worn her out, because after she said those words, she lay back down and closed her eyes. She continued to speak, though. "Christmas lasts through Epiphany. January 6. Look at any calendar."

Mrs. Drummond turned to Craig. "I don't understand why that woman's here at all." Then she leaned over and poked at the woman's brocade dress. "I expect she's a heathen with all that talk of the calendar."

Craig reached out so he could grab hold of the

older woman's hand and stop the prodding. No one wanted to be jabbed.

"The calendar is not a sin," Craig said to Mrs. Drummond. "The Good Lord doesn't care if we mark the days. Most would say He wants us to. In Psalm 90, it says, 'Teach us to number our days, that we may apply our hearts unto wisdom.'"

"Humph," Mrs. Drummond exclaimed, bristling. "Don't try to trick me, Craig Martin. I remember the reverend preached on that three Sundays ago."

"I know you pay attention in church," Craig assured her.

"Humph," she repeated, but she seemed satisfied and walked back to the kitchen table.

Craig turned to Vivian. While he wasn't looking, she had managed to sit up almost straight, but she still looked uncertain about everything around her.

"Don't worry," Craig said to her. "You're fine here."

He was going to say more to her, but he glanced up through the small window to the east and saw the storm outside was slowing. Everything was white except for a dark shape in the distance. Craig hoped that wasn't a lost cow. He'd moved his small herd before Christmas, four days ago now, into a sheltered ravine so they'd stay reasonably warm.

Of course, it had to be either a cow or a bull, he told himself as he looked again. If it was a buffalo, there would be a whole herd of them. He'd have to go out and check on the poor animal soon. Enough snow was still falling down the chimney to make the wood wet and the smoke worse, so he couldn't see much of anything inside, either.

"Just a minute," he said and then turned his attention to Vivian. He touched her forehead again. Her fever was definitely going down. He heard a sound behind him and turned to see Katy standing there, fidgeting.

Craig had to admit that he enjoyed watching the excitement on his daughter's face as she contemplated the woman.

"If she's a lady, maybe she knows a princess," Katy said hopefully as she looked up at him. "Don't you think, Daddy?"

"Maybe she does," Craig agreed with a smile.

He suddenly wished that he could take Katy for a visit to New York City when she was older. He'd spent most of his time there on the docks, but he'd passed through some of the fashionable areas. She would love looking in those store windows. And seeing the tall buildings. And all of the beautiful dresses coming out of some of the churches on a Sunday morning.

If he hadn't been worried someone would discover fourteen-year-old Finn had been with the longshoremen setting fires on the night of those riots, Craig would not have insisted they leave the city, at least not so soon. He never heard of anyone being charged for the chaos that night, and Finn had only been watching, but Craig wanted his younger brother away from those men who thought nothing of burning down homes.

"Why don't you put Kitty in that box by the stove?"

Craig suggested to his daughter as he let his mind return to his current responsibilities. The wooden box wouldn't.hold the beast, but the old tom didn't look too pleased to be squeezed in Katy's arms, so maybe he'd like to simply lie down for a rest. Craig knew the cat wouldn't scratch Katy, but it might take a swipe at the unsuspecting woman on the bench.

Once his daughter had left, Craig knelt to examine Vivian more thoroughly. He put his whole hand out to confirm what he'd thought earlier. Her fever was mild. She did have some light perspiration on what little he could see of her face, but that could be nothing more than the damp from being outside. Added to that, it was growing dark inside and the net she wore on her hat was hiding everything but her nose. A steady drip of melted snow was falling from her boots to the worn carpet he'd bought when Delores first moved into the house.

"Who is she?" Finn asked from where he stood at the stove stirring the pot of beans that he'd put on to cook earlier. They would have been eaten by now if there hadn't been so much activity.

"Except for her name Vivian Eastman—I don't know yet," Craig answered as he drew a clean handkerchief out of his pocket and dabbed at the netting that was plastered to the side of the woman's face.

"We talked on the way our here and she seems like a respectable lady," Reverend Thompson offered from his perch on a table bench where he was sitting next to his wife. The young girl who had come in with Vivian was sitting beside Mrs. Thompson. The reverend continued, "She's polite and well-spoken."

Craig decided all his visitors were accounted for, except Mrs. Drummond, who had not sat back down at the tables after all but now stood a few feet away from him. He'd need to talk to Mrs. Drummond some more, he thought, but other things came first. "I'm going to give Vivian something for her fever and then I have to go out and see to a lost cow."

"I bet it's that longhorn bull and not a cow," Finn said, reaching for a ragged cloth to protect his hand as he grabbed a kettle from the back of the stove. They usually made coffee in that pot. "The old fellow doesn't have much sense. The cows mostly do."

"Seems so," Craig agreed. He didn't move, though. He put his hand on the woman's forehead again. He wanted to be sure about that fever. She moaned and shifted slightly, raising a hand up to rest on his. She was wearing a dove-gray glove on that hand and it was stylish, but he noted it had been mended in several places.

Craig tried to gently withdraw his hand, but her fingers gripped him tighter. He knew she wouldn't be holding on to him if she were well. Delores had been appalled by his hands. They were too rough, she said. And it was true. His hands were calloused and the burn scars on his palms were deep red splotches. He did not have a gentleman's hands. He didn't want Vivian to see either one of them, so he tried again to withdraw the one she held. It only made her turn her face toward his palm, though, until her cheek was nestled right inside the cup his fingers made. Then she sighed as though she was finally comfortable.

"Easy now," he whispered, willing her to loosen her hold. "I'll get you some willow bark and you'll feel better."

She murmured but made no sound he could identify. Gradually, he slipped his hand away and then noticed the faint frown on her forehead.

"It was warm," she whispered in rebuke.

Craig wasn't sure how to respond. Clearly, Vivian couldn't mean she wanted to hold his hand against her face longer. It must be the fever making her say foolish things. Maybe her temperature was higher than he thought.

"Where's my manners?" Craig said, deciding what the problem was. "You need a pillow." He looked over to Robbie. "Can you bring us the pillow from the big bed? The good pillow?"

Robbie turned to do his bidding. It was the only goose feather pillow they had, and Craig was glad he had it for the woman to use.

"And I'll bring you some—" Craig began to repeat his offer of tea.

The woman opened her eyes partially then. "I hate willow bark—too bitter. Don't want it."

"Oh," Craig said with a frown growing on his forehead. He couldn't see well enough to know what it was, but there was something familiar about Vivian. It was like he'd seen a photograph at some point, but that was impossible. He'd only seen a half dozen of the things. He would remember this woman.

"She's talking," Finn announced quietly, sounding almost as impressed as Katy had been. He set one of their tin cups on the counter by the stove. "You got her to talk."

Craig ignored the comment. Vivian had known how to talk when she got here. Instead, he turned to where his brother stood.

"Use the rose china cup and saucer," Craig suggested to him. They were the only two such fine dishes they had. Delores had the set with her when she married him. No one had used either one since she had died, but this seemed to call for them.

"I don't like willow bark," the woman repeated, mumbling.

Craig wondered if she knew she'd already told him that. "I heard you, but it's good for you."

Then Craig announced to no one in particular, "I'll light a lantern, too. Then we can all see."

He didn't rise up right away to do what he said even though some light might bring everyone back to their senses. Vivian wouldn't want to be resting her head against his scarred hands then.

"I don't mind the dark," she mumbled and then tried to lift herself up on her elbows, her misshapen hat hanging crooked on her head and still shading her face. That black netting was halfway twisted around her chin. It didn't look one bit comfortable.

It was not light enough to be sure, but he definitely suspected Vivian might be smiling at him now.

"We'll get some lemon drops to go with the tea, too. That'll help with the taste of the willow bark,"

Craig said, deciding he really did need to do what he could to tamp down his warm feelings. Vivian did not belong here. He shouldn't get used to her.

Behind his back, Craig could hear Finn stepping over to the table. He'd apparently decided to spare Craig the chore of lighting the lantern. Maybe he sensed how much Craig wanted to stay beside Vivian.

In any event, Vivian wouldn't be so friendly when the lantern was lit. "We'll get you ready to travel in no time."

The woman swayed a little, perched as she was on her elbows. "I thought this was where Craig Martin lived. Aren't you him?"

A flare of sudden light showed that Finn had lit the lantern. The inside of the house was much more visible now.

Vivian had laid her head back as best she could, and Craig figured he didn't need to answer her question yet. Instead, he gently lifted the strands of wet hair off the half of her face that showed. She was sitting passively with her head resting on the back of the bench and her eyes closed. The netting covered the other half of her face, and he hadn't moved it to show he respected her privacy.

But once he'd moved her hair, he only needed to see a portion of her porcelain-white face in the light from the lantern to recognize her. He had to blink to be sure, but her image didn't waver. She looked exactly like the lady from the fire in New York City.

Craig was speechless. It couldn't be. He couldn't have been more shocked if she had been a princess with a crown waiting in her valise. He squinted then, thinking maybe the smoke was blocking his vision. But that didn't make any sense. Maybe, he thought, his mind was confused, since he'd just thought of that night. But he never saw people who weren't there. No mirages, either. He could see what was in front of him. Mrs. Drummond was right. Things were what they were.

"How did you find me?" he finally asked and had the satisfaction of seeing the woman's eyes flutter open. There was no doubt in his mind then. He'd know those violet-blue eyes anywhere. In fact, he had recognized them in dozens of his dreams over the years. But what was she doing here?

"The agency sent me," Vivian whispered. "Hard to place."

She started to struggle to sit more upright, and Craig put his arm around her shoulders to help her. She looked tired. Her face was white and a large red spot showed on the one cheek he could see. He wasn't so sure she was even steady enough to walk over to the table, but she seemed to do fine sitting.

"You can't be from that agency," he said firmly. "You would certainly not be hard to place. And they knew I needed a wife by December 24, Christmas Eve. I never thought anyone would be on their way here after Christmas."

The attorney he'd engaged to deal with Mrs. Hunt had said the judge, just like the sheriff had said he would, had given instructions to the older woman that she had until midnight on December 24 to come if she was going to pursue her claim. But, so far, she hadn't shown up. And now it was the afternoon of December 27. He understood that meant the court would not pursue her complaint against him. It seemed he wouldn't need a mail-order bride, after all. Maybe the children's grandmother had seen reason and withdrawn her demand.

"Of course, you wouldn't expect someone from that agency," Mrs. Drummond said, bristling. She had walked over and was standing close to him again. "Punctuality is important."

"The train was stopped." The voice came from the table. The thin girl with a solemn face who had been sitting beside Mrs. Thompson slid off the end of the bench and stepped out. She was not much older than Robbie and had brown straight hair. She bravely turned to Mrs. Drummond. "The snow stopped us. Too many times to count. We couldn't get here on the right day. Mama Vivian and I came from the bride place in Boston. We were four days off our schedule."

"Well, you're too late," Mrs. Drummond said emphatically. "Mr. Martin has made other plans."

With that, Mrs. Drummond stepped closer and took Craig's arm just like they were going to take a stroll down some fancy street in town. Or, Craig thought with a sinking heart, down a church aisle. He didn't know about those other plans that Mrs. Drummond was making, but it sure wasn't going to be the church aisle for him.

After Finn had sent the ad to the agency, Craig had carefully assured Mrs. Drummond that he respected her, but he couldn't marry her. She'd looked so disapprovingly at him that he'd mumbled something about her deserving more and him not wanting a hollow marriage. He couldn't bring himself to mention that he didn't want separate bedrooms, but he'd decided that if a mail-order bride came and he had to marry, he would make her his real wife if she was agreeable to it. He believed God would want him to have a true marriage or no marriage at all. Seemingly, Mrs. Drummond had not understood him, though. He'd have to speak to her in private, even if he had to take her for a walk in the storm outside.

But he'd deal with Mrs. Drummond later.

"You're sure which agency sent you?" Craig turned to Vivian. She seemed to be stronger now. At least there was some color in her cheeks.

"Of course, I know who sent me here," she snapped back at him. "It wasn't my idea to come, but I'm not without sense enough to know where I've come from." She pronounced the words precisely. "The Last Chance Bridal Agency on Tremont Street in Boston. Their motto is Hard-to-Place Brides. You wrote to them."

She looked defiant, Craig thought. He wasn't sure if she was proud or defensive.

"I'm surprised they didn't send a telegram," Craig said, frowning. It had just occurred to him.

"They did send a telegram to expect me on December 23," Vivian insisted. "At least, they were going to do so. And that secretary seemed very competent. I trust she did."

"Oh," Finn said, and Craig looked over at him. His brother looked guilty. "I forgot. Mr. Adler said he'd brought back some mail for us when he went to Cheyenne. And—"

Mr. Adler had stopped by earlier this morning with his daughter, Lizzie, to deliver their mail and give them a small Christmas cake. Finn was starting to court Lizzie, and Craig couldn't fault him for being distracted. Mr. Adler wasn't enthusiastic about the courtship, and Finn was nervous the man would stand in the way. Everyone had forgotten about the mail they'd brought.

Craig glanced at the corner cupboard and saw two envelopes sitting there. One looked like a telegram. He had taken only one step toward the counter when a hard pounding sounded at the front door. Someone was knocking so loud the frame was shaking.

"Who's that?" Craig asked as he stepped over and reached for the handle to open the door. If he didn't do something, he'd need to make repairs on the door after the thumping it was receiving.

Craig pulled the door back and a gust of wind blew inside. It was easy to see the snow-covered mountain of a man who stood outside, so blanketed with ice that even his beard had tiny icicles hanging from it. Craig wondered suddenly if the mistake with the mail-order bride had been discovered already and this was the angry groom demanding to know why his bride had ended up here. The huge man was old enough to be Vivian's grandfather, though, and Craig wasn't sure any mail-order bride of her age would want him.

Of course, they hadn't exactly wanted Craig, either, he told himself ruefully. Maybe that agency should be saying they had hard-to-place grooms.

With that, he glanced over at where Vivian was sitting and straightening her hat. He wondered if that man's last name was Martin, too. For all he knew, his first name might also be Craig. Miners were coming down from the hills in expectation of striking it big and he didn't know half of them.

The sudden thought occurred to him that the man could be one of those miners with a cabin full of gold. Money made a difference with some women— it would have with Delores.

He looked over at Vivian and almost sighed. He would have liked to know her better before she left. She would hardly stay, though, if she found her intended groom. And it was best that she did leave. He wouldn't feel guilty for not telling her who he was then. It would be like they'd never met.

Realizing it was inevitable, Craig opened the door wide.

"Come in." He made his voice as welcoming as he could.

The man outside was wearing a buffalo coat. His legs were like massive tree trunks and his muscled arms were raised to balance the heavy load he carried over his shoulders.

"Oh," Craig said as the man stepped completely inside the house. The burden on his shoulders was moving and wiggling most impatiently. It was wrapped in a blanket, but Craig didn't know what it was until everything jerked around and he saw a pair of feet clad in black women's lace-up shoes.

"Not boots," Craig muttered, knowing what it meant. This was no easygoing prairie lass the man had slung over his back like a hundred-pound bag of flour. Most women, at least most family women in the territories, didn't own lady shoes. The rocky terrain demanded boots, and that was what they wore.

He heard an indignant squawk.

Then the man lowered his burden to the floor feet-first. The blanket fell off. And there stood a middle-aged lady bristling and shaking herself more ferociously than the most excitable of Katy's banty hens.

For some reason, Craig looked over at where the mail-order bride now stood. At first, he was afraid Vivian was going to faint again. She was certainly pale enough. But she managed to stay standing and was already pointing at the woman the man had deposited on the floor. Vivian's finger trembled, and she had to move her mouth several times before any sound emerged.

"Mrs. Hunt?" Vivian finally managed to ask, her voice showing as much shock as Craig felt in his bones after he heard what name she'd uttered. How would Vivian know her?

"Mrs. Hunt?" he echoed the words in disbelief. He stared at the woman. This was Delores's mother? The woman who wanted to claim his children?

Vivian came over to where Craig stood, and together, they watched the blustering woman get her feet squarely planted. By then she was standing before them with a man's ragged undershirt wrapped around her head and her crooked hat somehow still anchored in place in the middle of it all. Her eyelashes seemed to be frozen together, because her eyes didn't open even though she was clearly struggling to make them work.

Craig figured it would only take seconds for the inside heat to melt the ice on her eyelashes.

"Is it really her?" he whispered as he stepped over to put an arm around Vivian. He told himself it was merely to steady her. She looked like a gentle breeze would tip her over. But he had to admit, it steadied him to have her standing there beside him, too.

"Do you know her?"

"Oh, yes," Vivian assured him. Her voice was solemn. "I know her all too well."

"But she's late," Craig said in bewilderment. The judge had said December 24, and even Mrs. Drummond agreed that Christmas had come and gone. Today was December 27. There was no need to hide the children, he realized in relief.

Vivian shook her head and added, "Mrs. Hunt has never done things in a predictable manner."

"But surely the judge—" Craig persisted. And then Mrs. Hunt was able to blink and her eyes opened.

The older woman looked directly at Vivian.

Craig still had his arm around her, so he felt the tremor that shook Vivian. He turned and saw she was looking even whiter than before, and he didn't think it was the fever this time. He instinctively wanted to protect her, but he wasn't sure from what. All he knew was that no one was going to hurt this mail-order bride even if she might not be meant for him.

What did he mean *might not* be meant for him? Craig asked himself in alarm. He felt like a swimmer going down for the third time. He didn't have to get married now. The children were safe. He needed to make it clear that he was not going to get married. She was not meant for him even if her being here hadn't been because of a clerical mistake.

Craig took a deep breath. Everything was a little murky now that he had this mail-order bride in his arms. The fuzziness would pass, though. He just needed to take a deep breath and relax. He smiled. He'd tell Vivian she was a wonderful woman and would find a perfect husband someday. He knew women were sensitive to rejection, so he'd be sure she knew it was nothing she had said or done. She might even cry a little, he told himself. He'd have to be gentle.

Then he glanced down and realized Vivian was so focused on that other woman that she had forgotten he was even in the room. Well, he told himself indignantly, he'd certainly been wrong about her hopes to marry him. She could not even remember him for two minutes. He should be grateful, he thought then. Yes, full of thanks and well-being.

He'd never known gratitude to leave a bitter taste in his mouth before. Vivian was upsetting his life, and he didn't care for it. And, look at her now—so taken with Mrs. Hunt that her hands had started to tremble again.

* * *

Vivian's knees shook. All of the warmth she'd felt when Craig had put his arm around her was gone. Maybe that was because he'd removed it. Not that it mattered She had other problems. She couldn't believe Mrs. Hunt was here looking at her as though she were trying to remember where and when she'd seen her last. Vivian hoped the woman had temporary amnesia. At least until she could slip away.

"Vivian Eastman!" Mrs. Hunt's booming voice was the same as it had been when she'd caught her eighteen-year-old son, Ethan, kissing fifteen-year-old Vivian behind the trellis in the Hunts' formal rose garden. They were supposed to be dancing in the ballroom or, at least, inside sipping sweet punch and giggling with their friends.

"Yes, ma'am." Vivian automatically curtsied and then realized she shouldn't have. She was none too steady on her feet right now. That long-ago kiss had been in the way of an experiment. And Ethan had been the one who dared her to do it. But afterward, she and Ethan had stood and stared at each other. And then they'd kissed again. That one had been real. For months, she'd felt a tingle in her toes remembering those kisses.

"What in the world are you doing here?" the reigning lady of New York City society demanded to know. "Hiding away with those burn scars on your face, I suppose. I heard about them."

Vivian swallowed and looked up at Craig. She thought he would be frowning, but he was looking at her almost like he was besotted with her. Or maybe he was confused. She could tell he was going to be no help in this. And she was right. Before Vivian could think of a truthful, but delicate, way to describe her situation, Craig spoke.

"She's going to be my bride," he said, his voice filled with sweetness even though his one eye was twitching slightly and she saw him mouth the word *please*.

"Oh," Vivian said, suddenly realizing he was attempting to wink at her. She tried to pat her hair down. She'd forgotten how ragged her manners and her clothes had become. He, on the other hand, was very neatly dressed. His clothes were plain, to be sure, but he wore them well. "It's my pleasure."

That would be general enough to pass for whatever he wanted, she hoped. It had been years since she'd received a proposal, even one as strange as this. But she'd gathered from the snippets she'd heard today that Craig needed to get married to solve some legal issue. She hoped it wasn't bankruptcy. Who would take care of the children if that was so? She needed to tell him that she wasn't marrying him, but there had been no time. He had every reason to think she would.

And then Craig smiled at her again. She was beginning to think the fever was affecting her nerves because she felt a tingle race down her spine—the same kind of tingle she'd felt with Ethan's kisses.

"No, the pleasure is all mine," Craig said.

Vivian made sure her veil was properly placed. She had marked down her reaction to Ethan's kisses as being due to her youth. She didn't know what her problem was with Craig.

"Oh, stuff and nonsense," Mrs. Hunt said, sweeping Craig's words and Vivian's vanity away impatiently as though they were nothing but troublesome mosquitoes. "Vivian Eastman had her pick of young men in Boston. My son among them. She wouldn't settle for you. Especially not with a weakhearted proposal like that."

"Your son never proposed," Vivian replied without thinking.

"Of course not," Mrs. Hunt said. "Ethan hadn't come into his funds yet, and I controlled his allowance. I still control most of it. Anyway, he told me he was planning to make an offer, and I forbade it."

"What?" Vivian squeaked out a protest. Ethan had given her every reason to expect he would ask to marry her. She would have accepted gladly. She had no idea back then that he was that tied to his mother's opinion. She wished he had told her, though. It would have been preferable to what she'd always thought— that he'd backed out because he heard how scarred her face had become in that fire.

"Oh, you were attractive enough," Mrs. Hunt said, her voice mild. "Back then, anyway. But your family had no money. Not really. Your brother had to marry that Waverly woman—Edith was her name, I believe. Horrible woman. But she had money behind her. I told my Ethan he should propose to her and he refused."

Mrs. Hunt gave a deep sigh but said no more.

Finally, Vivian asked, "And how is Ethan?"

"Oh, I don't know," the older woman said, her voice sounding weary. "I don't know why he's decided to do nothing that I tell him to do. He's not married at all. And here he is—thirty years old now. And with his money, he could have his choice of brides."

"I'm sure he could," Vivian agreed. She hadn't been the only woman to look at Ethan with stars in her eyes.

"I don't suppose you'd still be interested?" Mrs. Hunt asked tentatively.

"What?" Vivian exclaimed in shock. She had turned the key in that door and locked her memories away long ago.

Mrs. Hunt shrugged. "I'm afraid he's never going to make it to the altar." She sighed. "And me getting older every year." She looked at Vivian again. "You're not really here as a mail-order bride for that man, are you?" She gave Vivian a withering glance as she turned and pointed a finger at Craig.

"I—" Vivian didn't know what to say. She certainly didn't want to turn Mrs. Hunt loose on anyone, but she didn't want to lie, either. She smiled as sweetly as she could. "That's why the bridal agency sent me."

There, she thought, that was the truth. Until she had a chance to tell Craig that she was going to seek a job instead of getting married, it wasn't anyone else's business.

And then, before Mrs. Hunt could respond, Mrs. Drummond stepped forward.

"Don't pay her any mind," Mrs. Drummond said,

facing Mrs. Hunt before sending a glare in Vivian's direction. "She's the spare bride. Nothing more. Craig and I have been talking about marriage for some time now, but the silly boy thought I was too good for him, and so he sent for an extra…" Mrs. Drummond's words faded away, possibly because Mrs. Hunt's face was turning slightly purple.

Vivian stared in fascination at the two women. She was scarcely aware of Craig's arm tightening around her shoulders, although it did keep her steady. And his jaw had moved back into place, making him look determined. It was the rare man who could face down Mrs. Hunt. Her own son never did—at least not when Vivian had known him.

"I can explain," Craig said, his voice full and confident, until he was interrupted by a very unladylike snort.

"Two brides!" Mrs. Hunt faced Craig squarely. "The judge will be interested to hear about this. Two brides! What kind of a heathen home is this?"

"It's a perfectly fine Christian home," Craig responded firmly. "Now, I know it's made out of sod and not what you're used to, but I can tell you it's well made, and we pray within these walls every day."

Mrs. Hunt sneered. "You're living like moles in the ground! Walls of dirt. I've never heard of the like."

"But you don't see the dirt," Vivian insisted. The walls were hung with patches of old canvas in various hues, some golden, some slightly rusty and some definite brown. With the lantern lit and the light from the fireplace, the house, for all its humble nature, was really quite beautiful.

"And there are lovely wood carvings on the mantel and on the bench," Vivian continued. "I doubt you'd find finer carved frogs in Italy or even Portugal."

She'd also seen the dancing children, and curling vines, and hidden tiaras on the bench. And the figures on the mantel were in a light wood with deep, dark stains. She was going to ask how those pieces were made.

"Primitive carvings, all of them, I'm sure," Mrs. Hunt said, dismissing them with a sniff. Her black hat, Vivian noticed, had been squeezed into a point at the top, and the brim of it was wide and hanging low. "And I saw some interesting carvings of flying bats recently at the National Academy Museum that were more artistic than frogs would be."

"E'scusie," a soft voice said.

Vivian looked down and saw the tiny girl squeeze between her and Craig. Katy had a bit of trouble pushing aside Vivian's skirt, but she made it through even holding that indignant cat in one hand. The girl was staring in fascination at Mrs. Hunt.

"Are you the old woman who ate the lost little—" The girl started to speak before Vivian realized what she was going to say, and Vivian leaned down to whisper an urgent *no* in her ear. Given the girl's fascination with princesses, Vivian figured she knew the story of the children lost in the woods.

Mrs. Hunt glared at the girl like she suspected

what the question was to have been, too, but then her face softened.

"You must be Katy," Mrs. Hunt said.

The girl nodded hesitantly.

"How old are you, dear?" the woman asked.

"Four," Katy said and held up the right number of fingers.

"You can't like living here, do you, sweetheart?" Mrs. Hunt said as she took a step closer to the girl. "You need to be someplace where there's pretty things."

"I have my bench and my storybook," Katy answered solemnly. "And Daddy planted rosebushes for my mama. Lots of them. They're real pretty, but the roses need to sleep in winter."

"Trifles," Mrs. Hunt declared with a dismissive wave of her hands. "Have you been to Paris and seen a butler, wearing a black tuxedo and white vest, carrying a golden tray that has crystal glasses full of champagne on it? While sitting at a small table beside the Seine river and watching the birds fly by in the moonlight?" Mrs. Hunt sounded enraptured.

Katy shook her head, looking puzzled. "I've seen my baby chickens in the light of the moon, but I'm not supposed to be up at night and they can't fly." The girl's face brightened. "Sometimes I pretend they are flying. And they're real pretty then. My daddy doesn't let me go to the river by myself, though."

Vivian gave Katy a quick hug before Mrs. Hunt could issue a withering reply.

"I've seen some pretty birds in my life, too," Vivian said as she gently guided Katy behind her. That was the safest place for a tenderhearted child to be, and if Vivian knew anything about this household, Katy was beloved and happy here. "Unfortunately, some birds are not very nice. Like crows—always pecking at the baby birds."

"Why, I never," Mrs. Hunt protested, her face turning red.

Vivian nodded but didn't reply. Then she glanced up to see a surprised Craig.

"What?" she demanded. "I can protect a little one, too."

He nodded. "So it seems."

Vivian felt her face flush slightly and she looked away, her eyes going to the people sitting at the table. They were also regarding her like she'd done something remarkable. Really, she thought, didn't the people here know that young ones needed to be children and adults should shield them from bullies?

By the time she glanced over again, she saw a slow smile growing on Craig's face. She wondered what he was thinking.

"You like her," Craig said.

"Mrs. Hunt?" Vivian was alarmed at the thought.

Craig shook his head. "No, my Katy. You like her."

"Well, of course I do." Vivian said.

"Remember that's what our ad said, Daddy," Katy whispered from behind them both. "Our bride is supposed to like little children like me."

"Who wouldn't like you?" Vivian said as she turned and bent down to give Katy a hug. Fortunately, the cat was already lying on the floor beside the girl instead of being wrapped in her arms.

Katy hugged her back. "That's what my daddy always says to me and Robbie. He says everybody likes us."

Vivian glanced up at Craig. There was nothing dashing about that man. He was taller than most, but not by much. His features were even and he wore a neatly trimmed beard. His hair was dark brown, almost black, with a few strands of red here and there. One look at his face proclaimed him to be a man who spent most of his time outdoors. But his eyes—his blue eyes were kind and steady. There was nothing of the drawing room about him. And when he looked at his children, his eyes smiled.

"Your daddy is very wise," Vivian said to the girl and then rose to stand straight again. She wondered if she and her brother would be closer to each other now if they'd had a father like this man. Their grandfather, who had raised them, had been so reserved that it had been difficult to feel any warmth from him. Her parents had both died in a carriage accident when Vivian was only a few months old. She wondered with a sudden pang if she and her brother would ever see each other again.

Vivian saw Craig's stance shift and she knew he was turning to look at her. She wondered if there would be the same kindness in his eyes when he saw her.

But then, why should she care? She was a grown woman and didn't need the same tenderness a child did. When she lifted her eyes, though, she saw sympathy in his gaze. And a touch of what looked like appreciation, maybe even admiration.

Suddenly, she questioned if her fever was getting worse. Her knees felt weak. She needed to remember she was going to find a job. Mooning around over this man wouldn't help with that goal.

Chapter Three

Craig decided that if Vivian was a princess, she was a warrior princess. He had heard the fierce determination in her voice as she'd shielded Katy. It had only been when she'd turned her face that he'd seen the burn scars on her left side. He looked away then so she wouldn't see the distress in his eyes. If he hadn't already been convinced, those dark red patches on her cheek and neck would confirm as nothing else could that she had been the lady in that New York fire.

Even if she had been willing to marry a homesteader when she set out from Boston, he knew now that she would never wed him after he told her all of who he was. She'd stood up for Katy; there was no longer any question that he would have to tell her. He didn't want to bring Finn's name into it, but Craig needed to admit he had been there.

He'd tried to reason with the men he worked with that night, but the city had just passed a law saying immigrants would be drafted into the bloody War Between the States. They were frightened. They were not, they kept repeating, even granted the right to be citizens. Should they die for a country that did not want them? they asked.

Craig sensed that Vivian had taken Katy a step far-ther back. Which was prudent, he thought, because he could see Mrs. Hunt preparing to attack again.

She looked at the man still covered with snow.

"It's a good thing Mr. Gulch was able to bring me out here on his snow boots," she began, only to have the man himself interrupt.

"It's Dry Gulch, they call me," the man corrected her impatiently. "No *Mister* to it. Dry Gulch is where my diggings used to be. And when our wagon got stuck back a ways, I used snowshoes—shoes, not boots, to get here."

"Don't be ridiculous." Mrs. Hunt turned to the man. "Dry Gulch is not a name—not even for a dog. And everyone knows you need boots in the snow, not shoes."

Craig smiled as he saw the two older people stare each other down. Finally, Mrs. Hunt looked away and muttered, "You can call yourself whatever you want—that doesn't make it your name. Your mother would be ashamed."

"My mother would not," the mountain of a man declared.

"And what was her name?" Mrs. Hunt asked, clearly striving to ridicule him.

"Red Rosy," the man announced with a flourish. "Red Rosy with the Posy in Her Hands."

Mrs. Hunt gasped. "Why, she must have been—"

Craig was glad to see some sense of self-preservation stopped the society lady from finishing that sentence. He didn't want to have to brawl with Dry Gulch just to save a woman who was giving him nothing but grief.

He needn't have worried.

"Yes," Dry Gulch agreed with his head held high. "My mother always fancied Queen Victoria's posies, and her friends knew it. She worked saloons from Cheyenne to San Francisco. Well-thought-of, she was. When she died, hundreds of miners left their diggings and came out of the hills for her funeral. They each brought a posy of flowers just to put on her coffin. Oh, they gave her a rousing send-off."

"I see." Mrs. Hunt was clearly in shock, but she managed to be polite. "That must have been—ah— very nice for you."

The man shrugged. "Weren't me being planted in the ground."

But then Craig noticed a lone tear slide down the man's cheek into his beard. He still cared very much.

A long minute of silence hung over everyone until Reverend Thompson cleared his throat and turned to Dry Gulch. "I met Red Rosy, your mother, and she was a fine woman. Gave the church enough money to feed about twenty families through that hard winter we had some years back. Folks would have starved without her help. You meet anyone who gives you a hard time about your mother, you send them to me,

Reverend Thompson, at the church along the Crow Creek."

Craig had to admire Dry Gulch for not grinning at the idea of the portly reverend defending him when he was twice the size of the godly man and more than able to back down a group of men coming at him. But Dry Gulch was kind enough to say a proper thank-you.

It was good that Dry Gulch was quick about his gratitude, because Craig could see fury building on Mrs. Hunt's face.

"You." The society woman burst forth with the word like it was an accusation. But to Craig's surprise, she was not looking at him or Dry Gulch. She pointed her finger at Reverend Thompson. "You're the one that left me at the railroad depot in Cheyenne. I made arrangements to have someone bring me out here, and you picked up some man instead."

"Oh, I'm so sorry, ma'am," Reverend Thompson said as he stood up from the bench where he was sitting. "We thought that man here was the passenger."

The reverend pointed at the one they'd brought out in their wagon.

"Oh," Mrs. Hunt said as she looked at the stranger.

Craig sensed the two of them knew each other, but neither said anything. Instead, Mrs. Hunt turned back to Vivian.

"I still can't believe you put yourself up for being a mail-order bride when you could have had my Ethan," Mrs. Hunt said to her, almost pouting this time.

"Ethan has not talked to me in six years," Vivian

answered. "I don't think his heart was in pursuing me, not even back in the rose garden."

"Nobody wants to get married anymore," Mrs. Hunt said, sounding vaguely unhappy about that.

"Speaking of getting married," Reverend Thompson said to Craig. "If you didn't know Vivian here was coming, why did you give me the note telling me to come for a marrying? It doesn't sound like there's going to be a wedding."

"There will be a wedding," Mrs. Drummond said sternly as she stood up from the bench. She straightened her shoulders and took a step forward. Craig suddenly noticed that she was wearing her best Sunday clothes, a dark blue linen dress with a white lace collar. She even had a sprig of something in her hair. A woman wouldn't usually get herself up like that just to deliver a few pieces of fruit to a neighbor.

She continued to speak. "I sent you that note, Reverend. I came to marry Craig. I know he can't make up his mind—he's really quite shy—so I figured he needed someone to have a firm hand in all this. I decided to marry him as a surprise Christmas present to his family, even if I'm a bit late. Now no one needs to worry about finding the children a mother. We can all just be here together. Cozy-like."

"Oh," whispered little Katy as she gripped her cat tighter in her arms.

"Oh," echoed Robbie as he lowered his head.

"Oh," Craig added as he stared at Mrs. Drummond.

No one had called Craig shy since he'd been a tiny fellow no higher than his *mam*'s knees.

"Don't go getting all in a huff," the older woman said to Craig before he could gather enough wits together to figure out what to say to her. "I know you need to get married to—" she hesitated and looked over at the children "—well, let's just say to satisfy interested people that you have a good family life. I thought you and I could have one of those marriages like you had with Delores. She told me all about it."

Craig cringed. There had been a time or two when he'd come back to the house to find Mrs. Drummond's buggy out front and Delores and her drinking tea together inside. "I doubt she told you much."

Delores had never seemed to like Mrs. Drummond, but then, Delores had thought all of the people around were too common for her to call friends. Craig had been grateful that at least one woman would take time to visit with her. He couldn't imagine Delores sharing any secrets, though.

"Oh, but she did tell me things." Mrs. Drummond clicked her tongue. "No shared bedroom—at least not after Katy. You did the heavy wash and the cooking. Delores said they were the easiest years she'd ever had since she left New York. You even looked after the children. Not that they gave Delores much trouble."

Craig felt his face flush, but he had to defend his wife. "Delores was delicate."

Finn snorted but didn't say anything.

Craig figured he needed to stop this. There was no tactful way to say it, so he'd just let it out. "That doesn't mean I want to sign up for another marriage like that."

"Oh." This time it was Mrs. Drummond who was taken back. "My understanding was that the sheriff said you had to get married. For the sake of the children. I thought surely you would want to. You can't let those little ones down."

Craig cleared his throat. "I did have a judge to satisfy, but that ended on December 24." He nodded in the direction of Robbie and Katy. "We are all safe now."

"I'm not so sure about that." The stranger stood up from the table and exchanged a long look with Mrs. Hunt. "You should have received a letter from the judge."

"Letter?" Craig felt his heart begin to race. He hadn't even looked at the other piece of mail Mr. Adler had left.

Craig looked at the stranger. "I think you'd better tell me who you are."

The man put up his hands in a gesture of peace. "I'm Robert Cassidy. And I have been looking for a fatherless child. My child. I thought I might find the little one here. That's all. I'm not looking for trouble."

The whole room was silent.

"We have our f-father," Robbie finally said as he moved to put his arm around Katy.

Craig was proud of the two of them. And then he noticed the movement behind them. The girl who had spoken up earlier was slowly walking toward the stranger. She was quiet, but the look on her face was so full of longing that, without thinking about it, Craig stepped forward.

The girl stopped several feet away from the stranger. "Are you my father? I've always wanted to have a father."

Craig almost pulled the girl away from the man, but then he saw that the stranger was kneeling on one knee. He had a tender look on his face and was focused only on the girl.

"I don't know," he said to her quietly. "What's your name?"

"I'm Becky Eastman," she said, talking fast. "I was always Becky, but I wasn't always Eastman. I didn't have a second name 'til my mama died. She said I had to change my name because she couldn't take care of me any longer on account of she had to go to heaven to be with Jesus."

"Did she tell you who your father was?" the man asked.

The girl shook her head. "She just said I belonged with the Eastmans."

Craig looked over at Vivian. She was viewing the girl with proud approval and nodding silently.

"Well, I'm not your father," the man said, then rather sweetly added, "But, wherever he is, I'm sure he'd be proud of you."

"That's what Mama Vivian says." Becky nodded and stepped away.

She looked so disappointed that Craig almost went to her, but then she walked over to stand by Vivian.

The stranger stood up again and faced Craig. His expression was no longer tender or kind. Craig figured the man had more to say, and he didn't want to hear it, not like this in front of the children.

"I think you need to read that letter." Mrs. Hunt injected the words from where she stood beside the table. "I sent a telegram to the judge when it was clear our train would not make it to Cheyenne in time for his meeting. He said that, since the train schedule was not in my control, he would change the date of the initial meeting to tomorrow, Tuesday, December 28, at noon in Cheyenne. That letter is to inform you of the change in plans."

"I'll have my attorney challenge that." Craig hadn't considered the words before speaking them, but he wasn't willing to risk anything regarding the children. "These are my children. I know I'm not the first—ah..." Craig did consider his words now and he didn't know how to explain it without upsetting Robbie. So, he continued, "All I'm saying is that I was the husband to the woman who gave birth to both children, and I'm the only father either one has known. In my mind, that makes them my children. I am their father."

"You're sure about that?" Mrs. Hunt asked with a sly look on her face.

He didn't trust her expression, but he knew what he knew. "I am their father. Both of them. I was married to their mother."

"If your reasoning is that you are their father because you were Delores's husband, you will be mistaken," the older woman said triumphantly. "You were never married to Delores."

"Of course, I was," Craig answered impatiently. "Reverend Thompson performed the ceremony himself, and he's right here. He'll tell you."

"I did marry them," the reverend added helpfully. "Back in October of 1864. Fall ended early that year and winter was already starting. Gave them their marriage papers and everything."

"That marriage was not legal," Mrs. Hunt stated calmly.

"Just because it happened in the territories, doesn't mean it isn't legal all over the country," Craig argued back.

"No matter where you are, it's not legal if the bride is already married," Mrs. Hunt said as she then turned to the stranger, Robert. "Tell them who you are."

Craig watched in horror as Robert ducked his head in the direction of Mrs. Hunt.

"Delores and I were married in the spring of 1863," Robert said clearly.

"But she waited for you and waited for you in Cheyenne and you never came," Craig burst out. That had to count for something. "You abandoned her."

Robert grimaced. "I had an unfortunate encounter with the law. I thought I'd rig the cards a little in a poker game." He glanced at Craig. "Delores had expensive tastes, and I could never say no to her. I knew we'd need lots of money for winter and my pockets were almost empty. Anyway, I found myself held in a jail for a couple of years down in Arizona. I didn't know it would be that long, and I didn't want to write and have her know what had happened."

"So, you've been out for the past two years?" Craig asked.

Robert winced. "I did write to her before that. Told her what happened. She wrote back and told me about everything. Then, two years ago, I busted out of jail. I wrote again, telling her I'd be in Cheyenne for a day, and if she wanted to meet, I'd be there. Said to bring the boy. That we could start over and be a family someplace."

"That's where she was going then," Craig said. "That day when she was killed trying to ride that wild horse."

"I expect so," Robert said. "I actually couldn't stay in Cheyenne, so I would have been gone by the time she got there. Someone tipped off the law that I was there, and they came for me again. I ended up in San Quentin state prison in California. Hard place to be."

"For gambling and breaking out of jail?" Craig was surprised. "I didn't think they'd send you there for that."

Robert looked down. "Well, there was another gunfight and lawman. He tried to take me in, so I shot him."

"You killed him?" Craig guessed.

Robert shook his head. "No, but he was hurt bad. If he had died, they would have hanged me. They still wanted to. The Cassidy name means something in political circles back east, though, so my father tried to force the judge to go easy on me. Made the judge mad instead, so he sent me to San Quentin. He showed no mercy at all."

Craig was suddenly aware of the four little hands, two on each leg, that were holding on to him for dear life. Their eyes were riveted on the stranger. Craig squatted and opened his arms. Robbie and Katy both snuggled close.

"I wish my father hadn't interfered," Robert muttered. "I would have had less time to serve."

"You'd have been dead," Mrs. Hunt declared. "The courts needed to know who you were."

The man was an ungrateful cheat, Craig thought. He would never let him claim his rights. "You can't have either of my children. Even you must know it wouldn't be good for them."

"Oh, he'll sign all of his rights over to me," Mrs. Hunt said complacently from where she stood. "That was our agreement."

Craig looked up then. "What agreement?"

Mrs. Hunt smiled. "I pulled some favors and was able to get him released early from that horrid place." She smiled again at Robert. "Anybody can tell he never meant to hurt anyone. He and Delores were childhood sweethearts. Our families knew each other. They were a little naughty when they ran away to get married, but Robert has agreed to live in the Hunt household now. He'll be there to guide the children, too. A boy particularly needs a man in his life."

Craig looked down at Robbie. The boy looked confused and worried. Craig wasn't sure he understood, though.

Craig thought that Robbie needed a mother more than he needed a grandmother who bought anyone she wanted and an ex-convict for a father. Especially one who would likely sell him out to the highest bidder.

"I can't imagine the judge will allow any child to be raised by a man who almost murdered someone," Craig said. He would insist on that.

"That's harsh," Mrs. Hunt protested. "Look at Robert. He served his time. The law is satisfied. He's the perfect gentleman."

Craig did look. He saw a man who was carefully dressed to be a gentleman. His chestnut hair had been tended by a barber. His black suit was tailored, elegant and new. His vest was threaded with gold. And the wool coat he put over his shoulders was worth more than Craig's homestead ever would be. There was no way the man had made that kind of money in prison to buy clothes like that. Mrs. Hunt must be giving him an allowance, too.

"He has squinty eyes. He bears watching," was all Craig said. He knew it sounded petty before the words were out of his mouth, but he was desperate.

"My eyes are still getting used to the sunlight," Robert protested. "You'll see. I'll look honest and prosperous in a few weeks."

"Maybe," Craig said.

Clothes never had made a man kind, and Robert seemed to totter on the edge of something. Anger, perhaps. Regret, certainly. Craig had no doubt the man could become thoroughly unpleasant. And he didn't want Robbie anywhere around when that happened.

He didn't even want Robert around his children

now, but he nodded stiffly at the man. "I wouldn't put any man outside in this kind of weather, but it stays fairly warm in the barn. We have an old stove out there, and there's wood against the south wall, by the door to the large chicken coop. We use the barn for calving season, so it's snug. Once a fire is going, you'll be comfortable enough. You're welcome to stay there until tomorrow. There's a metal trunk in the second stall with some old blankets inside and plenty of hay to bed down in."

Robert nodded. He seemed almost relieved. Then he looked over at Mrs. Hunt. "That's where I'll be if you need me."

Everyone watched Robert as he opened the door just wide enough to step through and then closed it quickly behind him. A flurry of snowflakes made their way inside anyway, and it was clear the blizzard had taken a turn for the worse.

"I'd better go out and see that he doesn't take off with one of the horses," Finn said as he walked toward the peg that held his sheepskin coat. "A city man like him wouldn't know how to survive in a blizzard."

Craig nodded.

"Humph," Mrs. Hunt said sourly. "I might as well go out there, too. I'm clearly not wanted in here."

"That's not true," Craig protested. "The children and I appreciate that you came to visit. It's just that—"

"I know," she said with a weary wave of her hand. "You want to marry Vivian Eastman even if she's all done up as a mail-order bride. You think you'll have a happily-ever-after. But, just remember, a mother isn't all that children need. They need someone who can provide for them. They shouldn't have to grow up like tumbleweeds with no one to care about them."

"They're not tumbleweeds," Craig said, resisting the impulse to look over to where his children stood. Was their hair combed? The seams in their clothes straight? Did they even have their shoes on? They both had a tendency to prefer to go barefoot in the house. They might look like tumbleweeds to a stranger, but they were not.

Mrs. Hunt gave him a warning look and then reached for her cloak. Seeing that Dry Gulch already had the garment open and waiting, she let him wrap her in it. "I won't be long."

"I'll head out with you," the old miner said. "That cloak won't keep you warm, but my buffalo coat will keep the cold off both of us. I should have thought of it sooner."

Mrs. Hunt harrumphed, but she let him take her hand.

Craig watched as his house emptied right before his eyes. Even Mrs. Drummond, the reverend and his wife left for the barn with the excuse of seeing to their horses that were stabled there for the time being. Finally, Craig was alone with the children, the cat and the mail-order bride.

He looked at Robbie. "Why don't you and Katy take Becky to the big bedroom and all of you can take a nap?" Craig said.

"On the b-big bed?" Robbie asked in surprise.

Craig nodded. Delores had never let the children

even sit on it. "But get a wet rag and wash your feet off before you get on the bed." He'd looked and they were both barefoot. "And pull those quilts over you so you stay warm."

Robbie went to get a cloth and the two girls left to go to the back room. Finally, Robbie stepped inside the room and closed the door.

"They're gone," Vivian murmured.

"Yes." Craig looked up and wondered what she could be thinking. Of course, that was not difficult to know. She must be realizing she'd stepped into a tangle of grief and trouble.

Vivian didn't know what to do with her hands. She was just standing there, and she and Craig were looking at each other. When everyone had left so quickly, it had made the house feel suddenly intimate. Of course, it wasn't really private, she reminded herself. Not with the three children in the back room set to come out at any moment. Their little faces had looked so happy with a simple treat. Vivian felt an irritation, though, that was out of place with all of this sweetness.

Then she looked down at her feet and saw that cat. He was eyeing her like she bore watching, and she was relieved. At least someone here understood that they were in a delicate situation.

"I want to get a job," she blurted out without giving it much thought. She looked up at Craig. She knew he needed help, but it wouldn't be coming from her. "I'm sorry."

"Ah," he said, his voice mild. "Very sensible of you to find a way out of this."

His face wasn't looking happy or sad; it was just frozen like he didn't want to respond. Which annoyed her even more, since she wanted to know what he was thinking. If he showed any desperation at all, she would be tempted to—to what? She didn't know.

"I'm not trying to avoid anything," Vivian protested and then she hesitated. His face was starting to look a little bleak. He had to be worried. She could give him some assistance, she decided. "I do think Mrs. Hunt shouldn't be given the children. I will tell the judge that if you want me to. I have known her, and of her, for years. She expects people to do what she wants, but she can't do this. At least, I don't think so."

"I'm sure we will be fine," Craig answered, his voice sounding brittle.

He was lying and Vivian knew it. Well, maybe he wasn't telling a falsehood, she admitted, but he was certainly trying to spare her the knowledge of how bad things could be.

Then he turned his blue eyes on her, and they were so intense she had to look away.

"You don't want to be my mail-order bride?" he asked, seeming more curious than offended.

Vivian shook her head. "Oh, no. It's not just you. I only agreed to be a bride so I could get Becky out of my brother's house. I meant to go through with it, but on the train here I decided I couldn't. I've always wanted to marry for love. That's the first step in having a loving family. I know it sounds foolish, but—"

Craig held up a hand and interrupted. "It doesn't sound that at all. My *mam* married for love."

"She did?" Vivian asked.

He nodded and pulled a leather cord out from around his neck. A shiny gold ring hung from the cord. "My *mam*'s wedding ring. She gave it to me just before she died and told me to sell it and buy passage for myself and Finn to America. This ring was the most precious thing she owned. My father had given it to her when they married. I remember them every time I touch it."

"You didn't sell it?" Vivian asked. The band was thin and looked like it might have been thicker at one time.

Craig shook his head. "I couldn't. Whenever I was sick as a boy, I remember my *mam*'s hand rubbing my head. I could feel that ring on her finger and I knew all was well. It's all I have left of them."

"You must be pleased your parents married for love," she said.

Craig shrugged. "Our *mam* never said Finn and I should do the same. She could have married a man who owned a large farm, but she chose my father instead because she loved him. My father had nothing. He was a tenant farmer, and we went hungry many a night, especially after the potatoes started to rot all over the country. We had misery after misery. The man she could have married prospered. I know she had days she regretted following her heart. She would be alive today if she'd chosen the other man. She told me once to marry with my wits about me and not listen so much to my heart."

"And did you?" Vivian asked.

Craig shook his head. "My marriage to Delores was a disaster. She no more stepped off the stage in Cheyenne and I was smitten. I should have known better. I didn't have enough money to make her happy. Not that we ever went hungry. But we did go without the comforts she wanted."

"But you made her that lovely carved bench," Vivian protested. "Katy said you planted rosebushes. And the big bed you talk about sounds comfortable. You have a good stove and a sturdy table. And you had the ring to give her."

"I'm afraid Delores did not want to wear the ring," Craig said, his voice flat. "The other things were not enough to please her, either. As for the ring, she told me she'd wait until I could afford something with jewels in it." He lifted up the ring again. "And you can see the band is worn some. Delores wanted something new. Something worthy of her, she said."

"Oh, I see," Vivian said, and she was afraid she did.

Craig slid the cord under his shirt again. Vivian had seen enough of life to know that not everyone who married did so because of love for their spouse, but she had thought this man had done so. Of course, he had not said he didn't love his Delores—he'd said she didn't love him.

"I'm not saying you were wrong to send for a mail-order bride," Vivian said quietly. She knew she should stop talking, but her mouth kept going. "I understand. You needed a wife. But you don't anymore. So, things are good for you. And I'm going to look for a job instead—right here in Cheyenne."

"That's a sensible plan," Craig said, and his face did relax some. "You're not meant for homestead life anyway."

Vivian frowned. It was an excellent plan, but she thought she might have just been insulted. She studied the man's face and didn't see any malice there.

"Are you saying I'm not sturdy enough?" she asked. "I only felt faint because I had a bit of a cold and we hadn't had anything to eat since last night."

"You're hungry?" Craig asked in concern and glanced over to the stove. "Finn was—" Craig stopped and rushed over to the stove. "The beans are burning."

He grabbed a rag sitting on the shelf by the stove and pulled the large cast-iron pan over to the side of the stove away from the firebox. A trail of smoke followed him. Then he bent down to look into the pan. "We had the last of our bacon in there and some onions."

"I'm sure it smelled good," Vivian said, trying to be supportive. "I mean at first, before—well…"

No one could say it smelled good now, Vivian admitted to herself.

Craig looked up. "We should have eaten two hours ago. But with the company and all—the Adlers and then Mrs. Drummond. I sure hadn't counted on feeding Mrs. Hunt with those beans. She's likely to snatch the children right up and take them home to her French cook so they can be fed right."

"Her chef would never make beans and bacon— not if he was French or any other kind of nationality," Vivian agreed, deliberately adding a gentle tease to her voice. It must have worked, because Craig looked up and grinned.

"He might do it in revenge if he knew his pillow for the night would be a handful of straw and he'd be kept awake by the howling of wild wolves." Craig looked at her, serious again. "In the distance, that is. The wolves don't come close." He grew even more somber. "We don't have much in the way of comforts here, though. Our food is plain."

"And it's not a bad life," she insisted. "The children seem content. More than content—happy."

Craig nodded. "That's because they don't know any better. How do you think they'll feel when they become adults and realize what they could have had if I'd let them go with their grandmother? Instead of being excited to lie on a feather bed, they could have a castle full of feather beds and servants to smooth out every wrinkle in their silk sheets."

"Katy would love that," Vivian said with a grin. "But I don't think Mrs. Hunt is quite that wealthy."

Craig snorted. "She's offering tutors and travel— and there's the French food, of course. I'm not even sure what my *mam* would tell me to do."

"Well, French food can be burned as easily as those beans," Vivian said, hoping to make the man feel better. "Besides, if you have another pot, we can pour the beans out that weren't burned, and they might be fine with a little help."

Craig reached over and pulled a larger cast-iron pan off of a low shelf. "What kind of help are we talking about?"

He put the pan down on the stove and poured the beans that would go into it. She could see there was a layer of stuck, blackened ones on the bottom of the original pan. Those would have to be scrubbed away, but the other beans looked good.

"Becky has some spices," Vivian said. "The cook at my sister-in-law's house taught her a bit about how to use them. She'd be thrilled to have something like those beans to practice on. It'll be a challenge for her."

"I don't suppose she can make them taste like French food, can she?" Craig asked.

"If it's French cuisine you want, I can make *coq au vin*," Vivian offered. He looked at her with a question in his eyes. "That's chicken cooked slow in red wine," she explained and then remembered, "but I don't suppose you have any wine."

"There's an old bottle of wine that Delores kept in her trunk," Craig said. "I don't know where she got it, but it looks expensive. That's the easy part, though. We don't eat chickens here—well, just the tough old roosters."

"I'm not sure if anything tough would impress Mrs. Hunt," Vivian said. "Don't you have a young—"

"Daddy," a sweet voice said from behind them.

Vivian turned and saw that Katy had come out of

the bedroom. She was rubbing her eyes and holding her cat. Her curls were wild around her face.

"I'm not tired," Katy said. "And then I heard you talking about Mrs. Hunt wanting dinner. Is she hungry? Are we going to eat?"

The other two children came out of the bedroom, too. They both looked rumpled, but not the least bit sleepy.

"Wh-what are w-we doing?" Robbie asked.

"We're making a very special dinner for us and your grandmother," Vivian said.

Katy nodded, her face looking worried. "So Ga'ma will know we don't need to go with her and eat the French food." Katy added, "And so our bride can stay."

"Well, part of that is right, sweetheart," Craig said as he squatted down to be on Katy's level. "We do want to show your grandmother that we can feed ourselves."

"So she won't take us away," Katy persisted.

Vivian nodded. She hadn't been sure how much the little girl understood, but it sounded like she knew almost everything. As if to confirm it, Katy stood there for a moment, gradually looking wiser than her years.

"But we need a chicken," Katy said.

"Only if there is an old rooster," Vivian assured her.

Katy closed her eyes tight and scrunched up her face. It almost looked like she was praying. When she opened her eyes, she announced, "I have to go to the barn."

She set her cat on the floor carefully. Then Katy went over to the pegs that held an assortment of shawls and blankets. She reached high but was too short to grab what she apparently wanted.

"Let me get that for you," Craig said as he walked over and lifted an old army blanket off a peg. The scrap of blanket had been fashioned into a small shawl. He wrapped Katy in that and placed a knit scarf over her head. Then he tied a second scarf around her neck. "Don't stay long. And be sure and use the chore rope. That will take you right to the barn. I'll come out later to see about the rooster."

"I'll go w-with her," Robbie volunteered.

Vivian watched as Craig made sure they were bundled up and then kept his eyes on them as they opened the door and went outside.

When they'd left, Craig turned to her and said, "I'm not always sure I'm doing the right thing. I already wish she'd taken her kitty with her. That old cat knows a lot about handling trouble. He'd keep them both safe. I have to give Katy and Robbie some independence, though. I might be gone someday when they need to make the trip to the barn—or other trips. Or—" Craig choked and turned to Vivian. "I can't imagine them on a street alone in New York City. How do I prepare them for that?"

"Surely Mrs. Hunt wouldn't let them go on a street by themselves," Vivian said.

Craig shrugged. "She doesn't love them. Who knows what she'll do? Maybe not intentionally. She might just forget where they are. Or they could wander off. They're not used to cities."

Vivian searched for something reassuring to say to Craig, but her impression of Mrs. Hunt was not a positive one. The woman took advantage of people to gain what she wanted. She didn't pay much attention to taking care of them.

"She would always dress them well." Vivian offered what comfort she could. She was confident of that much. "You know they'd be warm and fashionable. They would not look like beggars."

But Craig wasn't listening. He stepped over to the window and looked through it.

Then he turned around. "They made it. They're at the barn."

"That's a relief." Vivian turned to her own little girl. She'd already seen Becky standing back by the cupboards. It looked like she'd been watching the other two children a little wistfully.

Vivian walked over to her. "They'll be back soon." She worried sometimes about Becky feeling left out. "And we need to get your spices out so we can fix the beans that burned."

Becky brightened at that thought and went to the far wall where the valise and trunks were lined up. Her small cloth bag was sitting beside the biggest trunk, and she opened it.

Vivian knew something was still wrong, though. She wondered how many times Becky had held back like she had done just now—staying behind when other children went ahead. But then, she hadn't been around many other children. Vivian had been her playmate as well as her mother. Maybe that wasn't all that was going on, though. She followed Becky over to where she stood.

"Did you want to go to the barn with the others?" she asked.

Becky shook her head. "I want to stay with you."

"Are you worried I won't be here when you come back?" Vivian asked gently. She wondered if Edith had said anything to Becky that she didn't know about. Or maybe one of Edith's servants had said something to make her feel insecure.

Becky shook her head again. "You might need me."

Vivian was puzzled.

"To help with your hat," Becky finished.

Vivian hadn't considered how often her hat had needed adjusting. Any time a breeze of any size blew by, it needed to be tilted again so the black net would be straight. And Becky was often there to do it. Vivian was chagrined that she'd never noticed that Becky was holding herself back from doing the things other children were doing because of Vivian's vanity.

"I'll have to get myself a different hat, then," Vivian said, trying to keep her voice steady as she bent over and kissed the top of Becky's head.

Then she looked over and met Craig's puzzled stare. "I have a thing or two to learn about being a parent, too," she admitted to him.

His face went from worried to amused in a flash,

and he walked over to where she stood. "Becky is blessed to have you."

"Thank you," Vivian replied.

Craig hesitated and then he added, "Of course, there's no need to wear your hat here."

"But—" Vivian protested. No one liked looking at her burn scars. They were ugly red patches of skin. She didn't expect anyone to like them. It was only polite to spare others from the sight.

Just then, the door to the house burst open. Vivian could see snowflakes blowing in on the wind. And then she heard the noise. Robbie was hushing someone and Katy was scolding someone, too. Then Vivian heard the squawking.

The children got themselves inside, and Robbie pushed against the door to close it. By that time, Vivian saw a few feathers, the same color as Katy's hair, sticking out from the bundle Katy carried.

"What's this?" Craig asked as he walked over to them. Vivian stepped closer, too.

Katy's face was rosy with cold as she reached up a hand and threw back the scarf around her head. Her copper curls were unruly. Her other hand clutched a scarf wrapped around something. Robbie looked like he wanted to stop Katy but didn't know how and was frustrated.

Finally, Katy walked over to where Vivian stood. The girl's steps left patches of snow all across the packed dirt floor, but Vivian didn't say anything. She had the sense that something important was happening.

Katy stopped in front of Vivian and lifted up the squawking, squirming bundle. "Ga'ma won't want to eat that old rooster. You can have my Gracie."

"Gracie?" Vivian turned to ask Craig, who was looking stunned.

"That's her favorite pet chicken." Craig glanced at Vivian.

"My best friend," Katy added mournfully. "Poor Gracie."

Katy looked down and watched as the hen managed to get her head free of the scarf. Then Katy took her hand and petted the chicken's head as fully as she could while the bird's neck bobbed and its beady eyes looked at everything.

"It's okay," Katy whispered to the hen.

Then she looked up at Vivian. Katy's lip trembled and her eyes blinked. "But it's not going to be okay, is it?"

Vivian reached out and touched Katy's cheek. "Are those tears?"

Katy shook her head vigorously and then looked away. "I don't cry. Bad things happen when I cry."

"Oh, sweetheart." Vivian knelt down and put her arms around the girl, who was now sobbing. "It's okay to cry. We all do that when we're sad. It doesn't make bad things happen."

"It doesn't?" Katy asked. Her eyes were wet and she was gulping air. "Once, I was crying, so Robbie couldn't go help mama and then she died. All because I wasn't a big girl and I cried."

Vivian enfolded Katy back into her arms and held

her close. Vivian looked up and met Craig's eyes. He was almost crying himself, but Vivian had to attend to his daughter instead of him.

"You didn't cause your mama to die," Vivian told the girl. "Your mama died because she did something dangerous. She was not careful. It had nothing to do with you crying."

"You're sure?" Katy asked as she backed away and wiped a tear off her face.

Vivian nodded. "And you don't need to worry about Gracie. We can make a good dinner with some of her eggs—and maybe the eggs of her friends, too. That's all we need."

"That's all?" Katy's eyes were wet, but she was looking hopeful. "I don't want Ga'ma to think she needs to take us away 'cause we don't eat right. Gracie would understand. She told me so."

"Gracie is your good friend," Vivian assured the girl. "But let's wipe your tears away."

No sooner had she spoken the words than Craig was at her side with a large white handkerchief.

Vivian turned back to Katy and patted her cheeks dry. "There we go. You can help me if you want. We'll make crepes."

"What's that?" Craig asked. His voice was more jovial than usual, and Vivian suspected he was trying to distract Katy and make her feel that all was well.

"Crepes?" Vivian said, matching his tone. "They're sort of like a French pancake. I know what Mrs. Hunt is used to eating. As long as we can get some flour, eggs, milk, sugar and a little butter—we'll make crepes. We'll fill them with sweetened apples, and if we have cream, we'll whip some to put on top of it all. Mrs. Hunt will think she's in Paris on the banks of the Seine river that she's so fond of."

"Sounds good," Craig said with a grin and turned to Katy. "You stay here with the others. I'll take Gracie back to her nest in the barn."

"Thank you, Daddy," Katy said, her face all smiles now.

As it turned out, all of the children wanted to help prepare dinner. Within minutes, they each had an old towel tied around their necks and had been given instructions on using their fairly dull knives to cut the apples. Vivian calculated there were still eleven pieces of the fruit in her valise. And then they had the four oranges, too.

They were a happy crew as they made the apples for the crepes and beat the eggs for the batter. When Craig came back from the barn, he even tied an old shirt around his neck to show the children they were not alone in needing aprons.

Finn was the first one to come over, and after some time, they sent him back to bring everyone over for dinner. They came as a group in the early evening. By then, Becky had not only gotten the beans to taste like a spicy Italian delight, she had also made a large batch of baking powder biscuits like the ones Edith's cook used to serve. Craig found a jar of wild honey in a cabinet to eat with the biscuits. And they had butter, of course.

Dry Gulch led the way to the table. Mrs. Hunt was

the last one to be seated. And she did not look happy to be sitting there.

"I should have brought dinner from the restaurant by the depot—the one at the Cheyenne Hotel," Mrs. Hunt said from where she was at the end of a table bench. Then she ran her gloved hand over the wooden table to check if it was clean. Vivian was glad to see the glove was spotless at the end of her inspection.

"You will like the Italian beans," Vivian said as she set a serving bowl of small red beans on the table and slid it in front of Mrs. Hunt as a sign of respect.

"And you'll want to taste some of the Italian biscuits," Vivian continued as Becky proudly put her plate of golden-brown biscuits on the table. They had been sprinkled with dried parsley flakes. "The recipe is from the Eastman family cook. Becky learned how to make them from her. It has some chives, too."

Becky beamed with pride.

Mrs. Hunt was silent. But Dry Gulch made up for it.

"My mouth is watering already," he declared with gusto.

Mrs. Drummond tried to be supportive. "Everything looks very healthy."

"We'll bless the food first," Craig said. He was the last to sit at the table, and he turned to the reverend. "Will you do the honors?"

"Gladly," the man said and bowed his head. "Lord, we thank You for Your provision to us and for us being able to sit down and break bread together. We ask Your wisdom as we talk about the future of this precious family. Let us each consider our hearts. Amen."

Vivian noticed that Mrs. Hunt seemed subdued at the end of the prayer. She at least took one of Becky's biscuits and ate a spoonful of the beans. She ate slowly, and the others finished before her.

"The biscuits are as light as I've ever seen," Mrs. Hunt remarked eventually. She'd eaten one covered with butter.

"Becky's going to teach me how to make the biscuits, too," Katy bragged. "Then you won't have to worry that me and Robbie are hungry. And my daddy gives us lemon drops. Lemons are good for you."

Vivian glanced over at Craig and he winced.

"I didn't want them to be unhappy like their mother had been," Craig spoke softly so only Vivian would hear. "I couldn't afford silk, but I could buy lemon drops. We all need some treats in life."

Meanwhile, Mrs. Hunt was shaking her head in a most disapproving way.

"You can't just eat biscuits and lemon drops." Mrs. Hunt gave Katy a small smile as though reminding herself to be kind. "There's more to meals than that."

"We have b-beans, too," Robbie added matter-of-factly. "And b-bacon."

Mrs. Hunt didn't acknowledge his words, which made Vivian worry that she might prefer Katy over him. The older woman never did seem to look at Robbie. And Vivian remembered that Ethan had once said his mother had always paid more attention to Delores than him.

Mrs. Hunt was still looking at Katy when she continued, "Wouldn't you rather have some ice cream? In New York City, we make it with pure vanilla beans from South America. In my house, we have it whenever we want. If you were there, you could have some right now."

"Robbie, too?" Katy asked.

"Of course," Mrs. Hunt said as she turned to give the boy a brittle smile.

After that, Katy and Robbie exchanged glances. They both looked puzzled.

"They haven't had ice cream," Craig said quietly. Vivian could see the defeat in his eyes.

Then Katy spoke up. "Sometimes in the winter, our daddy takes scoops of snow and puts warm honey and sugar on top of it for us." She was excited still at the memory.

"We don't kn-know where the b-bees come from that make the honey," Robbie added helpfully. "But they f-fly all over the world until they c-come to where we live. Maybe they even c-come from South America. And we can have that, too, a-any time we want if th-there's snow."

Mrs. Hunt was not pleased. "It's not right that a child shouldn't even know what ice cream is."

Robbie and Katy looked at their grandmother, uncertain of how to respond.

"I like snow honey," Katy said finally. "Have you ever had that?"

"Of course not," the woman said impatiently.

Vivian stood. One did not argue with Mrs. Hunt.

"We don't have either one for dinner. But we have French crepes with sweetened apples. You'll like them."

"Let me help you," Craig said, sounding relieved, as he stood up also.

Vivian walked over to the counter by the stove and Craig met her there. The crepes were in the warmer on top of the stove. The sweetened apples were in a cast-iron pan on the side of the stove away from the firebox. And the whipped cream with cinnamon was cooling by the window, which had been left slightly ajar. The frigid air seeped inside and the tin bowl was cold.

"I never want my children to grow bitter over what they don't have," Craig said when they were working together.

"They sound like they're happy enough with their snow honey." Vivian smiled. "And, of course, they have their lemon drops."

Craig grinned. "I buy a box every fall. And sometimes another one in the spring. Keeps us all sweet."

"I have a feeling you are what keeps your children sweet," Vivian responded. "Love makes everyone's life better."

Vivian blushed, surprised she'd been so bold as to make a personal remark like that to a man she barely knew. Craig sent her a guilty look and didn't smile back. Vivian tried not to take offense.

"It was only a remark," she said.

"I know," Craig answered. "It's just—when you know more about me. I, well…" He looked over his shoulder at everyone at the table. "We'll talk another time."

Vivian and Craig were only halfway through putting the crepes together when she heard someone muttering at the table.

"I've never been to a dinner where the hosts left in the middle of the meal," Mrs. Hunt complained softly. "It's horribly rude. Barbarian, even."

"Now, Margaret," Dry Gulch reprimanded her in a low voice. "You know most people around here don't have servants to fetch and carry for them."

"Manners are manners, no matter if one has servants or not," Mrs. Hunt responded. "And I didn't give you leave to use my first name."

"I figured that was an oversight," Dry Gulch said, his voice cheerful and unrepentant. "I told you I didn't hold with being a mister. I figure calling someone a missus is just as useless. A person only needs one name. Sometimes not even all of that. I could call you Maggie now that we're acquainted, so to speak."

Mrs. Hunt gasped in horror.

"Time for crepes," Vivian announced before war could break out. Then she hurried to start sending plates of apple crepes down the table. The dinnerware was an assortment of tin plates, some with turned-up lips and some without. They all had dents, but Becky had dampened them and then sprinkled sugar and cinnamon on them so they actually looked festive.

"I did the plates," Becky said proudly to Mrs. Hunt. "I learned it from the cook at where we were before—the Eastmans'."

Mrs. Hunt turned to smile at the girl. "Is their cook French?"

Becky shook her head. "She's Mrs. Cook. I don't know where she came from. I think it's Philadelphia, though."

"I see," Mrs. Hunt said, looking haughty.

At that point, the reverend and his wife entered the conversation to murmur thanks to Becky and then to Vivian when they got their plates. Mrs. Drummond nodded politely.

"Brilliant move to distract everyone with food," Craig whispered to Vivian as he reached past her to pick up two plates to deliver to the other side of the table.

Vivian answered with a smile. It felt good to work together with another adult. She supposed that was one benefit of marriage she would have appreciated. Not that she was planning to marry anytime soon, of course. It wasn't like she was saying no to him so she could say yes to some other man next week. She would make that plain to Craig when they had that talk that he'd mentioned. She still had to work at not taking offense at his reaction to her comments.

"More whipped cream, anyone?" she asked as she sat down on the end of one of the benches. Everyone was busy eating their crepes.

"Delicious," Robert muttered, a softness spreading over his hardened face. "I didn't have anything like this in San Quentin."

"Of course, you didn't," Mrs. Hunt said promptly.

"This is French cooking." She smiled over at Vivian. "And a very good attempt at it, my dear."

"Thank you," Vivian responded, trying not to smile at the grudging compliment. "Craig knows how to make these now. They have plenty of eggs and milk, too, so they can have them often."

"I doubt he'd be able to make these," Mrs. Hunt said with a frown in Craig's direction. "Most men wouldn't. I suppose he can make tea and beans, of course. But crepes take a light hand."

"What about your French chef?" Craig asked cheerfully. "He's a man."

"Yes, well…" Mrs. Hunt said. "But he's French. Cooking is in his blood."

"Irish? French? What's the difference?" Craig teased the older woman. "Potatoes are in an Irish man's blood. I can make those. Baked. Boiled. Fried. Creamed. You name it. You could serve my potatoes in a fine restaurant on Central Avenue."

"Nonsense," Mrs. Hunt countered. "There's a significant difference between these crepes and boiled potatoes."

Craig chuckled.

"They're sure good," Dry Gulch said then, and he smacked his lips. He had some whipped cream in his beard, but no one mentioned it.

It must be the lack of good lighting, Vivian thought. Imperfections were not as easy to see here. Even differences of opinions were muted. Maybe she could stop wearing her hat and netting inside this house. Maybe no one would even notice her scars.

The crepes were gone faster than Vivian thought they would be.

"I don't suppose you serve an after-dinner drink here, do you?" Robert asked when everyone had finished.

"Sorry," Craig said. "We run a sober house. But I could let you have a lemon drop."

"A what?" Robert asked in astonishment.

"A candy," Craig said. "A lemon drop. I keep them for the children. You could stir one into a cup of hot tea if you want. It's good when it melts."

Vivian wasn't sure what was happening, but she could feel the peace in the room crack and break. Maybe it was the suddenly fierce look on Robert's face.

"Delores loved sweets," Robert said. "She wrote that she asked for candy many times and you never bought any. It was such a simple request. She said you ruled with an iron hand."

Craig shook his head. "She wanted imported chocolates that they didn't even carry in the general store here. I did buy a box once. I had to order it from Chicago and it was very expensive. Plus, half of the pieces melted before they even got here. She only ate a few of them. She put the rest of the box on a high shelf so the children wouldn't get it and left it there until the ants came for it."

"Delores never was one to eat something simply because it was there," Mrs. Hunt said proudly. "Exquisite taste."

Craig hardly knew what to say. To him, every scrap

of food was precious. He guessed, though, that was what growing up in luxury did to a person. "We usually had lemon drops, and I learned to make taffy for Delores."

"You expect me to believe that?" Robert asked, his voice clipped and aggressive. "Delores also wrote that you drank alcohol until you passed out most every night. Whiskey. Wine. Tequila. She said that you were a mean drunk, and I worried about you being here with Robbie. She said you might hurt him. That's why I broke out of jail the first time. I didn't want my—"

Robert broke off as though he had suddenly realized what Craig said.

"You made candy for her?" he asked. "With sugar and a pan and—"

Craig nodded. "I even tried my hand at pralines a few times. They were pretty good, too."

Robert looked at Mrs. Hunt. "Delores lied about him and the candy. Was she telling the truth about the alcohol?"

Mrs. Hunt shrugged and looked down. "I don't know."

Robert grimaced. "I guess the answer is that she probably did lie, then. She wanted to see me riled up. I should have known. It wouldn't have been the first time. It made her feel important, I suppose."

"I'm not a drinker," Craig assured him. "I don't have a taste for alcohol. Never have had. I've seen what it does to some men. And I'd never hurt either one of my children—or any child."

Vivian watched Craig speak. He wasn't dramatic

about it, but he was confident. Steady. He knew who he was and who he was not. He wasn't lying. Those children were his and they were safe.

Mrs. Hunt gave a distressed grunt. "But they were Delores's children, too."

Craig glanced at her and nodded. "I make it a point to remember Delores to them. I want them to know their mother. She and I had our troubles, but I loved her and the children loved her."

Mrs. Hunt quieted herself and then gave Craig a long look. "The best way for them to really remember their mother, though, is to give me the children to raise. No one knew Delores the way I did."

"The children need to know me, too." Craig forced himself not to point out that Delores had cut off all ties with her mother, so it was doubtful Delores would have wanted the children to be with her mother.

They were both silent for a minute.

"I guess we'll see what the judge decides tomorrow," Mrs. Hunt finally said.

With that, the woman rose from the table. The other guests followed.

Vivian stood up as well. The spark had gone out of the day. As she looked around, she saw it was darker inside the house as well. And colder. It was early evening and not the usual hour to go to sleep, but she was exhausted. She had not slept well last night on the train.

Finn went to one of the windows and announced, "The snow has stopped. We might be able to get out tomorrow after all."

Vivian went over to the stove. Craig was pouring water into a small basin that sat on an opening in the firebox. They'd do the dishes when the water was hot.

"I'll snowshoe my way up to the top of the rise," Dry Gulch said as he went to look out the other window. "See what the country south of here looks like. Might be the snow has blown off the road."

"I'll go back out and build up the fire in the barn stove," Finn offered as he went to take his sheepskin coat off of the peg by the door. "It'll make it more comfortable tonight for the men who are staying there."

"Mrs. Drummond and Mrs. Thompson," Craig said as he turned away from the stove. "I figure the two of you can share the big bed for tonight." He looked at the third older woman. "Mrs. Hunt, you can have the side bedroom."

Then Craig turned to Vivian. "I'm hoping we can make that bench comfortable for you for the night. The bed in Mrs. Hunt's room is small or—"

"No, no," Vivian said. "I'm good with the bench."

"We have enough quilts to go around," Craig said. "And we have a bear skin that can go on the bench to make it softer."

"It will be fine," Vivian said. Truthfully, even if the bench was hard, it was preferable to sharing a bed with Mrs. Hunt.

"The loft is big," Craig continued. "Katy and Becky can have one side of it. Robbie and I will bunk on the other side."

Before long, the dishes were washed and the beds

were made. Vivian was wiping off the top of the table when she realized that the children needed to look their best when they went before the judge tomorrow.

"Clothes," she stepped over to the stove and whispered urgently to Craig. "Do the children have their good clothes ready for tomorrow?"

Craig winced. "They are wearing all they have. It will have to do."

Katy was wearing a threadbare brown dress that was so tight the seams were almost splitting. Robbie's shirt was scorched on one sleeve and ragged throughout. Its original color had been green, but it had been washed until it looked grayish yellow.

"I—" Vivian said and then stopped. Craig's face had shut down like he didn't want to talk about the children's clothes.

"It's not your fault," she said softly.

Craig looked up. "I'm their father. Of course, I'm responsible for their lack of dresses or shirts."

"But—" Vivian started to comfort him, but she didn't have a chance.

"I should go out and check on everything in the barn," Craig said stiffly. With that, he went over to the pegs by the door, brought down his coat and wrapped several knit scarves around his neck. Then he walked out the door.

Vivian shook her head. She knew all about a man's pride. In fact, she knew about a woman's pride, too. There might come a time soon when she wouldn't be able to buy even a new shirtwaist for Becky. And children grew so fast that it wasn't always true that their clothes would last for more than a year.

With that thought in mind, Vivian walked over to the smaller of her two trunks. It had been packed at her grandfather's house after he died, and she'd put everything in it that belonged to Becky. Lately, she had added the valise to the top of the pile of things in the trunk because of the Deringer it contained. It was best to have the gun locked in the trunk. Her grandfather had insisted she take some lessons on the gun after he gave it to her, and she knew the importance of safety.

After she moved the valise slightly, Vivian slid her hand down the side of the trunk. She could tell Becky's dresses by the feel of the fabric. Finally, she found the one she sought and pulled it up. It was wrinkled, but she could iron it before she went to bed. A light blue sprigged calico, it had dark blue flowers embroidered around the edges of its broad white collar. It had been Becky's favorite dress a couple of years ago and was clearly too small for her now. Vivian had kept it, planning to use the fabric in a quilt someday.

"Becky," Vivian called softly up to the loft. The children had not prepared for bed yet, but they were giggling about something as they got their covers sorted and ready.

Becky peered over the loft and grinned. There hadn't been a loft in any of the houses where they'd lived, and Becky was enjoying this one.

"Come here a minute, please," Vivian said.

When the girl was down and standing beside her, Vivian started to explain that Katy needed a new dress because she was going to see the judge.

Becky understood quickly. "So their grandmother won't be able to take them away."

"It might help," Vivian said.

"She can have all my dresses," Becky declared as she spread her arms wide. "I want her and Robbie to stay here. They need to be with their daddy."

"I think one dress will do," Vivian said as she held up the dress she'd pulled from the trunk. "This one should fit her the best. It's too small for you now anyway."

Becky nodded, her eyes still smiling. Then she motioned for Vivian to bend down so she could whisper in her ear. "They like me. Katy and Robbie. They like me. Even Kitty likes me."

Vivian turned to whisper in the girl's ear. "And do you like them?"

Becky nodded emphatically.

Thank You, Father, Vivian prayed silently as the girl raced back toward the ladder, the blue dress clutched in her hands. *Becky has some friends.*

There was excitement in the loft as Becky stood up with the dress and offered it to Katy so she could try it on. Vivian could see the children's shapes as they chattered, and that set her mind to thinking about what Robbie could wear.

Finally, she remembered a plain white blouse that Becky hated to wear. It had a pointed collar and could almost pass for a boy's shirt. She went to the trunk and pulled that garment out, too, then called up to the loft to ask Becky about the blouse. When the girl said it was best to give it away, Vivian asked for the dress to be thrown down so she could iron both pieces of clothing.

By the time she'd pulled the small iron from her trunk and heated it on the stove, the children were in bed, as were all of the rest of the guests in the house. Craig was still out in the barn, likely being sure everyone there had enough blankets or quilts to keep warm for the night.

Vivian had finished with her ironing when Craig came back inside. She was glad she'd finished, as her back was beginning to ache. She watched as Craig took off his coat and unwound the knit scarves around his neck.

"It's clearing up out there," Craig announced softly with a smile for her. "I agree with Finn and Dry Gulch that we'll be able to travel tomorrow."

Craig walked over to one of the benches by the table and sat down.

"I have clothes ready for the children," Vivian said as she nodded toward the dress and shirt she'd laid out on the bench on the other side of the table.

Craig was pulling off his boots and didn't look over at the dress and shirt Vivian had ironed until he was finished. Then he stood up and lifted the chore lantern so he could see the garments better.

"These don't belong to my children," he said, clearly puzzled.

"They are things Becky doesn't wear any longer,"

Vivian said. "She is willing to give them to Katy and Robbie."

A muscle moved in Craig's jaw. "I'll pay you for them."

"There's no need," Vivian said. "They're too small for Becky now. She's grown."

"But you've already done so much for us," Craig said, his voice low. "I've spent years trying to figure out why Katy stopped crying, and she fell into your arms like sobbing her heart out was the most natural thing she could do. I don't know how you did it."

"Well, she was upset about Gracie," Vivian said. "Her emotions took over."

"Oh, it's never been that she didn't care," Craig said. "I could see things were bothering her something terrible, and yet she wouldn't shed a tear. I'd ask her about it and she wouldn't tell me. You're the one she told. I never realized that Robbie's guilt from that day had landed on Katy, too. I should be buying you a new dress instead of letting you give us anything."

"If it makes you feel better," Vivian said, "Becky wants Katy and Robbie to have the clothes. She likes both of your children."

As she spoke, Vivian felt the muscle twist in her back again, and she put her hands on her hips and turned slightly to ease the discomfort.

"I can iron a shirt for you, too, if you'd like," Vivian offered. "Impress the judge."

"The judge knows me," Craig said. "A few wrinkles won't change his mind."

Craig kept looking at her, his head cocked like he

was trying to determine something, until he finally seemed to reach a decision.

"Come over to the bench by the fireplace," Craig ordered her. "You've got the same pained look on your face that I get when I've spent too many hours in the saddle. I know how to make that better. Our *mam* taught both me and Finn. She knew a Chinese woman who showed her. Now we both know how to care for our backs."

Vivian was curious and walked over to the bench. Craig was waiting there.

The first thing Craig did was take Vivian's crushed hat and ragged veil off her head and set them on a box by the bench. "I don't suppose you would want to give those away?"

Vivian looked up to see the teasing in Craig's eyes.

"I know they are in bad shape," Vivian admitted. "I have new ones in my trunk. I just haven't taken the time to switch them."

"You don't need a hat or a veil here," Craig said and then indicated she should sit down with her back toward him. Once they were both settled, he told her to lean her head forward. She usually wore her hair pulled back from her face, but after the wind's whipping it around earlier today, her hair hung down. He pushed all of it to one side and put his hands at the back of her neck. Then he began to move his hands.

"Ahh," Vivian moaned. She'd never felt anything so good as the motion of his hands. "What is this called?"

"Our *mam* never got around to naming it for us," Craig said as he kept up the pressure of his hands.

"It's heavenly," Vivian whispered.

"That it is," Craig answered. "I usually have to back up against a corner in the wall to get relief. Our *mam* taught us how to do that, too."

By then, Vivian had felt the tension leave her back. She sat with her head down, the flames in the fireplace growing low and leaving the room in gathering darkness. Vivian was so tired she almost dozed off. But she didn't. At some point, Craig stopped and they sat on the bench together.

After a few minutes, Vivian felt a warm breath on the back of her neck. A gentle kiss followed.

She turned to face Craig. "Did your mother teach you that, too?"

He grinned. "No."

"Well," Vivian began to protest, but then stopped. "I guess it was harmless. Like a grandmother kissing a baby good-night."

Craig winced. "No Irishman can let a challenge like that go."

Before Vivian knew it, Craig had gently cupped her face. All of her face. She panicked.

"No," she whispered.

Craig released his hands and brought them back to his lap. "I'm sorry."

Vivian felt foolish. "It's just that no one touches my scars. I—"

Craig gave a short nod. "I know how you feel."

"I doubt it," Vivian retorted.

Craig leaned closer to the light from the fireplace. "Look at my hands."

He opened his fists and she saw the scars. They were the same color as those on her face.

"My wife didn't want me to touch her with these hands," Craig said. "It was like she thought the scars were contagious. I know how people are."

"I'm sorry," Vivian said. "Your scars don't bother me."

Vivian wanted to say more, but she didn't know what to say to comfort this man. And then—like a bolt of lightning—she remembered where she'd seen him before.

"Are those scars from that night?" Vivian whispered. She hadn't forgotten the flames of that night. And the strength of the stranger who helped her. "When you lifted that beam off me?"

Craig went absolutely still for a moment and then he nodded. "I don't hide my scars. You don't have to, either."

"Oh, I'm so very sorry," Vivian said. He hadn't admitted it was him, but she knew. She realized she'd never really thought about the price that man had paid to save her life. If her burns had gone deeper, the doctors said she would have died. If he hadn't moved the beam when he did, she wouldn't be here. "I owe such a debt to you for that night, and here I am making a fuss about you touching my face."

Vivian forced herself to lean closer to him. "I won't pull back this time."

Craig shook his head. The teasing light had gone

out of his eyes. "You don't owe me. I—" He stopped and swallowed. "There are things you don't know about that night. Finn and I are Irish immigrants. I worked as a longshoreman. That night we—"

"I'm sure you weren't the ones who set our house on fire," Vivian said lightly. "You don't need to apologize for working with some horrible people. I suppose every job has a few people who aren't nice."

Craig looked like he wasn't finished with what he wanted to say, but he was silent.

"Now, you were saying about your hands," Vivian reminded him. She did not want to hear his confession. She supposed he'd heard the men talking about burning buildings and hadn't reported them to the police. He probably hadn't even thought they were serious.

He did not respond right away, but after a few moments, he continued.

"I don't want you to think all of my scars came from that night," he said. "I wouldn't have the hands of a gentleman anyway. Besides, any man would love to touch your face. You're beautiful."

Vivian hated to talk about her scars. She never did, and she didn't know why she was telling this man about them. She certainly didn't want him to pity her. "I know the one side is all right."

"I mean both sides." Craig reached out his hand and lightly touched her chin until she was looking him in the eye. "You are a beautiful woman. All of you."

Vivian shook her head. "You're too kind."

She didn't like men pretending she was pretty when she was not. But she thought he meant well. She moved away from him on the bench. "I'm tired."

Craig nodded and stood up. "Morning will come early."

With that, he turned and walked over to the ladder going to the loft. She watched until he was lost in the darkness above.

Then she heard Craig say softly, "Sweet dreams."

"The same to you," she whispered back.

A soft chuckle floated down to her ears.

She smiled a little, wondering how she was going to have any kind of tolerable dreams after this. She'd been wrong that the kiss on her neck had been small and of no consequence. Maybe that was why she didn't want to hear a full confession from Craig. It was the first time a man had kissed her since the fire had destroyed her looks and her chances for marriage. She'd reconciled herself to the fact that a man could not find her attractive. And now this. She felt like this man was turning her life upside down.

But, she reminded herself, she couldn't trust he was serious.

None of the other men she had known had felt that way after her accident. Her sister-in-law had been right about one thing. All of the proposals had stopped after she'd gotten her scars. Ethan's withdrawal had been the one that hurt, but there had been others. The few visits she'd had from men after she came back from the hospital had been full of curiosity and pity. They'd soon ended, too. She wondered if

Craig felt compassion for her and that was why he'd kissed her. Well, she reminded herself, it was a very small kiss. More like the kisses on the back of her hand that men used to give her in a greeting. That was all. Not something to worry over.

With that, she gathered up the quilts that had been left in the room for her bedding and made a comfortable nest for herself. She would sleep well. It wasn't until she had almost nodded off that she remembered she'd have to take the opportunity tomorrow to look for work in Cheyenne. After the judge's proceedings, she'd see what the town had to offer for her and Becky.

Chapter Four

Craig woke abruptly. It was almost totally dark. His nose was cold even though the rest of him was warm. It took him a moment to realize where he was. He was in the loft of his house, sleeping next to Robbie. A couple of quilts were on him, and he had a thin mattress beneath him. Then he heard the sound again. Someone was crying. Or moaning. He wasn't sure. He raised himself on his elbows and looked at the other side of the loft. He could see from their shapes that Katy and Becky were asleep. They were not tossing or turning. He rose as high as the ceiling would allow and crawled to the edge of the loft. He could see the glow coming from the smoldering pieces of wood in the fireplace down below.

He couldn't see Vivian from where he was—the back of the bench blocked his view—but the sounds appeared to be coming from her. She must be having a nightmare, he thought as he swung his legs onto the first rung of the ladder.

He was glad he'd slept in his clothes, since the air was freezing. His socks kept his feet warm as he made his way down the ladder.

Everyone else in the house was sleeping, and it was still dark outside. He didn't want to scare Vivian, so he was careful not to bump into any furniture as he worked his way toward the bench. He knew what half of the problem was when he got close enough to see that Vivian had thrown the heaviest quilt off of her during the night. He picked it up and tucked it around her.

He became worried that her fever might have come back, so he bent over and lightly put his hand on her forehead. Her awful black hat and netting were still sitting on the box by the bench, so he could feel the full width of her face. To his relief, he felt no extra heat on his hand.

"Humm," Vivian murmured as she turned her face toward his hand. He imagined it was his warmth that drew her. Within moments, she was breathing hard, and he had the sense she was reliving bad memories. She frowned and her legs jerked.

"Vivian," he whispered, his voice low. He did not want to startle her awake. "Vivian."

Her eyes opened. It took her a minute to focus.

"There's a big fire," she mumbled as she started to rise up from the bench. She obviously couldn't see well; it was still dark. "We have to get out of here." She looked up in alarm. "Where are the children?"

"Easy," Craig murmured as he put his hands on her shoulders to steady her. "It's okay. There's no fire.

Just the wood burning in the fireplace. The children are sleeping in the loft."

By now, Vivian was squinting as she tried to see all of the house. "It was so real."

Craig nodded. "I used to have nightmares about fires, too."

He wasn't sure whether she wanted to keep talking about her nightmare or if she wanted to be distracted, so he waited for her to say what she would.

"Is that because of the fire where you rescued me?" Vivian asked. "Your bad dreams?"

"No, they're from before that," Craig admitted and then hesitated. "It's cold out, but I think the snow has moved on."

Vivian gave a rueful smile. She was sitting upright by now with the quilt wrapped around her shoulders. "You can tell me about your fires. You know all my secrets by now. I may as well know one of yours— you know, like we are friends."

Craig wondered how a few words could make him feel so good. She moved over on the bench so he had a clear space to sit, too.

"To earn passage for me and Finn to come over here from Ireland," he started as he settled down, "I took a job stoking the furnaces on the ship we were traveling on. I was thirteen—but I told the ship captain I was sixteen. I don't know that he believed me, but I was desperate. Turned out the ship's captain was, too. His ship was sailing the next day, and two of his firemen had gotten into a brawl of some kind and were in jail. And they weren't getting out for a month. The captain knew he was in trouble. It's hard to hire stockers. Nobody wants that job—at least no one who has done much work on ships."

Craig took a moment to pull Vivian's quilt over her left shoulder. He knew that was where some of her scars were, but they were not visible. She wore a long-sleeved nightgown and her hair hung down.

He continued, "Sailors call the furnaces the pit. Each man usually feeds four furnaces—lined up in a row. It's so dirty and smoky down there that we could not get the soot and coal dust off of us no matter how much lye soap we used. We took four-hour shifts, and the heat was unbearable. Not many men could handle it. My job was to add coal every three minutes to each furnace. If I didn't go fast enough, the furnace doors would flap behind me, leaving awful burns on my shoulders and back. That only happened once with me. I learned, but I heard stories of other stokers."

"How horrible," Vivian gasped. She looked a little pale.

He smiled grimly. "It was almost easier for me than some of the others. I was young and could move quick. Plus, I'd worked on my family's tenant farm in County Clare in Ireland since I was four years old, so I was strong.

"But you were scarcely more than a boy," Vivian protested.

"I learned to make fire work for me," Craig said as he pointed to the mantel. The burning wood in the fireplace did not give off much light, but the shape of a cross and a few of his other pieces could be seen.

"I've never seen any carvings like those," Vivian said. "I looked at them earlier. They look burnt and yet they're beautiful."

"One of the other stokers on that ship taught me about *shou sugi ban*—it's an old Japanese way of preserving wood and making sculptures," Craig said. "You char the wood surface until it turns black, then you cut out pieces to make it look like these. All light and dark. Japanese culture seems to pair opposites like that. It's that way with these wood pieces. You finish it off with some oil. It always reminds me of how God can bring light out of what we see as hopeless darkness."

"They are works of art," Vivian said.

Craig nodded. "Learning to make them helped me make peace with fire." He paused and then offered, "I can show you how it's done sometime."

"I'd like that," Vivian said. "Maybe I will see fire differently, too."

"I think you will," Craig agreed. "The Bible says 'He shall baptize you with the Holy Ghost, and with fire.' That's in Matthew 3:11. So fire can be used for good. That's what I learned with *shou sugi ban*."

He didn't add that they needed fire to live on the prairie—for food, for heat and sometimes for protection. It probably wasn't a good plan for Vivian to sleep by the fireplace, though. Maybe tomorrow night they could change places. There would be room for one more on the girls' side of the loft.

Of course, he suddenly realized, he would likely not have as many visitors the next night.

He stood up from the bench. "We best get some sleep. Tomorrow will be a long day."

Vivian nodded.

Craig slept for another four hours. As was his habit, he got up before sunrise so that he could warm the house before the children came down.

He was putting the coffee on to boil as dawn started to shine through the frosted windows. He'd already sliced some bread for toast. He was moving softly, but Katy climbed down the ladder from the loft before he saw her. Her hair was tangled and she was in her nightgown. She rubbed her eyes as she stood there.

"My eyes burn," she said, frowning up at him.

"I know," he answered. "The wood got wet and it made smoke inside the house. But the air is better now. Your eyes will feel better soon."

Katy nodded and walked over to lean against his leg.

Craig put his hand on her head and cuddled her close. He enjoyed greeting the children in the morning.

"I have a new dress," she said, a smile on her face.

"I heard," he said.

"It's so Ga'ma will think I'm pretty," she added softly.

"Your grandmother thinks you're pretty no matter what kind of a dress you have on," Craig said firmly before he stopped to think about it. He rather doubted those words were true. He'd taken to defending the children from any slight and automatically reassuring them.

"I think you're always pretty," he added. Now, that was the pure truth.

Katy's mind seemed to be elsewhere, though.

"Is the girl Becky going to be our sister?" she asked. "Robbie said she is."

"Maybe," Craig said, unsure himself. He certainly didn't want to mislead on this one. "We will have to wait and see."

Katy thought a minute. "Because of the wedding?"

"I don't know if there will be a wedding," Craig said.

"A bride needs a wedding," Katy said firmly. "On account of the beautiful dress she gets to wear."

"We have to be patient," Craig said. He did not know how to explain to Katy that there was no storybook romance unfolding here. He was surprised that she didn't pursue her talk about the dress, though.

"Becky says her Mama Vivian is her second mama," Katy informed him. "But she likes Becky just as much as her real mama did. Becky said Mama Vivian would like me, too."

There was a scramble of more footsteps as Robbie rattled down the steps of the ladder.

"And me," Robbie said as he came to stand by Craig. "Becky s-says Mama Vivian doesn't c-care about a little bit of dirt." He paused a bit. "I think she sh-should be our mama, too."

Craig smoothed down the wayward brown hair on Robbie's head.

"And we sent for her," Katy added confidently. "We didn't ask Mrs. Drummon' to be our mama."

"You don't need to worry about Mrs. Drummond," Craig said in a low voice, because the woman was sleeping in the big bedroom. He was grateful he could assure his children on one thing at least. "Now get dressed and come have some breakfast."

"When do I put on my new dress?" Katy asked.

"After we have our oatmeal," Craig said. "Wear your old dress for now."

"Will Mama Vivian be able to eat breakfast with us?" Robbie asked. "I could make her some toast."

Robbie was proud of his ability to toast a slice of bread in the fireplace.

"I think she would like that," Craig said. "In fact, you can make some for everyone. I sliced enough." Robbie started to walk back to the loft ladder. "But get dressed first. It's going to be another cold day. Put on double socks."

Craig reminded himself that the children both had two pairs of socks. They might not have many clothes, but he did not deprive them of truly important things. They had mittens and scarves, too.

"I can make some sugar tea," Katy said, excitement in her voice. "I can scrape the sugar off the loaf for Mama Vivian and everyone."

"Dressed first," Craig repeated. "Then I'm sure she would like that, too."

Craig hoped Vivian would appreciate that the children were doing everything they could to serve her.

He could have saved his worries. By the time

breakfast was ready and everyone in the bedrooms was awake, Vivian had praised the children until he should have been worried that they might be puffed up with pride. But he figured Vivian was doing it partly to distract the children from what was going to happen later in Cheyenne.

"Thank you," he managed to murmur as they both cleared the table. The men would be in soon from the barn.

Vivian looked up at him with a question in her eyes.

"You're keeping their minds off that meeting with the judge today," Craig added.

"I think we all need to trust God that the judge will be wise," Vivian answered. "I think you said you've met him."

"I know him," Craig replied. "He's a good man, but he'll stick to the law. There's no telling how he'll decide. And with Mrs. Hunt and this Robert claiming Delores and I weren't even married, I don't know what he'll do."

"Well, I can't think he'll send them off to be raised by an ex-convict," Vivian said. "I don't care who was married to who—that can't be the right thing to do."

"Mrs. Hunt will make her case," Craig said.

The children's grandmother had been quiet through breakfast. But then, so had the other two older women. Maybe they hadn't slept well. There was nothing to be done about that now, though.

Craig and Vivian worked together to wash the dishes. Finn went out to hitch the horses to their wagon. Reverend Thompson did the same with his wagon. Mrs. Drummond decided to leave her buggy here. She'd drive it home later today, she said. Before long, they were all ready to leave.

There had been no new snow during the night, but the air was so frigid everyone's breath came out in puffs of white smoke. The children's cheeks were pink; their noses, too. Even Katy's kitty was subdued and anxious to keep burrowed under the quilts and straw that had been placed in the bed of each wagon. Everyone had a coat and gloves or mittens. Most had scarves wound around their necks.

Craig and Vivian helped the older women and the children up into the wagons. Mrs. Hunt, Mrs. Drummond and Mrs. Thompson settled in the back of the reverend's wagon. Robert sat beside Reverend Thompson on the seat. At the last minute, Dry Gulch decided to go along, lifting himself into the back and sitting close to an alarmed Mrs. Hunt.

Craig was surprised Finn climbed up into the back of his wagon with the three children. Usually, Finn sat beside him on the seat. But then Craig realized his brother was allowing Vivian to sit in his place. Craig was sure his brother had matchmaking on his mind when Finn reached over and placed a quilt on the back of the seat. It would be there, ready to pull up over their shoulders when the wagon started to move. Craig realized he would need to tell Finn just who Vivian was. His brother had not seen her the night of the fire, although Craig had told him about her.

"May I?" Craig asked as he held out his hand to

help Vivian up to the wagon. She had her gray gloves on her hands and a new black hat firmly attached to her head. The veil coming down was reinforced on the hat brim. He was disappointed she was not ready to give up that veil yet, but he would give her time. She hadn't worn it for breakfast, and that was progress.

"Thank you." Vivian smiled at him as she took his hand. He helped her up into the seat, moving his hand to her elbow for the last part of the way.

Craig was seated beside Vivian and ready to take up the reins when he casually brought the quilt from the back of the seat up to cover their shoulders. Vivian had to move closer to him for the quilt to fit over them both. Craig decided he needed to thank his brother later.

"You can duck your head under the quilt, too," Craig said as Vivian squirmed to get herself settled. "Your hat will be fine."

By the time Vivian was warmly tucked in, she was sitting thigh-to-thigh close to Craig with her hat pushed back and her head almost resting on his shoulder. He couldn't help but smile. He wondered if there was any hope this woman would really be his bride. Could she forgive him for his small part in what had happened? It sure felt good to have her beside him.

"I'm going to need a new dress," Vivian murmured softly, her head covered by the quilt except for the space that was close to him.

"Oh." Craig felt his hopes of a happily-ever-after falling fast. He had forgotten all about the difference in their financial lives. He did not need to marry another woman who wanted a new dress every time she turned around. He knew by now that that kind of a woman had a deep unhappiness he could not fix.

"I'll need something serviceable for when I find a job," she continued. "The ones I wore in the sickroom with my grandfather all had to be thrown out. They were that badly stained. And I want to save my other clothes—the ones I wear in public. Who knows if I'll be able to afford clothes like that again. No, I need a simple cotton dress if I'm to find a job as a cook—or maybe as a maid in that hotel."

Craig was speechless. Delores would not have dreamt of finding a job. Or of wearing a dress made of cotton.

"You want to work?" Craig asked.

"I'll need to provide for Becky and me somehow," Vivian said cheerfully.

Craig realized he didn't know this woman at all. He could not keep comparing her to Delores. Delores never considered getting a job when she ran out of money—not when she could marry a man to provide for her. These two women might be as different as night and day. Still, there was no need to rush into anything. The fact that Vivian was set on getting a job meant she didn't want to tie herself to someone like him.

They rode the rest of the way to Cheyenne in silence. Craig reminded himself that he shouldn't get used to Vivian sitting beside him. It probably wouldn't happen again unless he had to drive her to Cheyenne when she left. He didn't want to think about that day at all. Enough trouble crowded his mind today.

Vivian hadn't gotten tired of snuggling close to Craig and wasn't ready to see the buildings of Cheyenne come into view in the distance. It was quite a sight, though. The roughly boarded structures and the leaning tents started out small and gradually grew in size. They were all covered with so much snow that the only way to tell the difference was that the tents curved as they leaned inward and the slapped-together wooden buildings tilted in straight lines.

When the wagon got closer, Vivian saw that all of those buildings had a stove pipe sticking up from the roof with a trail of black smoke drifting out. As best as possible, the stores were all laid out in a straight line with businesses on both sides of the icy road. There were no trees to keep the wind and the snow away.

False fronts rose up bravely from a few buildings. Vivian could only see the back of them at first, but even then, she remembered from her trip out of town how colorful the fronts were painted. Yellow swirls. Green lettering. Blue background. The general store had such a high front, and the hard scrapple saloon was another. She wondered if that one still had the sign in their window asking for a cook.

The closer the wagons got to Cheyenne, Vivian thought, the more the snow seemed to sparkle and the bluer the sky turned. She wouldn't have minded traveling a few miles farther in the warm cocoon

Craig had made for them with that quilt. She realized, for the first time, how fortunate a woman would be to marry a man who knew how to make so much out of so little. He had made a house out of dirt and a romantic space out of an old quilt. Most men she knew would be lost without a servant to bring them heated bricks or jugs of hot tea in cold weather. Her own brother wouldn't have a clue about how to survive in the territories.

Finally, Reverend Thompson pulled his wagon to a halt at the front of the saloon she'd just noticed. Vivian peeked out from behind the heavy quilt and saw that the sign asking for a cook was still there in the window. She wasn't sure if she should ask about that job or look around more first.

Then she saw seven men standing around in front of the saloon and decided it would be best to look elsewhere for a job. A woman could get a bad reputation working around so many men—especially ones like these. Some of them were dressed in buffalo coats, and a few made do with old army blankets cut to serve as ponchos. None of the men had shaved in weeks. She doubted they'd bathed more recently than that. Their hair hung down in uneven clumps, and they all had hats sitting on their heads, often tied down with bandanas or other strips of material. She saw one piece that looked like a foxtail.

The only bright spot for Vivian was that she realized her own hat wasn't so outlandish in these circles. She doubted anyone would remark on it, even if the men were all looking at her curiously.

"Let's get everyone inside," Craig said as he set the brake on the wagon. She wondered if he'd seen the men sizing her up. Then he carefully moved the quilt so it covered more of her and less of him. She figured that meant he knew. He looked at her and continued, "Keep yourself covered. I'll come for you last and carry you. No sense in you getting your shoes wet."

"You don't need to—" Vivian started to protest, but Craig had already walked to the back of the wagon and was carrying Katy and her cat to the door—of the saloon. Vivian realized where they were headed. For some reason, she thought they'd be going to a building beside the drinking place. But, when she looked, there was no such building. At least, there wasn't anything but what looked like a storage shed or maybe a shelter for horses. But it was not that close to the saloon, either. What did they call the place anyway? she asked herself as she tried to read the sign. She had to twist her head sideways to see.

"'The Big Dipper,'" she read aloud. There was a picture of a glass of beer on the sign, so there was no mistaking the business done in that rickety old building. A scantily clad woman was shown in the back of the glass of beer, too, so there was no doubt about the low morality of the place.

"The children can't go in there," she hissed as Craig walked by. "The judge will see and—"

"The judge knows," Craig turned to say. "This is where he does his business on the days that he's in Cheyenne hearing cases this time of year."

"In the saloon!" Vivian protested.

"This time of year, they don't heat up the church except on Sundays," the reverend stopped to explain. "Takes too much wood and coal. So, the judge uses the back half of the saloon. It's the only building that is always heated and is big enough to hold everybody who wants to see what's going on. And there are always those who want to know."

"But—"

"The bartender doesn't sell drinks when court is in session," the reverend continued. "But after the judge leaves, he does a booming business. It pays for the extra coal. And if anyone gets disruptive, the judge fines them or sends them to the jail. That puts money in the town coffers, too. They don't waste much heat in the jail, either, this time of year, so the men pretty well behave. And they're harmless."

Vivian took another look at the men gathered around the side of the building. She wasn't sure about them being safe.

"Well, I never." Mrs. Hunt's voice was loud and she was protesting Dry Gulch carrying her into the saloon. The waiting men were grinning as they watched. Dry Gulch said something to Mrs. Hunt in response, but Vivian couldn't hear it. The society woman did get quiet, though. And then the door closed behind them.

"Best get on in there," Mrs. Drummond said as she walked by Vivian, who was still sitting in the wagon. "Dry Gulch just picked up Mrs. Hunt to hear her squeal and give those other miners something to talk about. No one's going to come and carry you. Leastways, not if you act like a lady."

"I'm going to carry her," Craig said quietly as he walked back to the wagon. "And she's always a lady—it's not an act."

Vivian didn't think Craig sounded happy about any of it, but she kept silent.

"Humph," Mrs. Drummond said and, despite the cold air, put one hand on her hip and shook her other finger at Craig. "We'll see if she's a lady. You're just trying to sweeten her up so she'll tell the judge she's going to marry you. Well, it won't work. You can't trust her. You'd have to be deaf to not know she grew up around Mrs. Hunt—in New York City. They sound just like each other. Vivian's not the kind of wife you need. If you want the judge to know you have a decent country wife waiting for you, you just mention my name. He knows me and knows I'll stick to my word. I'll be right inside there, so I'll be ready when you need me. And I expect you will."

With that, Mrs. Drummond glared at the men standing by the door until they stopped talking. They almost saluted when she walked past them with her dress held out of the snow and her nose high in the air.

Once the older woman was inside, Craig motioned for Vivian to move to the edge of the wagon seat. He held out his arms and then lifted her off of the seat. She buried her nose in the heavy wool of his coat.

The men around the front seemed to all gather their breath and give a long, low whistle as Craig carried her by. She lifted her head slightly and looked at them closely enough to see they were all smiling. The scarred side of her face was turned against Craig's chest, so all they saw was the pretty side. She wondered how they would react if they saw her full face.

The door swung open and Craig carried her through. Vivian felt the heat even before Craig set her upright on the floor.

"Oh." She breathed in the warm air, suddenly aware of just how cold it had been outside. She looked around and brushed some of the snow off of her coat with her gloved hand. The walls of the huge room were gray planks of wood, turned brittle with their age. The ceiling was high in most of the room, and a narrow staircase hugged the left side of the room. She figured the low ceiling over the counter and the back room indicated several rooms on the second floor. Four windows, all of them fly-specked and smoky, lined up like sentinels, looking out to the street. The floor was made of wood planks that were scuffed and water-stained.

She saw several men—different ones from those outside—standing at a long bar some distance in front of her. They were leaning on the counter and had their backs to her. Out of habit, she reached up and adjusted her hat and veil anyway. Those men could turn around at any moment, and she didn't want to hear any comments from them about her face.

A long mirror hung on the wall behind the bar. The counter below the mirror had dozens of brown and clear bottles of what must have been various liquors. A row of short glasses was laid out on a towel in front of the bottles. And then, on the floor at the end of the counter, sat a small saucer of milk and Kitty lapping it up. Robbie was watching the cat.

It took a minute or two before she saw the man who must be the bartender and a cat lover as well. A stout, grizzled man in a white shirt and apron, he appeared to be in an intense conversation with the man at the far end of the counter.

"No, I can't give you any breakfast," the bartender was saying impatiently. "I don't have a cook and I'm too busy at the bar to go back to the kitchen."

"You brought out breakfast for that old cat," the man argued.

"Milk, I can give you," the bartender said.

"I always have eggs and a slab of ham when I come here and you know it," the rough-looking man said. "Sometimes you add biscuits and honey."

Vivian thought he looked like he'd been living in the bush for a month. She wasn't sure if she'd seen him before and then she realized he reminded her of Dry Gulch.

"I have my stomach set for breakfast," the man added, growing more adamant. Vivian decided that, if he was like Dry Gulch, he wouldn't hurt a fly.

"I'm sorry, I—" the bartender tried again to explain.

That's when the bushy man reached across the counter and grabbed the white collar on the man's shirt and lifted the bartender high. Or, at least, enough off the ground that the bartender's feet were no doubt dangling behind the counter.

"Oh, my," Vivian said as she saw the bartender's face turn red and then blue. Apparently, the man could hurt someone bigger than a fly. In any event, she couldn't let this continue.

"I can cook you breakfast," she said loudly as she stepped toward the quarreling men. "Don't fight. It's not gentlemanly. Your mothers would be ashamed."

Both men turned to stare at her. Admittedly, the bartender was looking at her sideways, given the grip the other man had on his shirt collar.

The bearded man was the first to speak. He slowly let the bartender down and then turned to Vivian.

"I do beg your pardon," the man said before giving a deep bow. "I find myself in a predicament. You see, my stomach has near given up on me. It's been that long since I've eaten."

"I understand," Vivian said as she walked over to the counter. She could feel the eyes of everyone in the room looking at her back, but that only made her walk straighter. She was used to men staring at her. Maybe it hadn't happened in years and maybe it had never been because she'd offered to cook, but she still knew enough to ignore it.

"If you have food in the kitchen, I will cook some breakfast for this man," she said to the bartender, who was still rubbing his neck.

"You follow me back yonder and I'll set you up," the bartender said, and that's when the cries of "Me, too" and "I was here first" started.

Vivian followed the bartender into a back room with a black stove and lots of counters. The windows in this room were no cleaner than the ones in front, but they did look like they would open. Faded yellow curtains hung on them, and an old black-and-white photo of a man was hanging from a nail.

"Cook up everything you find," the bartender said. "I'll pay you wages and I'll put a cup out for tips. You keep all of what's collected."

That was the best news Vivian had heard in days. She'd heard miners were very generous with their tokens of appreciation, but she had no idea if that was true or not. As it was, though, she couldn't even afford to buy a meal for herself and Becky, so any contributions would be welcome.

"How many miners do you think will want breakfast?" Vivian turned to the bartender with her question.

"All of them," he answered. "And they'll want lots of it."

"We better ask Becky to come back and help me then," Vivian said to the bartender. "She's the girl with the brown hair standing with the reverend and his wife."

If Becky hadn't looked so approvingly at her when Craig suggested she sit on the wagon seat with him, Vivian would have protested and sat with Becky in the back of the wagon. She and Becky had made this far together, and it was a little unsettling to be apart so much. She wasn't sorry for the separation—not when she saw how Becky blossomed with her new friends—she just missed the girl being at her elbow.

Vivian looked around and pulled two metal basins

filled with eggs off one of the shelves and a slab of bacon off another. She saw a bag of Pioneer Steam Coffee from Seattle and sat that on the counter along with a bag of flour. She found some spices and sugar still on the shelf. There was some soft butter, too, in the wooden box insulated with tin in the corner. A basin of snow stood in the top section of the box now, but it would be an ice block in summer.

She circled the room more carefully and saw a couple of aprons hanging on a peg by the window. There were some buckets for water on a low counter, so she guessed there had to be a well nearby.

Five minutes had not passed before Becky came. Then Katy came, herding Craig and Finn in front of her.

"Robbie and the bartender are watching Kitty," Katy announced.

"The sheriff came to say the judge would be late," Craig added. "We have almost an hour before he starts. So, we all decided to help you make breakfast."

Vivian thought Craig looked too pleased with himself to not have influenced the judge to wait. "What did you do?"

"Nothing." Craig flashed a grin. "I'm guessing he heard about the number of men here wanting breakfast and decided to give them time enough to eat. The judge tends to be cranky in the mornings though so it is best to let him drink another cup of coffee"

"That sounds wise," Vivian said. "But how did he hear about all the men here?"

"I may have told the bartender to send his helper

over," Craig confessed. "I figured you might need help serving up the eggs and bacon."

"But you don't want to get your clothes dirty," Vivian protested.

Katy giggled. "We can wear aprons."

The girl had one of the aprons that had been hanging on the peg wrapped around her shoulders like a cape.

Vivian bent down. "You'll get your dress all messed up with it that way. Here."

Vivian untied the cape and folded the apron so it was the size Katy needed to protect her dress.

"I already have my apron," Becky announced. She had gone into the kitchen before Katy.

"And the judge wouldn't notice a spot on me anyway," Craig said.

"Or me," Finn added as he stepped through the door.

Vivian was so pleased when she saw them all here that she almost felt like crying. It had been a long time since she'd had so many people volunteer to help her. She could almost pretend they were her family. They certainly were more willing to work on her behalf than her brother had been, and he was the only family, outside of Becky, that she had left.

"Thank you," Vivian said softly. Then, before she could even get a speech together in her head, the door opened again.

Mrs. Hunt stepped inside. "I didn't want you plotting against me in here."

The words would have stung, but Vivian didn't

say anything because the older woman, the reigning queen of New York society, was walking over to the peg and pulling down an apron.

"Tell me what to do," Mrs. Hunt said.

Vivian was stunned. The woman didn't seem to be joking.

"I am getting everything ready to fry the bacon," Vivian said. "But if someone wants to slice it, that would be good. I'm going to see if the bartender can send one of the men to the general store for another large slab. Then I need a volunteer to crack the eggs. We'll need a bucket or two of water for coffee. And someone can start to make some batter for flapjacks. We'll need lots of batter."

The door opened again and Dry Gulch appeared. "What can I do?"

"Go out there and tell the men that they need to be patient, but we'll have breakfast for them in twenty minutes or so," Vivian said. "We have a whole crew working on it."

"They'll think they've died and gone to heaven," Dry Gulch said and then he left the kitchen to spread the word.

It took a few minutes more than they had expected, but finally they had freshly washed dishes to serve the three dozen men outside. Vivian had fried seventy-five eggs and ten dozen slices of bacon. Becky and Katy had made over a hundred and fifty pancakes with a cinnamon flavor to them thanks to the tin of the spice they found in one of the cabinets. There were several small jars of honey to go around. Finn made two big pots of coffee. Craig had been outside most of the time cutting more wood to keep the kitchen stove blazing away.

After the food was boiled or fried, Craig carried in the last load of wood and went to stand by the kitchen stove. He took off his mittens and stretched out his hands to absorb the heat. Then he looked at Vivian and frowned. "You have that pain in your back again. I can tell by the way you're standing."

She shrugged. "It's not so bad."

"Not good enough," Craig said as he walked over to her and put his warm hands at the top of her back.

Vivian sighed as his hands started to rub her neck muscles. She closed her eyes to savor the sensations. Her whole back relaxed.

And then she heard it.

"What's going on?" Mrs. Hunt demanded to know, her voice broadcasting throughout the kitchen.

Vivian's eyes flew open. All hope of stress relief was gone. She craned her head and saw Mrs. Hunt standing there with her hands on her hips and outrage in her eyes.

"Just a few things my *mam* taught me for dealing with back pain," Craig replied mildly. He did drop his hands, though.

"Totally innocent," Vivian choked out the words.

"I should hope so," Mrs. Hunt said, but she didn't give up her stance—or the sharp look in her eyes.

Vivian felt her face blush, but it was indignation that was surfacing.

And then Craig shifted his legs and turned as someone called his name.

"Here's my attorney," Craig said as he walked over and shook hands with a short man in a wool coat. And then the judge came into the kitchen and everyone froze in place.

Vivian expected Mrs. Hunt to complain about Craig's actions to the judge, but she didn't. Slowly, Vivian's fist relaxed at her side. She didn't know what she would have done with her fisted hand, but it seemed like the natural response to being unjustly accused.

"I'm wondering if you have any breakfast left for a poor old fellow," the judge said with a smile.

"We do." Vivian stepped over to give him the plate she'd been saving for herself and Becky.

Becky saw what she'd done and nodded her approval. "We already ate some at home anyway."

Vivian nodded back, trying not to flinch when Becky called Craig's place home. She'd have to talk with Becky, but it could wait.

The judge stood at one of the kitchen counters and finished his pancakes and eggs quickly. He drank half of his coffee and then said he'd return the cup later before walking out of the kitchen.

Finn offered to do the dishes, and Vivian was surprised when Robert brought his empty plate back and said he could help with the washing up.

"I haven't eaten so well in a long time," he offered by way of explanation after Vivian looked at him quizzically.

"We all have things to be thankful for," Vivian said.

"I surely do," Robert said. "I surely do."

The man looked pensive, and Vivian was tempted to ask him what he meant, but there were so many other problems to fret about right now.

The kitchen emptied quickly. Even Finn and Robert went out to the area the judge has set aside. They wanted to reserve a seat for themselves for when they finished the dishes. Finally, there was only Vivian and Craig left.

Vivian untied the apron she'd been wearing and walked over to the peg to hang it back where it had been. She'd already moved the tips she'd received from the pocket in her apron to the velvet purse she wore attached to her belt.

Vivian adjusted her bag so it was secure and then turned around to see Craig watching her. He was quiet and his eyes were focused.

He seemed to be waiting for her to say something and so she did. "I suppose you know I was showing what I can do in the way of breakfast just in case the bartender wants to—"

"He already told me you have the job if you want it," Craig said, his tone even but his voice tense for all that.

"Well, he should be speaking to me about that," Vivian protested. She felt her face blush, though, and she reached up to adjust her hat and veil. She was appalled that she had not thought to do so earlier. She didn't know why it was that, when she was around

Craig, she kept forgetting to check to be sure her scars did not show.

Craig was still looking at her. "Bill, the bartender, thought you were going to be my wife. Dry Gulch told him you were a mail-order bride who'd come to marry me."

"Oh," Vivian said. "But I'm not now—a mail-order bride, that is. At least, not exactly."

"I know," Craig said. "But Bill didn't want to cause trouble between us. He's a good man. I've been trying to get him to come to church on Sunday. Reverend Thompson has a church out by where we live. I told Bill he's welcome to come and spend Saturday night in the barn with Finn if he wants."

"I expect he's working most Saturday nights," Vivian said.

"Says he's hiring someone to take over for him one night a week so he can get some sleep," Craig said. "Said it might as well be Saturday night."

"Well, then," Vivian said.

Craig nodded. "We'd better get out to the judge's corner."

Craig didn't move, though, and she didn't, either.

"Maybe we could say a prayer before we go," Craig said.

"I'd like that," Vivian said as she took the hand he held out.

They bowed their heads.

"Father," Craig prayed aloud. "You know what is happening today. We pray you give the judge your wisdom. Help the children to know how much they are loved. Be with us all. Amen."

Vivian nodded.

They walked together back to the main part of the saloon, and Craig did not release her hand until they made a turn and came to several old army blankets that hung from a rod. They were held up by a series of strings connecting pegs in the ceiling. Vivian didn't get a good look at how the blankets floated so evenly but decided she'd come study it later. The girls might like something like that in the loft. Craig let go of her hand so he could brush aside the blankets. Then they walked to the other side.

"Oh," Vivian said in surprise. There were two small windows on the far side of the room, but they didn't give much light. And there had to be sixty people in the crowded space. Only a handful of them were women. Two of them were dressed like she would expect saloon girls to be attired. One had a startling bright purple feather in her hair. Another had a dress that sparkled. She noticed Katy and Becky had turned in their seats on the front bench and were looking at the two women with interest. The girls both stood up and started walking closer to the back of the room where the women were sitting. Vivian quickly stepped over to steer them back to her and Craig. She smiled at the two women, hopefully showing she was not opposed to them being here. She just didn't want the judge to think Craig didn't keep a close eye on his children. Of course, he might not even be looking at the children. She glanced up to the plank platform where the judge sat at a table. A set of stairs off to the side led up to the low stage. The judge not only wasn't searching for the children, he was looking down and adjusting the sleeves on his long black robe.

"I didn't expect the robe," she said quietly to Craig.

"The judge likes a bit of drama," Craig said with a smile. "He feels it give his position more authority if he dresses the part."

Vivian nodded. She supposed the man was right. The courtroom was certainly equipped to look impressive. The United States flag sat on the platform behind the judge's table.

"There's so many people," Becky whispered to her.

Vivian reached down to pull Becky closer since she seemed a little nervous.

Katy was excited, though.

"Lots and lots of people," Katy added, her eyes wide with wonder. Vivian asked herself if this was the most people Katy had ever seen in her young life. Finally, Katy stopped looking and fixed her gaze on the judge. She turned to Vivian. "What's a judge?"

Vivian glanced up at Craig.

"You can do the honors and answer," he said with a grin, like it was a dare.

So, she squatted down until she was level with Katy.

"Is he a dancer?" Katy asked in growing excitement before Vivian could speak. "I've never seen a dancer. I think they wear robes like that sometimes. They have big feet, though." Katy stretched to stand taller. "I can't see his feet. Are they big?"

"He's not a dancer," Vivian assured her. "He's probably closer to a constable."

"A stable?" Katy frowned trying to figure out the word the only way she could. "Like in the barn?"

"No, not a constable," Vivian said as her brain scrambled for what kind of people Katy knew—which wasn't many except for the characters in her book. "Maybe more like a king."

Katy gasped in pleasure and her eyes went wide. "The father of a princess?"

Vivian looked over at Craig and saw his grin widen.

"Well, I don't know if he has any children," Vivian admitted, returning her attention to Katy. "But he's like a father, because he only wants the best to happen to all the children. You don't need to be afraid of him. Or be nervous that he means you harm."

"He knows how to rule the kingdom," Katy said confidently. "Unless the other dancers stop him 'cause they're jealous."

"I don't think there are any dancers around here," Vivian said as she stood up. She didn't know where Katy got her ideas. *Please, Lord*, she added silently, *give the judge wisdom and let him know how to rule in this situation.*

"What happened to the king's crown?" Katy asked with a frown. "Did he lose it?"

"He doesn't need a crown," Vivian answered. "He can rule without it."

Katy's face stayed crunched in a frown, like she wasn't sure.

Vivian looked up at Craig.

"Katy likes things to have all the parts," Craig explained. "You'll learn that when you've read her a few stories. She wants details—the right details."

Vivian rolled her eyes at Craig and he smiled.

And then Katy tugged on her sleeve.

"There were kings in the Bible, too," Katy said as she reached out and took Becky's hand. "I don't think they always wore their crowns, either. Sometimes they fought battles without them."

With that, the two girls went back to the front benches where the reverend and his wife were sitting. The older couple moved closer together so there was room for both girls next to them.

"Maybe someday Katy will know more people than the ones in her storybook," Craig said pensively. "She'd like that."

"She's only four years old," Vivian protested. "She has enough people and places to see right now with you. She has time to see the world later."

"Thanks," Craig said. "I'm not sure it's true, but thanks. I can't imagine my life without them, but I don't want to hold them back."

Together, they started walking toward the front.

Along the way, Vivian could tell that the number of spectators had grown since breakfast. Even the men she did not recognize nodded and bobbed their heads to her. Four long benches were lined up on each side of the aisle.

Finn stood and waved Vivian and Craig over to the front bench.

Once they were seated, Finn leaned down and whispered to them. "Save room for me and Robert. We're going to go back and tackle those dishes, but we'll be finished before too much can happen."

With that, the two men hurried away.

Vivian resisted the urge to grab Craig's hand. It was not rightfully her battle, but she cared deeply what happened to these children of his. He was a good father, she told herself. That should be enough for him to keep his children.

She glanced over and saw a muscle in his jaw move. And then she felt his hand searching for hers. He found it and held it close.

They were almost friends, she told herself. Of course, he would feel they were in this together. All was as it should be.

And then the judge raised his gavel and brought it down on the table. His face was so solemn if made her anxious. What was the man planning to do?

She glanced over at Craig. It was clear he didn't know what was going to happen, either.

Chapter Five

"Court is in session," the judge proclaimed, and Craig felt the sweat break out on his forehead. He'd never been one for playing poker, but he felt like he was in the middle of a high-stakes game and didn't know how his cards would match with the others at the table. His win would be big or his loss devastating. His children were what he worked for. They owned his heart. He definitely had more on the table than he could afford to lose.

"The lawyers will take their respective places," the judge declared, and Craig watched his lawyer seat himself at a side table on the main floor. Craig had not been able to talk to the man since he'd read the letter changing the date by which Mrs. Hunt could come to Cheyenne, but Craig hoped his lawyer would argue that it was not fair—nor legal. He wasn't sure what else he had to stand on now that his marriage to Delores was in question.

Across the room, another lawyer was seating himself. He looked more confident than Craig's lawyer, and that didn't put Craig at ease. Though the judge was not generally impressed with credentials.

"Because this is a civil and not a criminal case," the judge continued, "I am going to have the principals in the case introduce themselves to the court." He looked out into the audience. "Is Mrs. Margaret Hunt present?"

Mrs. Hunt rose up proudly. "Yes, Your Honor."

Craig figured the judge would be pleased with her. She was not all frilly and feminine like someone given to vapors and moods. Instead, she stood straight-backed, looking out at the audience like a general surveying her troops. Dressed in a wool navy suit with gold braiding along her shoulders, she had neatly pulled back her slightly graying brown hair in a serviceable bun. Under the brim of her hat, he could see her face was unlined and she looked remarkably youthful for a woman of her years. The braiding wasn't the only gold she wore, either. She had a brooch that looked expensive enough to feed an army for a year—maybe more than that if one considered the dismal rations the soldiers were said to have been fed in the recent War Between the States.

When Mrs. Hunt turned to face the judge, Craig saw that the crown of her navy hat was circled with some kind of a gold chain that he'd guess was real. If she had wanted to sway the judge in her favor, Craig suspected she had done so. It was clear that she had dignity and money.

"Mrs. Hunt," the judge continued. "I know you

have brought this case as the grandmother of the two children involved. Do you have anyone present who could speak to your character?"

"But I didn't know to bring someone," Mrs. Hunt said, suddenly flustered. "Although I would think my character is obvious to everyone."

She turned to look at her lawyer. He shrugged his shoulders and shook his head. Then, apparently giving up on him, she searched the audience frantically, as though hoping to see someone she hadn't expected to be there. The room was silent for several moments while she scrutinized every face. Craig wondered if he should run to the kitchen and bring Robert back.

Finally, Dry Gulch surprised everyone by standing up and taking off his fur cap—which left his hair flying wildly. He lifted a hand to press it all down and then cleared his throat. "I reckon as I know her better than anyone else here after carrying her over my back for what must have been five miles if it was anything. And through a freezing cold blizzard at that—"

"Really, Mr.—" Mrs. Hunt tried to stop the man. Her face was flushed, and Craig knew she was embarrassed. "It's not like you had to carry me. I was perfectly able to walk."

Dry Gulch snorted. "Not in those shoes, you weren't. You would have lost all your toes to frostbite."

"My toes!" Mrs. Hunt exclaimed as she poked her foot out from beneath her dress and looked down at it.

"Those lady shoes of yours aren't worth anything here in the snow," he said. "After five miles in that freezing ice, your toes might have turned black and fallen off."

"No!" Mrs. Hunt looked up, aghast.

By now, the men on the benches were poking each other and whispering. In resignation, Craig figured they should have sold tickets for this show. He supposed Mrs. Hunt was his enemy in all of this, but he meant her no harm. He didn't like seeing her ridiculed, even if Dry Gulch wasn't intending to do that.

"Despite that—" Dry Gulch cleared his throat and continued "—I have to say on her behalf that Margaret here is a stout, hearty woman. Reminds me of my own dear mother, Red Rosy."

Craig could see the men at the side of him nodding their heads solemnly. At least the chuckling had stopped. They all clearly respected Red Rosy. He thought Mrs. Hunt was going to faint, though. Her face had gone from pink to purple, so he wondered if maybe she wouldn't erupt instead.

"Many of you knew my mother," Dry Gulch continued. "A finer woman—"

"Enough," Mrs. Hunt bellowed as she slapped her hands over her ears and then moaned. "Enough. Enough."

The judge must have agreed. "You may sit down now, Mrs. Hunt."

"I'm nothing like that Red woman, your honor," Mrs. Hunt said before she did as the judge requested and reluctantly sat down.

"And Dry Gulch," the judge continued speaking to the man who was still standing. "As you know, your mother saved my parents in that bad winter ten years ago. The blizzards stopped even the regular freight wagons from coming through. There was no railroad connection then, and I had no way to get back to Cheyenne. My parents told me later they had been out of food. Your mother had a big heart, and she provided for them and some of the other families that were caught with nothing to eat. She used her own money, but you were the one who hitched up some mules and went to Denver to bring back food for the lot of them. I can never thank both of you enough. I will enter your recommendation as to Mrs. Hunt's character as positive in the case file."

Craig almost shook his head. Delores's mother clearly didn't know whether to accept the good words Dry Gulch had said on her behalf or to stick with her pride. In the end, she simply nodded to the judge when he asked if that was acceptable.

"We will proceed to Craig Martin, the father of the two children," the judge announced. "Many of you know him."

Craig expected Mrs. Hunt to object to him being called the children's father, but she didn't. She probably needed time to rest before speaking again.

Reverend Thompson stood up and cleared his throat. "Craig Martin is a good Christian man. He, along with his brother, have been part of my congregation for six years now, first in Cheyenne and then now at my church near the old Crow Creek. He practically raised his brother, and Finn has become a good young man who will soon be setting up his own homestead when he turns twenty-one years old. I know Craig loves his children and will do good by them, too."

The reverend sat down, and no one said anything for a moment.

"He's my daddy," Katy stood up then and repeated in a clear voice. "I'm glad he's my daddy."

"Thank you, dear," the judge said kindly. "I will have more questions for you and your brother later, but you can sit down now."

Craig had kept Vivian's hand in his, so he was not prepared for the loss when she moved her hand away until he saw she had stood up.

"My name is Vivian Eastman," she stated. "I came to Cheyenne recently to—well, that's not important— I just want to tell you that Mr. Martin is indeed a good father. And he's the bravest man I know. Why, he's a hero. He saved my life in a fire in New York City some years ago. Not many men would have done that. I am confident that the children would always be safe with him. And, he has made a lovely, lovely home for them."

Craig was struck speechless. He was no hero. He needed to tell Vivian the whole story of that night of the fire, but—he looked around—he couldn't do it right now. He hadn't missed the fact that Vivian had made no mention of her scars. He didn't want to embarrass her. No, this conversation required a private moment.

And then he saw Finn in the back of the room, looking as uncomfortable as Craig felt. Neither one of them had been proud of what happened that night in the fires.

Craig turned back to the front of the room as he heard Mrs. Hunt muttering something.

"That house is *not* lovely," Mrs. Hunt declared forcefully as she started to stand. She had obviously recovered and was back to her commanding self. "Why, the walls are made of dirt—dirt! He could just as well dig a hole in the ground and call it a palace. And, he goes so far as to have heathen symbols all over. That can't be good for his children. He's not raising them to be Christians, that's for sure. He even reads them stories about frogs and princesses."

Craig was shocked and more than a little confused.

He heard Katy's soft gasp, too, from where she sat on the other side of Vivian.

He'd acknowledge that his walls were dirt, but— "My children are not being raised to be heathens, and you know that. I take them to church and I read the Bible to them every afternoon before they have their nap and—" Suddenly, Craig realized what she was aiming at. "Remember, you gave them that storybook. Well, you gave it to Delores, who left it for the children. I read that book to them in the evenings because it reminds us all of their mother. I'll not say that is wrong."

"I doubt that is the book I gave to my little Delores," Mrs. Hunt retorted as she faced Craig. "That was a long time ago, but I don't remember any imaginary animals in it. As I recall, the first story is about a sweet old woman who takes care of orphans. I'm sure she'd be the perfect example of a loving grand-mother."

"You mean the woman with the shoe?" Katy asked from where she sat on the bench. Craig looked over and saw his daughter wrinkle her nose. "I didn't like her. She had all of those children and didn't know what to do. She wouldn't make a very good grand-mother." Then she studied Mrs. Hunt. "Would you know what to do with all those little children?"

A wave of friendly laughter ran through the room.

"I'm sure she's a perfectly fine woman," Mrs. Hunt protested, glaring down at Katy. "Those children should be grateful they had someone willing to provide for them. They didn't live in a no-account town in a hole in the ground."

The room went totally silent at that. No one seemed to know what to say, and then the sound of glass shattering came from the other side of the saloon. Following that, the air erupted with a vicious bark, followed by a snarling, snapping meow. The echoes of those sounds hadn't faded when a sharp yip of pain rang out.

"Kitty!" Katy shouted as she jumped up from her seat on the bench.

Craig reached out to catch his daughter, but she was too fast for him. She was racing toward the blankets that separated the rooms. By the time Craig was up and running, Katy had disappeared through the folds in that makeshift wall.

It sounded like an army of hard-booted men were following Craig into the front of the saloon, and he was grateful for them when he reached the other side and saw the scene in front of him.

"Katy, don't move," Craig commanded quietly. A disheveled Katy, in her pretty new dress, had crouched down beside the old tomcat, who was spitting defiantly at a large dog standing there. The canine was tall as a late-spring calf. Craig glanced around and didn't see any man who claimed the dog, so it must have been a stray. It looked hungry, and the cat's dish still held a few scraps of toast, no doubt left over from breakfast.

"Scoot back close to me," Craig directed Katy.

Craig heard light footsteps come up behind him and glanced over to see Vivian.

"What can I do?" she asked quietly.

"Be ready to take Katy from me," Craig whispered back. Then he looked over at the bartender, who was standing there with his mouth open in surprise. Craig turned to him. "Do you have another slice of bread for the dog?"

The bartender shook his head. "Everything I had was used for breakfast. We wouldn't have had those old crusts if Sammy Goodnight had had better teeth. He can't hardly eat anything anymore." The bartender stopped. "No milk left, either. I do have whiskey. And beer."

"Any other scraps of food at all?" Craig asked as he inched closer to Katy. Normally obedient, she must have reached some limit, because she hadn't come. Instead, she sat with her hand on her furry friend's arched back and did nothing to stop the tears streaming down her face. She looked up at Craig, her eyes filled with misery. "Kitty's in trouble," she said.

"We'll help him," Craig whispered as he moved closer yet. He wanted to be near enough to grab her up and into his arms. Then he'd see about corralling the stubborn tomcat. The fierce little beast didn't know when to make a retreat, and Craig wasn't so sure Kitty would relish being rescued.

"That mutt might like a bit of coffee," Craig said, loud enough for everyone to hear. "If he's a miner's dog, he's drunk plenty of that before."

A few men snorted and then laughed.

"I do have some cold coffee back here," the bartender muttered as he turned to the counter behind him. "I'll just put it in a saucer for the animal. Looks like a wolfhound to me."

Craig was in place now. He wanted to distract the two combatants before he grabbed Katy. That tomcat might protest the sudden movement, not knowing Craig's actions were to help. And no one knew what that dog would do.

"Wolfhound, you say." Craig said smoothly as he kept his eyes on the strange animal. "That would make you Irish, m'boy. Did you know I'm Irish, too? No wonder you're hungry. Seems like we always are now. You mind your manners here and I'll see what kind of grub I can find for you."

The dog cocked his head at Craig, seeming to like the talk.

"You're probably just cold and tired," Craig continued, making his words sound sympathetic. And, the truth was, he did feel sorry for the mutt. He didn't know how the animal survived in this kind of a winter.

Then he looked down and Robbie was scrunched down beside him, looking like he was assessing the danger himself. Craig knew he had to move before the boy decided to take action.

"Poor old d-doggie," Robbie said, continuing Craig's conversation.

Robbie's voice was high and young. The mutt moved to stare at the boy, and that was the moment Craig was waiting for. He reached out and grabbed Katy around her waist, lifting her up high. It wasn't until he had her high enough to see that he realized Katy had wrapped her arms around the cat as he'd started to lift her. Now he had his daughter ready to give to Vivian, but there was a hissing cat attached to the bundle.

Craig looked over at Vivian.

She nodded. "I'll take them. I have my gloves on."

The dog was growling now, seeing that his opponent was out of reach, so Craig had no choice. He handed Katy to Vivian, deliberately knocking the cat back to the floor as he did so. The cat landed on his feet with a huff and an indignant scowl for Craig.

The dog took a step toward the old tom and started to sway. Craig realized then that it was in no shape to fight. It was almost passing out from hunger. The animal's ribs were apparent even though its dark grayish hair was thick for winter.

"Here now," the bartender said as he quietly set another saucer on the floor and pushed it within reach of the animal.

The dog didn't even hesitate. It stumbled over to the saucer and began to lap up the coffee.

Craig turned and stepped close to Vivian. He wrapped his arms around her and Katy and then, missing Robbie, noticed the boy wasn't where he had been.

"Where...?" Craig said as he twisted slightly only to see that Robbie had settled himself close to the dog and was petting it.

"Robbie?" Craig called to his son softly. He didn't want to make any sudden sounds or moves that would take the dog's attention away from the saucer that was emptying too quickly for Craig's peace of mind.

Robbie looked up. "It's okay, D-Daddy. The doggie is j-just scared. He's not a b-bad boy. And, if he b-brings dirt in the house, he can s-stay out in the barn. I'll stay with him."

"No one's staying in the barn," Craig replied. The dog had finished the saucer of coffee and did seem to have given up the fight. It looked very content lying there and being petted by Robbie.

"The dog can't come home with us though." Craig knew he had to make that clear. "He must belong to someone, and they will miss him."

"We can take him home until the sheriff tells us they've found him," Robbie countered reasonably. "He won't be any trouble. I'll feed him and pet him."

Craig hesitated. There was no point in waiting for

the dog's owner when it was clear the animal had been abandoned.

"I'm sure the bartender will give the dog a good home," Craig said with a pleading glance at the man. "I can pay for all the food it eats." *Within reason*, Craig added to himself.

"Now, we need to go back," Craig said as his heart went back to its normal beat. "We need to talk some more to the judge."

"But I want us all to go home," Katy wailed from her place in Vivian's arms. "Can't we just go home? I don't like the mean dogs here."

Craig walked over to Vivian and opened his arms to Katy. She leaned over to him and laid her cheek on his shoulder before he took her completely. Then he rubbed her back until the tears stopped.

Craig carried Katy back into the judge's side of the room, and Robbie followed them, carrying Kitty. Vivian seemed to herd them all toward their benches. They settled down, and the benches behind them filled.

Finally, the judge cleared his throat and shuffled a couple of papers on the table. Then he looked out at the audience.

"I want to talk to the children now," he announced.

Craig noticed Mrs. Hunt's lawyer starting to rise, likely to object, but she shook her head at him slightly, and he sat down again.

"Will Robbie Martin and Katy Martin come up to the table here?" the judge asked.

Craig was still holding Katy on his lap, and he felt her stiffen.

"The judge is a nice man," Craig whispered in her ear. "You don't need to be afraid of him. Just answer his questions the best you can. Can you do that?"

Katy nodded her head. "Who's going to protect Kitty while I'm gone? Maybe that dog will come in here."

"Robbie is going to bring Kitty over to me," Craig said. "You'll be able to see that he's safe. I won't let anything bad happen to him while you're talking to the judge."

Katy nodded again and then crawled off of his lap.

The whole room stirred as heads craned to see the children.

"Thank you for thinking of those clothes," Craig leaned over and whispered to Vivian. "It's too bad they got them dirty crawling around on the floor with that cat and dog."

Craig knew how women were about cleanliness. He regretted now that he had not told the children to wear their old clothes until just before they were called to speak to the judge.

"A little dust—and that's what it is, really—isn't important," Vivian declared. "They both stood up for other hurting beings, and you should be proud of their good hearts. I think the judge is smart enough to make allowances for their clothes."

"I think so, too," Craig said softly. He had to admit to himself, though, that he was surprised that a society lady like Vivian would be so tolerant. Mrs. Hunt would not be. He could see her from where he sat, and she was frowning as she watched the children. He wouldn't be surprised if she spoke up and demanded they return to their seats until they could get the dirt off of themselves. But then, even she would not defy the judge.

Robbie walked up the steps first. Then, from his greater height, he looked down to where Katy still stood. He motioned for her to come, and she did. Together, they walked over to the judge and his table. When the children reached him, the man stood and lifted each of them up to sit on the edge of the table.

Then he turned to those on the benches and said, "This is just between me and the children. I'm going to ask them to speak quietly so no one can hear what they say except for me."

Craig watched as half of the men behind him stood up to stretch and walk out into the other part of the saloon. This was the intermission in the play for them. And, like as not, they wanted to see if anyone had claimed that dog. Then a number of the men would order a drink in hopes that the bartender would comply and the judge would not notice. If they had two drinks, they'd likely know better than to come back into the courtroom.

His eyes kept drifting back to his two children, though.

"They'll be fine," Vivian muttered from where she sat on his left side.

Craig nodded and forced another smile. "The judge

probably just wants to know what they had for breakfast."

"Robbie will tell him all about how to make toast," Vivian said with a smile.

Craig nodded. He realized she didn't need to say anything else. She was one hundred percent on his side. Apart from Finn and, long ago, his mother, this was the first time he could remember having someone support him with no questions asked.

He wasn't sure what the judge's decision today would be, but he did know he had a friend sitting next to him who cared.

Vivian kept forgetting about adjusting her veil. She had been so caught up in the battle with the animals and now with the expression on Craig's face that she'd forgotten about keeping her scars covered. Fortunately, there were lots of shadows in the saloon, so her face wasn't clear most of the time. All of the men here who said they were so grateful for breakfast would turn away from her if they got a good look at what she really looked like. She could feel the weight in her purse of the coins the men had given her as tips for the meal—that was in addition to the payments they'd made to the bartender for the food itself. She was beginning to think this was the job she wanted. She didn't want her face to interfere with that. She hadn't counted the money, but it would provide for her and Becky for a few days at least—maybe even a week if she was frugal.

Vivian carefully adjusted her veil, anchoring her hair pins securely.

Becky was sitting beside the reverend and his wife, and the girl half rose off of the bench when she saw what Vivian was doing, but Vivian waved her back. She could handle the veil herself.

A tiny giggle came from the stage where the judge sat, and she looked up. Katy was sitting there explaining something to the judge. Remembering that Katy had just been in tears, Vivian marveled at how the girl could change in a moment. Now her arms were waving this way and that way, so Vivian figured she was well into her story. And then Vivian heard the words *bride* and *Christmas* and *king*. The judge was grinning and Robbie was even nodding along, so Vivian knew the story was keeping them interested. She wondered if the word *princess* had been mentioned, but, if it had been, she hadn't heard it.

The children and the judge were all smiles when he sent them back to their benches. Vivian glanced over and saw the sour look on Mrs. Hunt's face. She felt sorry for the older woman, but she couldn't imagine the children would be happy living with her. Mrs. Hunt wanted something from the children. Vivian was sure of that. But Vivian wasn't sure the older woman wanted their happiness.

Then the men were filing back into the courtroom and were noisy. Two of them had even started to sing a song. The judge lifted his gavel and brought it down on the table sharply. "Order. There will be order in the court."

The men all looked guilty and settled into their seats on the benches. It was silent.

"I now call Craig Martin and Vivian Eastman up to my table," the judge said solemnly. "Again, we will talk quietly and privately."

The grumbling was clear to hear again. Finally, one man yelled up at the judge, "We missed out on what the kids said, but we don't want to miss what the mail-order bride says. That's our business, too. If she don't have a hankering for Big Craig, she might want one of us."

"Yeah, who's she going to marry?" another man called out.

"I'm not running a matrimonial service," the judge snapped back. "If you want to marry the bride, ask her."

"What?" Vivian said, her voice squeaking. She had already risen from the bench and was preparing to walk over to the stairs.

"You just want to keep her fer yourself," another man scolded loudly from the back of the room. "After eating that fine breakfast, I—"

"Mrs. Hunt helped with that breakfast, too," Vivian turned to say to the men. "In fact, I'd say she was the most important cook. She'd make some man a wonderful wife."

"Me?" Mrs. Hunt was looking up in panic. "Married to—"

Vivian nodded with a grin. "I want to give praise where it's due."

"But—" Mrs. Hunt started to say something, but

then she turned to look behind where she'd been sitting and stared in horror. A few dozen men were making their way toward her with determined looks on their faces—at least it looked that way, but it was hard to tell since they all had bushy beards.

"Oh," Vivian gasped. She hadn't meant for this to happen—at least not with so many men. She was even alarmed. Not one of those men looked like he'd had a bath in the last year. Nor a proper shave in half that time.

"I forgot she burnt the toast," Vivian called out in an effort to spare the older woman. Then she remembered that Robbie had made the toast, and she didn't want any confusion. "In New York, it was. Years ago."

Mrs. Hunt's son told her that his mother had almost set the house on fire the only time she tried cooking breakfast. The horde of men didn't break rank at her words. They didn't look like they would have cared what Mrs. Hunt had charred.

Vivian didn't know what else to do. She turned to look at Craig. He was looking worried, too.

"We need to—" Craig began and then stopped.

Vivian looked down and saw that Dry Gulch had turned to see what was happening. He quickly put his arm around Mrs. Hunt's shoulders and moved her closer to him. The older woman didn't look happy, but she didn't complain. Then Dry Gulch gave a level look that Vivian could not see to the men heading toward them. They were all standing tall, and Dry Gulch was sitting on the bench. But he stopped them cold. Whatever it was, it had the men gulping and stammering and finally turning around in defeat.

Relieved, Vivian hurried to the short set of stairs as fast as she could, the heels on her shoes making a tapping sound on the wooden floor as she went. Craig was beside her all of the way, and she was grateful for that. Vivian figured they would both rather face the judge than the belligerent men who were now standing at the back of the room grumbling to each other. Vivian wondered if the men would have still backed off if they'd known how much money the widowed Mrs. Hunt would bring with her to a marriage.

The judge invited both Craig and Vivian to sit on the table, facing him, like Robbie and Katy had done earlier. Vivian hadn't sat like that in years, and she let her feet swing free like she had as a child.

"Let's talk," the judge said as he stood up so he was level with them. Vivian was glad the judge had turned his attention to Craig first. She didn't know what she could say to make the situation better.

"Before we go any further," the judge said to Craig. "I need to ask if you knew Delores was already married when you exchanged vows with her."

Vivian felt a jolt. It had never occurred to her that Craig would have acted in any way dishonorably in all of that confusion.

"No, of course not," Craig said, his voice shocked. "I knew she was waiting for the man who was Robbie's father, but she never indicated that they were married. Quite the opposite, in fact. And, when he never showed up, I assumed he was either dead or had changed his mind about coming for her." Craig paused. "I don't think she even mentioned that they were thinking of a wedding. I assumed she had probably been hoping he would make her his wife now since they'd had the baby, but she never mentioned it."

"You expect me to believe you married her without asking about the man who had fathered her son?" the judge demanded to know.

Craig winced. "I never said it had been a sensible thing to do. I'll admit I didn't want to know about that other man. I was still so amazed she agreed to have dinner with me that first day she stepped off the stage. A lot of men were inviting her to join then. But she only ever ate with me. I thought she was starting to care about me—when she singled me out like she did. I decided to let the past stay the past. That man could have been dead for all I knew. Besides, the Bible calls us to forgive each other. I thought, in time, she would love me as much as I was coming to love her."

The judge nodded. "Yes, well, I suppose you're not the first man to rush into things without getting all the facts."

Vivian straightened her spine. She knew how fickle men were about marriage. She remembered the days when she was receiving proposals and how quickly the men withdrew them after she'd had her accident with the fire. Ethan Hunt had been the main example of someone who had been hot turning cold. But she'd never considered that the same could be said about women. Even if Delores believed Robert was dead or not coming back, she had no right to pretend Craig had had her heart when he clearly hadn't.

Vivian wondered if the judge was thinking the same thing.

"You do believe Robert is Robbie's father, though?" the judge asked Craig. Vivian could see he was hitting all of the important points.

"I don't think there's much doubt about that," Craig said. "Having been around him some, I do think Delores would be attracted to a man like that. A gambler. Charming. Someone who lived on the edge. And, from what Mrs. Hunt said, Delores and Robert knew each other while they lived in New York City. So, it makes sense that they got married and she hid the truth from me. I never did know what was happening in her mind."

The judge was silent for a minute, obviously debating something. "Did you or Delores ever tell Robbie that you weren't his father?"

"I sure didn't." Craig looked appalled. "I don't think she ever said anything. Robbie would have surely said something to me. And I certainly never saw him as anything but my son."

Vivian felt uneasy with that answer. What little she knew of Craig's late wife indicated the woman would tell Robbie something like that—thinking she was getting even with Craig and not realizing, or not caring, how harmful it would be to her son. The fact that Robbie had never said anything to Craig might indicate only how deep that hurt could go.

"It will be something of a shock to the boy," the judge continued.

Craig nodded "He very likely is questioning who his father is. Robert and Mrs. Hunt have hinted at their relationship, but haven't said anything direct."

"He hasn't asked you about it?" the judge asked Craig.

"No." Craig shook his head. "Usually, Robbie needs to take time to think about things before he's ready to talk. I'll make a point to spend some time with him when we get home—just the two of us."

The judge stepped away from Vivian and Craig, his attention captured by the back of the room. Vivian twisted around to see, too. The place was partially empty. The children were all sitting on the bench with the reverend and his wife.

Vivian's heart went out to Robbie and Katy. They sat there silently; their hands tightly clasped together. They looked anxious. And then she saw Robert come back into the room. That wolfhound was following behind him, and the sight made Vivian nervous. The dog didn't appear to be asking for a fight, though.

"Robbie needs to know the man, at least a little." Craig must have seen him enter as well. "I don't know how he'd adjust if—" He didn't continue.

Vivian understood that he couldn't say the words.

The judge nodded, too. "Some days, I feel like Solomon. There is not always an obvious answer as to what is best."

"You've always been a fair-minded man," Craig said, his voice low.

The expression on Craig's face was so bleak that Vivian had to reach out and touch his hand. When she did, she felt his palm open and enclose her smaller hand.

When Vivian looked up, she saw the judge looking at her quizzically.

"The children are somewhat confused," the judge said to Vivian. "They think you came to be a mail-order bride for their daddy—and to be their mother—even if you're not a princess, although you have princess hair." The judge's eyes twinkled. "I must say they are delightful children. But they also say you want to get a job cooking breakfast for these men." The judge waved his arms to include the men at the back of the room. "Do those sweet children have the right of it?"

Vivian heard a shift in the muffled sounds of the men behind her. It had been a low hum, but more men must have come back to the benches, because the volume rose.

Vivian concentrated on the judge and nodded to him. Without thinking, she replied at a normal volume. "I'll admit I did set out from Boston in answer to a mail-order bride ad, but I decided on the train ride here that I want to marry for love and not convenience. And I was just offered the job as breakfast cook here. So, yes, I am likely to take a job."

A loud whistle from the back of the room was the first sign that she'd forgotten to speak softly. And then Vivian heard a raucous voice call out, "Lady, if you're looking for love, look no further. I'm at your service."

Vivian turned in alarm and faced the men in the benches. They were all grinning and preening like a flock of wild banty roosters, combing back their feathered hair and lifting their chins to show off their beards.

"Stop that," she hissed at the lot of them. "Can't you see we're talking about serious things up here? These little children need to know who's going to be their parent."

The voices grew still. Vivian heard one of the men murmur to everyone, "Poor babies." That seemed to stop the ruckus.

Vivian stopped to swallow and then continued. "With all due respect, Your Honor, I have to add that the children deserve a better life than the one Mrs. Hunt has planned for them. They love their daddy, and Craig is very good with them. I don't see how you can let her have them."

"It is a difficult decision," the judge admitted, nodding his head. "But she does offer some advantages."

Then the man tilted his head and continued to address Vivian. "I understand you have said you'd give the children a party for Epiphany—December 6. Is that right?"

Vivian had forgotten all about that in all of the commotion. "Yes. They missed Christmas, you see, and—"

"Good," the judge said decisively. "You have stated that you want to take the job at the saloon here, but we can get that postponed for a week or so. No one has answered that advertisement for a month, and this time of year, they're not likely to get another applicant. To be safe, I'll ask them to hold it for you, though."

The judge swallowed and continued, "The job I'm hoping you will take, meanwhile, is to stay and be the court's representative at Craig Martin's place. I want those children to have time to get to know their grandmother and for Robbie to become a little comfortable with Robert. You will be the referee. I want you to make sure the children are not bullied or unduly influenced. You'll be paid a good salary of twenty dollars for the nine days. Mrs. Hunt has already agreed to cover expenses in all of this. I've included some for supplies as well. You may as well eat well while we see how this goes."

The judge turned to Craig. "I'll try to make a couple of visits out to your homestead to see how everyone is doing. You'll report to me how everything is working out. We'll meet at the Martin homestead on Friday, January 6. I'll announce my decision after the party. I hope this is all right with you. You're far enough out of town that I think it would be best for Mrs. Hunt and Robert to stay with you at the homestead. Do you think you can manage that?"

Craig nodded. "I want what is best for the children. Both Mrs. Hunt and Robert will be welcome. I do have to tend to my cattle, though, so they'll have to entertain themselves. As for meals—"

"I'll do the cooking," Vivian interrupted him. "It will be good experience for when I work as a breakfast cook. We'll have to stop at the general store before we leave and get supplies."

"I'll pay for the food," Craig said. "They'll stay as my guests. And, you're my guest, too. I don't want you to do the cooking."

"I don't mind," Vivian protested. "I'll want to do some baking for Epiphany anyway."

"Regardless of whether you cook or not, you came out here because of my ad. That makes you my guest. I'm responsible for seeing that you have a pleasant time."

"I came here to save Becky from the workhouse," Vivian said without thinking. And then she saw the shocked expression on Craig's face.

"How?" he asked, his voice sharp.

The judge was frowning, too.

"I should not have said anything," Vivian muttered. "My sister-in-law said she would send Becky there, but she never did, so forget I said anything."

Craig eyed her knowingly. "She never acted on the threat because you had sense enough to get on that train and come to me."

Vivian nodded her head. "My brother wasn't any help, either. He did not have the spine to stand up for what was right. He didn't care what happened to us."

A hero like Craig was so far from the kind of man her brother was that the two wouldn't even be able to agree on anything. Vivian was glad she had answered that bridal agency ad even if she wasn't going to marry Craig. It was still a privilege to have met him and realize not all men were like her brother.

"Well, Vivian, I'm glad you ended up here," the judge said heartily as he looked out at the assembled men. "Folks here might be too boisterous at times, but they mean well. They will treat you and your Becky right."

Vivian nodded. She hoped the judge was right. She and Craig walked back to the benches, and the judge hit his gavel against the table, ending the court session.

The whole room stood and adjusted themselves, ready to leave.

"We get to go home now?" Katy jumped up from the bench and walked over to Craig. She had her cat gripped in her arms.

"We'll have to talk to Bill about that dog first," Craig said as he motioned for Robbie to join them.

"That dog's not nice," Katy said, her lip out. "He tried to hurt my kitty."

"That cat of yours was right in there getting ready to fight, too," Craig said.

Vivian put her hand on the girl's shoulder. Someday, Katy would make a great mother. She would protect a child from anyone.

"I'm sure the dog will be safe now that he's had something to eat," Vivian said, assuming that the bartender had come up with something more substantial than a few scraps to feed the mutt. "Sometimes people are more cranky than ordinary when they are hungry."

Katy seemed to consider Vivian's words. Then

she motioned for Vivian to bend down so she could speak in her ear.

"Is Ga'ma cranky 'cause she's hungry?" Katy whispered.

"I don't know," Vivian said, forcing herself not to chuckle. Then she stood up. "We should go buy some food at the general store so we can fix her dinner, though. Then nobody will have that problem."

Katy nodded solemnly as she opened the curtain between the two sides of the saloon and peeked through it. "I don't see that dog."

Katy sent a grin over her shoulder as she stepped through the divider.

The girl is adorable, Vivian thought to herself as she looked back to see where Craig was. He was in an intense conversation with Robbie, but they would be following shortly. She knew the judge was trusting her to be impartial, but Vivian was going to have a hard time not encouraging the children to stay with their father. No amount of money would give them a better life than being with the man who loved them.

Vivian felt a jump in her heart. A woman might not have a better husband than Craig Martin, either. Not that she was planning on marrying him. He'd been heroic that night in New York, but she couldn't claim it had been personal. He didn't know her at that point. And, although he clearly loved his children; she had seen no indication he felt anything for her, except for that brief kiss on her back. She was sure he would be kind to any wife he had, but she wanted more than impersonal kindness, and he'd given no indication he felt anything more.

No, she'd rather have a job making breakfast for a thousand scruffy miners than marry a man who didn't love her. At least with the miners, she'd know where she stood.

She did look behind her. Craig and Robbie still hadn't come through the blanket wall. She'd take Katy and wait outside for them. They'd be through soon.

Chapter Six

A solemn Robbie walked beside Craig as they made their way toward the curtain that separated the judge's courtroom. Vivian and Katy had already gone through a few minutes earlier and were probably outside by now. Voices were coming from the other side as well as gusts of cold air that indicated the main door had been opened several times.

"We can give some money to Bill at the bar to feed the dog," Craig assured the boy as they neared the opening to the main room of the saloon. Robbie had wanted to take the dog home with them, and Craig had said no. "And we will ask about you coming to visit the dog when we get to Cheyenne next."

"Thanks." Robbie's voice was flat and his shoulders slumped.

"The dog is wild," Craig continued as he opened the curtain. "He probably has his favorite places to sleep and everything. He might not like it in our house."

"He could stay in the barn," Robbie offered. "With me."

"It's too cold for you out there," Craig said. Finn and Robert had fashioned warm beds in the straw, but Robbie was little. His body heat would leave faster than that of the men.

Robbie slipped through the opening, but he didn't answer.

Craig stepped through the blankets, too, before letting them close behind him. He felt guilty. Robbie asked for so little, and he'd wanted a dog even before Katy got her kitty. But, at least, the cat scared the mice away. Craig was unsure what a dog could do that would justify his care. And he didn't trust a wild dog with Robbie any more than he trusted that old tomcat with Katy.

"We'll see about getting you a tame dog," Craig said. He put his hand on Robbie's shoulder as they stepped inside the saloon. He wasn't about to let the boy stroll through there unprotected.

"I w-want this dog," Robbie said.

"Oh," Craig said. The room was darker this side of the curtain and smelled of alcohol and tobacco smoke. The plank flooring had been scuffed with work boots and scraped from fights. The windows were frosted over, but the dirt showed plain on them. For the first time, Craig understood why the judge wore that robe. It was important for people to respect the law. The saloon didn't help that feeling.

Craig decided he'd call together some of the home-steaders and find a way to get more wood and coal for the stoves at the church. The community needed to show it respected the courts and the law if they expected the children to be raised to do the same. The church would have more dignity than this place. And they needed to build a school, too.

Already, dozens of miners were milling around in the saloon, trying to arrange themselves into friendly groups. The entertainment for the day was over, but they weren't ready to go back to their diggings. Craig didn't blame them. It was too cold to work anyway. Several of the men were getting set to play checkers. A table of six sat there arguing about something. Their coats were ragged; their hats had holes in them, sometimes from what looked like bullets.

Robbie stopped and Craig nudged him forward with a gentle pressure on his shoulder. He wanted them both to get out in the fresh air even if that they would be cold. But the boy didn't move. Instead, Craig felt the muscles in Robbie's back bunch up to resist going forward.

"I don't s-see him," Robbie spoke.

"Who?" Craig asked although he suspected.

"The d-dog."

"The bartender likely has him in the back room," Craig said. That's what he'd do with a wild animal anyway. "The mutt probably doesn't like so many people around."

Robbie nodded. "I d-don't, either."

Craig recognized his mistake. He didn't want Robbie to think the dog was like him. Robbie was a mild-mannered boy; that wolfhound was a raging beast—at least when he was hungry. They had nothing in common. But, then, if Robbie saw the dog again, he might understand that.

Craig was tall enough to look over the heads of some of the men so he could see Bill standing behind his counter, waiting for the next drink orders. Craig motioned for the man to meet them at the end of the counter.

"Let's go see the dog," Craig said.

At that news, Robbie happily started to walk.

Craig managed to dodge most of the drinking men, and soon he and Robbie were standing at the corner of the counter. Bill had a dish towel draped over his shoulder and he was clearly doing good business.

"Robbie here wants to see the dog," Craig said when he got close enough. "Is he in the back room?"

Bill shook his head. "He's gone."

"Gone?" Craig was surprised. "Did he run away?"

The dog was feral enough to just shoot out the door if it took the notion into its head. Craig hoped Robbie knew enough about animals to understand they did not all like to be enclosed.

But the bartender was shaking his head. "One of the men that came in with you took the dog."

"That came in with me?" Craig asked. The bartender knew Finn, the reverend and Dry Gulch. Craig didn't remember any strange men that the bartender wouldn't know entering the saloon around the same time as they did, but there had been so much confusion that it was possible.

"The d-dog wouldn't leave," Robbie said, his voice

cracking. He was close to tears. "He knew I'd be b-back for him."

"I'm sorry, lad," the bartender said. "I didn't know you wanted to take him."

Robbie looked up at Craig, but he wasn't accusatory. Still, Craig regretted not having the bartender keep the dog for Robbie. They could manage one more mouth to feed.

"Maybe the man who took the dog is still around," Craig offered. "Let's go outside and look."

Craig looked down at the boy. "Here. Let me get the scarf around your neck better. And pull down the hat on your head. And mittens. Remember your mittens."

Craig felt for the coins in his pocket. Any man in the saloon would sell that dog to him for a two-bit piece, and he had several with him. If he had to, he'd go higher. But he had no doubt he could buy the dog for Robbie once he found the man who had acquired him.

When they were both bundled up, Craig led Robbie out of the saloon. The boy was fairly bouncing with excitement.

"Should I c-call the dog?" Robbie asked when they reached the saloon door.

"Let's look around first," Craig suggested. "We don't want to scare him."

"He w-won't be afraid of me," Robbie said with confidence.

Unless his ears were playing tricks on him, Craig thought that Robbie's stuttering had lessened. If it was the prospect of having a pet that was doing that, Craig wished he'd found a dog for the boy earlier.

The icy wind slammed into Craig and Robbie as they stepped through the saloon door. Gray clouds hung in the sky and the snow kept falling. Craig looked at his wagon, hoping Vivian and the girls had gone down the street to the general store. The wagon was empty. He looked at the ground and saw footsteps that appeared to belong to them.

Craig shifted his legs so that he took the brunt of the wind and then pulled Robbie close to him. "Let me look for a bit and see if I can find that dog."

Craig searched the street up one side and down the other. There were only a few people out and most of them were moving fast. It was clear no dog trotted along beside them. The tracks were so scuffed in the snow along the street that he could not tell if a dog had walked there recently. Then he noticed the reverend's wagon was still standing on the road up from the saloon. If he wasn't mistaken, Robert was crouched down in the back of that wagon, huddled in a mountain of quilts. Craig figured the other man would have seen anyone leaving the saloon with a dog.

"Keep your head down and let's go see what Robert knows." Craig tipped his head down so the snow wouldn't hit his face and Robbie did the same as they walked the few yards to the wagon.

"Robert," Craig called as they drew near. The man's face appeared in an opening in the quilts. Irrationally, Craig noted that the man looked every inch a gentleman even though he was buried like a ground-hog. "We're looking for that dog. Have you seen—"

Craig stopped the moment he saw an animal's leg sticking out from the second pile of quilts Robert had arranged in the wagon.

"You have that dog?" Craig asked Robert. What would that man from back east do with a dog?

"He has the dog?" Robbie echoed in excitement.

Craig nodded and then addressed Robert. "I'd like to buy the dog from you."

"It's not for sale," Robert said as he slipped the quilts off his head and sat there looking more like the judge than Craig appreciated.

"Why not?" Craig had to ask even though he was already beginning to suspect he wouldn't like the answer.

"He's a present for my son," Robert said smoothly, turning his attention to Robbie. "What do you say, Robbie? Would you like your father to give you a dog?"

Robbie's face went white and Craig knew it wasn't the cold.

"Who's your son?" Robbie asked quietly, look-ing stricken.

"Name your price," Craig interrupted, his voice harsh. "You've got no call to do this." He didn't want any man teasing Robbie. Or maybe *tormenting* would be a better word.

"A man should be able to give his son a dog," Rob-ert said with a malicious smile. "It's one of those things a boy will remember when he's a man."

Craig figured Robbie would remember this, all right.

"What do you say, Robbie?" Robert asked. "You're my son. The dog is for you."

After a distressed glance up at the man, Robbie kept his eyes down. Then he shook his head and backed away, reaching out until he found Craig's hand.

"Well, maybe later," Robert said, revealing little emotion. "I plan to bring the dog with me, so if you change your mind, let me know. He's a noble animal, and I don't think it's right that he has to go around begging for food from every stranger he meets."

Robbie took another step back. "He doesn't b-beg. I've seen dogs c-crawl on their bellies and h-he doesn't do that.

Craig knew good intentions when he saw them, and there was nothing worthy about the eastern man's plans. He didn't blame Robbie for being tempted, but what a coldhearted thing for Robert to do to a child, especially one he wanted to claim as his own.

"Let's go find your sister and Becky," Craig said to Robbie. He added Vivian's name in his head just for the pleasure of remembering it, but he didn't want to say it in front of Robert.

They both turned and walked. Their boots crunched as they walked through the packed snow. Craig expected Robbie to turn and look back at the dog, but the boy didn't. He was a good soldier, but it was a sorry state of affairs.

"I'm sorry," Craig said. "I love you as my son, but

Robert has claim to you, too. That's one of the reasons we are meeting today. To see who the judge thinks should be your father."

"I want it to be you," Robbie said.

Craig put his hand on the boy's shoulder as they walked. He had never felt as helpless in his life. He'd prayed until his heart was weary and he had no peace. How could he expect Robbie to accept this when he couldn't?

Craig stomped the snow off his boots before opening the door of the general store so that Robbie could enter before him. The warm air was a relief, and the twin smells of spice and pickles floated over them. The small windows lining one side of the building were frosted from the cold; the ones in the front were scraped clean. A thin light filtered in, showing off the merchandise that filled the shelves. Bolts of fabric were laid out on a table. Craig took off his mittens so his hands would take in the heat quicker. Then he tugged off Robbie's mittens and unwound the scarf that was wrapped around the boy's face.

"I think we should each have a stick of peppermint," Craig said as he turned Robbie slightly and pointed him toward the glass front on the counter. There were licorice whips, lemon drops, horehound drops and the peppermint sticks both children loved.

Robbie picked up his step at that. Craig assured himself he wasn't bribing the boy. He did know that a piece of candy wouldn't win out over Robbie's desire to have that dog around, but he wanted to offer some solace.

"Me, too, Daddy," the bright voice of Katy sounded before he noticed she had come from behind to stand beside him. He turned then and saw Vivian and Becky next to Katy.

"Of course, you, too," Craig said as he bent to give the girl a quick hug. He'd never been more grateful for his two children than he was today.

"You're welcome to have one, too," Craig said to Becky. "The children love the peppermint sticks, but you're free to choose whatever candy you'd like."

Becky eagerly joined the other two children at the counter.

"You, too," Craig said softly when he and Vivian were alone. He reached out and took her hands, and they stood there, looking into each other's eyes. He wouldn't have taken her hands if he'd thought about it. She'd made it clear she wasn't interested in marrying him. But he still wanted to please her.

Vivian turned her face up and smiled.

"I'll take a peppermint stick," she said finally, but she didn't move.

Maybe she would change her mind about marrying him, Craig thought uncertainly. Since the sky outside was overcast, there were many shadows within the store. Craig wondered if that was why Vivian had swept her veil back further than she usually wore it. He hoped she would wear the veil less over time. It was true that her skin was a dark red where it had burned all those years ago, but she was a beautiful woman and the scars did not take away from that. And her smile warmed a man's heart.

Craig was content. He knew that Mrs. Hunt could give the children more expensive presents than he could ever hope to, but he did what he could and he offered it with love. He had to trust that that would be enough to keep them with him. As for Vivian's place in his future, he figured there was no need to ponder that. He needed to confess everything that had gone on in New York on the night she'd been injured. Once he did that, she would likely leave. And he wouldn't be able to blame her for doing so.

"Be careful with Kitty," Vivian said as she stood behind Katy at the counter. The cat was looking around like he was picking out his own treat. If he ever settled on anything, he could bound away from Katy before anyone could stop him. Fortunately, the hams were hanging from the high beams of the store.

"I thought Mrs. Hunt would be with you," Craig said as he followed them over to the counter. A box of crackers sat under the sweets. An open barrel of pickles sat in front of the counter with the smell of vinegar strong around it.

"Oh, she's been here," Vivian said, an edge to her voice. The woman had purchased a doll for Katy that was the most expensive one in the store. "She bought every toy there was on the shelves for Katy and Robbie. And then she went down the street to send a telegram. Probably to ask for more money."

"Nothing for Becky?" Craig asked.

Vivian shook her head. "Not that we would expect it."

Craig winced. "She's wooing my two, I guess."

Vivian grunted. "She says she's making up for every Christmas there ever was. Only she's not waiting for Epiphany to give the gifts to the children. She says she wants them to experience the presents for a longer time. Whatever that means."

"It means she's trying to buy their cooperation for going to live with her," Craig said. "She wants them to get used to having elaborate toys. By the time Epiphany rolls around, she's hoping they will have their trunks already packed."

Vivian could see how concerned Craig was.

"Don't give up yet," she said, fighting the urge to reach out and take his hands again. She needed to temper her feelings if she was going to be as impartial as the judge wanted in her role. "The children may surprise you."

"They're just so young," Craig said, looking down. "I can't expect them to withstand the temptations she is offering."

Vivian knew his fears, and she worried about the same thing. Would the children even understand what they were giving up by agreeing to go with Mrs. Hunt? Katy seemed to know what was at stake, but she was only four years old. She could be swayed by some new fancy toy and not realize the decision was permanent. That might be part of Vivian's job as the court's representative for the next nine days.

"Where's Finn?" Craig asked.

"He went to talk to the reverend," Vivian said. "We ordered so many cooking supplies and then Mrs. Hunt added the gifts for the children. We can't haul everything and us in the wagon. We're hoping the reverend will agree to follow us home with his wagon.

"She's buying that much?" Craig turned to her.

"Mrs. Hunt is paying for all those gifts she wants," Vivian answered. "A doll for Katy that is almost as tall as she is. A case of cast-iron soldiers for Robbie. A top that twirls for Robbie. A small necklace for Katy. And more. I didn't know how to stop her. But I did say you wanted the food to be added to your account so her bill was separate."

"Thank you," Craig said. "A man needs to have some pride. And we needed supplies anyway. I would have needed to come to Cheyenne today with or without the judge's order."

By then, they were up to the counter and paying the storekeeper for the peppermint sticks. Afterward, the five of them headed to a wooden bench along the left wall of the store. They sat there and enjoyed their candy.

Vivian and Craig were in the middle of the bench, and she liked the way it made her feel to be sitting shoulder to shoulder with him. His arms were strong, and she relaxed, sensing she was protected. She even slanted her hat away so that the brim didn't interfere with them being close. He had seen her face, so she didn't worry overmuch about her veil.

"Should we buy a peppermint stick for Ga'ma?" Katy asked as she sucked on the hard candy she had in her hand. She and Becky sat on the other side of Vivian.

"What do you think?" Craig turned to Vivian.

She smiled. "Mrs. Hunt will fuss and spit and then she'll say you shouldn't be ridiculous and then she'll accept it and put it in her purse to give to Katy later."

Vivian looked at the girl, who shook her head. "Ga'ma will like it."

"Maybe we should buy one for the man with the dog, too," Robbie said.

Craig stopped smiling, and Vivian watched all of the happiness fade from his face. Something was wrong and she didn't know what it was "Who's the man with the dog?"

"Robert," Craig answered in a clipped tone. Then he angled away from Robbie so only Vivian could hear. "He took ownership of the dog from the saloon knowing Robbie had grown attached to that big mutt. Robert said he wanted to give the dog to his son. *His son.* I think Robert is trying to tempt Robbie to agree to go back east with him and Mrs. Hunt. All Robbie needs to do is accept that he is Robert's son."

"But that's not right," Vivian insisted. "He might be Robert's son, but you were the one who raised him. He shouldn't try to make that kind of a bargain."

Craig shrugged. "Robbie won't even say the man's name now. But what he's doing is legal."

The door to the store burst open, and Mrs. Hunt stepped back inside. A thin layer of snow clung to her cloak and hat. Cold air had come in with her, and she stomped her feet on the plank floor to rid them of the packed snow on the bottom of her black shoes.

"I don't see how anyone can live in such as freezing place as here," the older woman declared as she looked around glaring into the shadows. "Why, my bones are even feeling it."

"It's cold in New York City, too," Vivian replied mildly.

"Yes, but it's so much more civilized," Mrs. Hunt protested. "I didn't have to go out and tromp through the snow just to send a telegram."

"That's because your servants did it for you," Vivian reminded her.

"I suppose," the other woman said thoughtfully. "I should have bought my maid with me at least."

With that, the woman shook her skirts, dislodging some stray snow. She looked at the storekeeper. "Do you have everything all boxed up and ready for us?"

"Yes, ma'am," the man said. "Just have someone pull the wagons around back and we'll load them up."

"Ga'ma." Katy walked up to Mrs. Hunt and tugged on her skirt. "I got a peppermint for you."

Vivian saw the shock on the society lady's face. She'd likely never had a sticky-fingered child offer her a sweet before, at least not a candy that was probably still a little sticky itself.

"You eat it for me, sweetheart," Mrs. Hunt said with a gracious smile.

"Okay," Katy said as she withdrew her hand. The girl walked back to the bench, but she didn't look happy.

"She didn't want it," Katy said softly to Vivian as she stopped in front of her. "Will you keep it for me?"

"I'd be honored," Vivian said as she slipped a

handkerchief out of her purse and wrapped it around the peppermint stick.

Mrs. Hunt went behind the store's counter after saying that she wanted to double-check to be sure all the gifts she ordered were being loaded onto the reverend's wagon.

"I had planned to get some presents for the children for Epiphany," Craig said. "Do you think Mrs. Hunt left anything?"

"She didn't even look at the books," Vivian said, a note of conspiracy in her voice, as she stood. She looked around and saw all three children were looking at the plow blades and shovels.

"Don't touch things." Vivian called out the reminder to the children as she motioned for Craig to follow her.

The books were all sitting in an open wooden crate that was easy to overlook because it was in a corner behind some of the bolts of fabric. Vivian breathed in deeply of the scent of new books. The spines of the books were facing upward and a person only had to bend over the crate to make their selection. They didn't have much time, but they managed to pick out *Flower Fables* by Louisa May Alcott for Robbie, *The Little Match Girl* by Hans Christian Andersen for Katy, and *Alice's Adventures in Wonderland* by Lewis Carroll for Becky.

"I can help pay." Vivian repeated her offer for the third time as they walked to the counter.

"You save your money," Craig replied.

Vivian gave up on convincing him. Truthfully, she

was touched that he'd included Becky with his children and had seemingly done so without thinking about it. The girl would be delighted. Actually, all three children would be. She already knew that his two little ones loved the storybook that they claimed as their own. They would feel rich to each have their own book. Not even Becky was able to read the books on her own, but Craig would read them aloud in front of the fireplace and everyone would enjoy them.

Finn was standing with the three children beside the front counter when Vivian and Craig walked back to the main part of the store. They all looked excited, and Finn was carrying something heavy in a gunnysack.

"Don't ask," Vivian advised Craig quietly before they got close enough for the others to hear her words. She guessed someone had purchased a Christmas gift for Craig and would want it to be a surprise. "Children love their secrets."

Craig greeted the children with a hug and nary a question about the sack that Finn held.

"You got the supplies you need to feed everyone for a few weeks?" Craig asked.

Vivian nodded, using her fingers to count off the foodstuff. "Two big smoked hams. Three good-sized wheels of cheese. A dozen cans of peaches. Another dozen of tomatoes. Sugar. Some raisins and nuts to add to our king cake."

"That's for Epiphany," Katy announced in a hushed voice. "For the party."

"A bag of potatoes. Another of onions. Four

squashes. Three slabs of bacon." Vivian kept adding what she had purchased. "Enough flour for several dozen loaves of bread or biscuits. A package of
Horsford's Bread Preparation. Bags of dried beans.
Dried apples. Cornmeal. Five jars of home-canned
beets. Three of sour cabbage. Another one of green
beans. Coffee. Oh, and two jars of homemade relish
that will go well with the hams."

"Good," Craig said with a nod. "We won't go hungry—that's for sure."

Vivian scarcely had time to buy a bolt of white
muslin and a few yards of lace before it was time to
climb up to the wagon. She planned to make a new
nightgown for Becky for Epiphany. She had some
floral soap she'd also give the girl. They had been on
the train for Christmas, and while they had read the
Christmas story in the Bible, they hadn't exchanged
presents. Epiphany would be good for them, too. This
time, she'd like to read the Christmas story from her
grandfather's Bible. As she recalled, his Bible had
gorgeous pictures depicting the angels and the shep-
herds. The children would love to see them.

And, Becky might find it comforting to know that
her grandfather had listed her mother in their family
Bible. At least, he had told her that he had noted the
death of Becky's mother.

The bolt of white muslin would provide enough
fabric so she could also make monogrammed hand-
kerchiefs for Craig, Finn and Robbie. She had plenty
of embroidery thread in her trunk and could decorate
them with their initials in different colors. She could

make a matching nightgown for Katy, too. The girls would like that. She could even embroider their initials on the front of the gowns.

It was midafternoon before all of the supplies were loaded and the children were all bundled up and placed in the back of Craig's wagon. Mrs. Hunt and Robert had decided to travel back in the reverend's wagon. Vivian could hear the dog growl and bark from the back of the wagon. Every time the animal made a sound, Robbie flinched and turned to look anxiously at the other wagon.

"That m-man is m-mean to the dog," Robbie whispered over the edge of the wagon to Vivian. He was scowling. "He should be nice."

Vivian caught herself before agreeing with the boy. "Sometimes people don't do what they know they should," Vivian said. She had to be content with that. The judge said she should be impartial and not take sides. She'd leave Robbie to make his own conclusions. The boy was bright; he'd see what Robert was like behind his gentleman's clothes.

Vivian stepped over to where Craig stood ready to help her climb up into the front of the wagon. The same quilt they had used on the way into Cheyenne was waiting for them for the way home. Vivian was glad for that. What sun there was had gone behind the gray clouds. It was growing colder.

She put her gloved hand in Craig's, and he swung her up so her right foot could find a hold to help her take a step forward and settle into the seat. Before she knew it, Finn had climbed into the back with the children and Craig had made his way into the wagon seat beside her. He swung the quilt around until it covered them. The fabric was cold but would warm quickly.

Craig adjusted the quilt around her head. "Keep your hat brim down and you'll be safe from the wind."

It seemed to Vivian he was giving her most of the quilt. "I want you to keep warm, too."

Craig grinned then. "Don't worry about me. I stay plenty warm just sitting here beside a beautiful woman."

Vivian blushed. "Oh, you."

Craig chuckled as he took up the reins and set the horses to walking.

Vivian discovered that a compliment from the right man could keep her from being cold, too. It took her a minute, but then she realized in astonishment that a man had said something nice and she had accepted him at his word. Not once had she told herself that he couldn't mean she was attractive because he knew she had scars.

"Thank you," she whispered softly.

Craig turned to her, a question in his eyes.

"For seeing me and not my scars," she said.

He nodded. She wasn't sure he understood, but he seemed to. He put the reins in one hand and held her hand with the other. For the first time since she had stumbled into his house, she wondered if she hadn't been hasty in saying that she wouldn't marry him. And it wasn't just that he accepted her scars. She was beginning to rely on him. He was steady. And he'd rushed to her aid when she'd needed help. He was a hero. Most men she'd known wouldn't have headed to the fire to save her; they would have run the other way. She thought of Ethan Hunt. She'd been convinced he cared about her, and he'd shown otherwise after her face was no longer perfect. Craig Martin was a completely different type of man. Yes, she decided, she could trust him.

She snuggled closer to him with each revelation she'd considered until finally her cheek was practically resting on his shoulder. The cold wind slipped into the gaps between them and the quilt.

"We'll be home soon," Craig whispered.

Vivian nodded.

Chapter Seven

The sunlight was fading as Craig drove his wagon to the top of the rise in front of his homestead. It had been a long day. Snow was blowing low against the ground. Gray patches of land showed here and there where the drifts had not collected. There was no smoke rising from the chimney of the fireplace, but he suspected there would still be some hot embers there. He was glad they had been able to buy plentiful supplies. He should have made a trip into Cheyenne weeks ago to restock the root cellar and the cabinets. They could face a long cold spell now and not worry.

"Whoa," he called out to his team of horses as he pulled them to a stop next to the door of his house. He looked at it with new eyes after Mrs. Hunt had denounced it so. It was a good home. He prayed she would see the benefits of having a house like this in the frigid winters here on the Wyoming plains. The thick walls held in the heat in the winter and kept the place cool in the hot summer. No plank-built cabin could do that. Plus, the sod building blocks were easy to cut, and he had been able to build a house that had two bedrooms—one for him and Delores and the other, a smaller size, for Finn. Both bedrooms had precious plate-glass windows. And the loft had a sturdy ladder and could hold a dozen children if they had enough quilts.

"I'll get the children inside," Finn said as he climbed down from the back of the wagon. "You see to the lady."

Finn's voice was peculiar, Craig thought, as he tried to puzzle it out. His brother sounded offended. That wasn't like him. And he knew Vivian's name; there was no reason to call her *the lady*.

Craig worked his way down from the wagon and walked back to where Finn stood. They were far enough away that no one could hear them, and Vivian and the children all seemed to be sleeping, but Craig didn't want to be overheard. "You upset that you were sitting behind with the children?"

Normally, Finn would be sitting up front with him, but nothing about today was ordinary, including the extra passengers they had.

"No," Finn said curtly and then looked up at Craig. "When were you going to tell me?"

"Tell you what?" Craig asked, trying for patience.

"That she was the woman from the fire." Finn nodded his head toward Vivian. "The one you told me about that night—the one who got burned."

Craig felt the jolt go through him at Finn's words. He should have told his brother. At first, he hadn't been sure Vivian was that woman and then, he supposed, he thought to protect him from the truth. But Finn wasn't a boy any longer. He needed to face the past, too.

"You're right. I should have said something," Craig admitted. "I didn't know she was going to mention it to the judge."

Craig had cringed at that moment, too. Over the years, he had practically forgotten about that night of rioting in New York City. He and Finn had moved thousands of miles away, and neither one of them had expected to ever need to think of that day again.

Craig had wanted to break off any connection Finn had with that rough gang of men, so he had decided it was time to move. They had paid the full month in advance on the room they were renting, but that didn't stop Craig. He'd packed their meager belongings the next day, and they'd slipped away that night. That gang of men would have followed Finn to any street in the city, trying to force him to join in their devilry again, but Craig knew they wouldn't travel much farther than the state border. He'd bought horses and a wagon and headed west, keeping off the main roads in case they were being followed. He hadn't suspected that either of them would face that night years later in Wyoming Territory.

"I'm sorry," Finn whispered, his voice hoarse.

Craig understood his apology was to cover all of it. The hurried leave-taking, the goodbyes left unsaid, their combined sense of guilt. "You were young—fourteen years old—and you foolishly chose to follow

some men who thought violence solved every problem. I'm sure they looked like exciting men, but you
learned they were not. I know you regret having been
there, but you didn't actually do anything but watch."

"Still," Finn said, and the word hung in the air.

By that time, the horses were getting restless. The
wind was much less powerful on the protected side of
the building, but it still blew hard enough. Craig remembered when he'd debated where to put the front
door on his house, trying to consider the force of the
wind. The truth was, there had been no place that was
calm on a windy day.

"It's over and done," Craig said to his brother. That
much he knew. "God has forgiven you. I have forgiven you for going out that night when I told you to
stay in our room. Those men you were with are not
worth worrying about."

"But when I think of what I could have done..."
Finn muttered.

"Praise God that you didn't," Craig said.

Finn nodded and peace returned to his eyes.

"Now, let's get everyone inside," Craig said as he
walked back to the front of the wagon and nudged
Vivian's shoulder gently.

"I'll take the children," Finn said cheerfully as he
set about waking them.

The reverend's wagon rattled up next to them. It
had started to snow again, and there was a layer of
white over all of the passengers and packages.

"I s-see the d-dog," Robbie said in a hushed voice

as he stood up and yawned while looking toward the other wagon.

Craig nodded. He was afraid the dog was going to be too much temptation for a young six-year-old boy. Craig wondered if he should find a pony for Robbie. That might be enough to make him stay home. Of course, he realized that would only make Robert and Mrs. Hunt show up with an elephant. There was no way to win at that game.

"We're home," Vivian said softly as she looked around.

It warmed Craig's heart to have her refer to his place as home. He was grateful that the judge had ordered her to stay here until January 6. He prayed she might change her mind about marriage in that time. He'd seen her read her small Bible. God might direct her to stay.

"I'll carry you inside," Craig offered as he held his arms up. She leaned forward, and he scooped her up with the quilt still around her. Finn had already carried the girls inside, so the door was only loosely closed.

Once inside, Craig built up the embers in the fireplace until they were steady flames. Finn had gone to bring in Robbie. Vivian and the girls were all still huddled under the quilts and sitting on the carved bench. To heat the house more quickly, Craig went to the kitchen stove and built up a fire in that, too.

Then he went out to bring in the food supplies. He wanted everything to be inside before the night turned completely dark. The sounds of the wolves had been closer last night, and he didn't want those hams to tempt them. He didn't think they could smell the meat, but he wasn't taking any chances.

The door was opened time and time again as the men brought in both the supplies and the packages Mrs. Hunt had purchased. The older lady herself sat down at the table and asked that everything be brought to her.

Craig noted that the reverend helped carry in the food but didn't offer to bring what Mrs. Hunt had purchased. Robert and Dry Gulch were happy enough to carry for her, however.

Craig was even more confident that the action was deliberate on the reverend's part when the man muttered, "No child needs that many toys."

Craig snorted. "Those aren't toys. Those are weapons in her war to win the children."

The reverend nodded. "Precisely. And I don't approve."

"It will be difficult for the children to resist," Craig said, feeling weary suddenly. He wondered if he was being too polite. The judge had more or less ordered him to offer Mrs. Hunt and Robert hospitality, but he was hard-pressed to give it. How was a young child supposed to know that fancy clothes and toys didn't really satisfy a person?

Finally, everything was unloaded, the wagons had been driven to the barn and the horses had been rubbed down and fed. Craig laid a small fire in the stove in the barn as well so that it would be warm when it came time for Finn and Robert to go to bed.

The reverend and his wife had decided to spend the night with them again as it was an hour to their home. Craig had urged them to do so, concerned with them driving their wagon that far in the cold darkness.

Since Mrs. Drummond had decided to stay at her home in Cheyenne rather than coming back with them, the larger of the bedrooms could be given to the reverend and his wife. Craig was glad the preacher wouldn't have to spend another night in the barn with the other men. He was of an age where a comfortable bed was most appreciated.

As the chill left the house, Vivian unwrapped from her quilt and moved to the kitchen. She peeled and sliced potatoes, carrots and onions and fried them in the big cast-iron skillet Craig used. Becky offered to make her biscuits, and Katy eagerly helped her. To add to the supper, Craig fried a few eggs as well. Vivian put some beans on to soak for the next day as they worked, and there was talk of baking bread the next day.

Craig hoped all of the activity meant a few days of good eating. Nothing would make Mrs. Hunt and Robert more difficult to deal with than their having empty stomachs.

And, he thought as he put the spices in the cupboard, he liked watching Vivian bustle around his kitchen like it was her own.

"I'd like to talk to you privately," he told Vivian as she started to peel potatoes for supper. He was putting more wood in the stove. "Maybe after supper?"

He could tell she was pleased as she nodded.

Five hours later, he realized there was no way that conversation would happen tonight unless he asked Vivian to walk outside with him in the bitter cold. Snow was coming down again. After supper, Mrs. Hunt had insisted the children, who were already tired, be given all of their gifts, which seemed to set them all on edge one way or the other. The children were overwhelmed and the adults, except for Mrs. Hunt and Robert, were dismayed.

Finally, Craig announced it was time for everyone to go to sleep, and Vivian was the first to head to the loft. She was spending the night with the girls so Mrs. Hunt could have the small bedroom again. Vivian looked worn out, and he didn't blame her. Tomorrow would be soon enough to explain about the long-ago riots, he told himself. Still, when he settled in with some quilts on the bench by the fireplace, he fretted. He did not want to see the disappointment in Vivian's eyes when she realized he wasn't the hero she'd thought he was in those fires.

Vivian woke up slowly and stretched under the heavy quilts. She was warm and cozy—not at all inclined to get out of bed and climb down the ladder. When she looked over the edge of the loft, she saw the frost on the dark windows. That signaled it would be another cold day. It was also, she noted, her first day of duty for the court. She smiled just thinking of herself in that capacity. The judge had to know she had a soft feeling toward Robbie and Katy and was not at all impartial when it came to their well-being.

Lord, give me wisdom to help those two little ones, she prayed. *You know the future that is best for them. Guide us all.*

Then she lay there thinking that she might have more decisions to make than she wanted. Ever since Craig had said last night that he wanted to talk to her in private, she had known it was something serious. She recognized the signs. The flushed face, the downcast eyes that couldn't stay down but kept looking up with intense feeling, the softness in the voice and in his eyes. He was going to propose, she'd told herself last night. That was why she'd hurried to the loft when everyone was heading to bed. She wanted to think about what to say to him before he asked.

Then, as she had been drifting off to sleep, she realized he'd never said he loved her. And if he didn't say it, she could hardly ask him if he did. How would she ever know if he'd spoken the truth?

It wasn't until she heard footsteps out in the kitchen that she slipped out of the warm bed and faced the cold morning. She climbed down the stairs and, while shivering, rummaged through her trunk until she found a wine-colored wool dress that was one of her winter favorites. She wanted to look her best when Craig proposed—assuming, she reminded herself, that was what he was anxious to speak about. It was only respectful to treat the moment as important.

She felt a sudden hitch in her breath. Could she be wrong about what Craig wanted to talk about? She couldn't think of anything else that would require privacy. Unless—her heart sank—maybe he wanted to bribe her in some way to hurt Mrs. Hunt's case with the judge. He did love his children.

Vivian didn't move for a few minutes, but then she slowly shook her head. No, she refused to believe Craig was a dishonorable man. He would never ask her to do anything that wasn't right.

She climbed back up the ladder and knelt in the back corner of the loft. Her fingers were stiff and the buttons on the dress were awkward, but Vivian managed to get dressed fairly quickly. She brushed her hair into a bun at the back of her neck and started to settle her hat on her head. Then, in a defiant gesture, she set the hat back down on the floor. She wasn't going to wear her veil today. If a man was going to ask her to marry him, he would have to take her as she was. She climbed back down the ladder with her head high and feeling lighter than she had in years.

The main room of the house was in shadows. The windows there were frosted over as well, and the sunrise was only beginning to throw light into the day. The fireplace was ablaze, though, and that lifted the darkness partially.

Vivian, a smile on her face, looked around. "Where's Craig?"

Finn was shoving wood into the stove, and he turned to answer. "He had to go out to the barn. Robert was ready to shoot that dog."

"What?" Vivian gasped. "What did the dog do?"

Finn shook his head. "Nothing a normal dog wouldn't do in the circumstances. He prowled around all night, growling soft like he heard something outside. I opened the door a couple of times and never saw anything. But a dog needs to make peace with a new home. Robert was just upset because he didn't get a good night's sleep."

"Well, that's no reason to kill a dog," Vivian exclaimed.

"That's what I told the man," Finn said. "But he kept asking to speak to Big—I mean Craig. Not that he would allow something like that on his property anyway. But Robert insisted."

"You call him Big? Your brother?" Vivian asked. She remembered the clerk at the railroad depot in Cheyenne had also called him that. She wanted to know more about Craig, and no one could tell her more than his brother.

Finn shrugged and then closed the door to the firebox on the stove. Turning to her, he said, "I was pretty small when we came to America. About the size of Robbie. And I had some trouble with older boys who didn't like that I was trying to get delivery jobs right along with them. I started calling Craig Big because he was my big brother, and they thought he was a fighter, so they left me alone. The name stuck. Big always looked out for me."

Finn paused and looked uncomfortable. Then the words poured out of him. "I am so sorry about the fire that night. I never thought anyone would be hurt. Everyone was so upset about the draft laws that had passed. They didn't want to fight in that war and thought it was unfair the city wanted to force them into it. I was too young, but I agreed it was not right and—I'm just so sorry."

Vivian was frozen in shock. "You were there? With the rioters?"

"They were men Craig worked with and they asked me to go along with them," Finn admitted, his voice low. He was looking at the floor. "Craig told me to stay home, but I—I went. And I'm so sorry for it."

"These were men Craig worked with?" Vivian kept her voice even. She wanted to be sure she understood this. She knew Craig had said he knew the men. That they were all longshoremen. But that implied a distance between them. From what Finn was saying, it sounded like Craig worked with them—side by side, day by day. Was he then part of the group that set fire to her grandfather's house? If Finn had gone out after had Craig told him to stay home, that must mean Craig had already gone out. The truth was that Craig might not be a hero. The guilt on Finn's face told her all she needed to know. Craig had thrown the beam away from her that night, but he likely had helped cause the fire in the first place. He might not be the man she had thought he was.

"Excuse me," Vivian said. She'd been well trained in the polite world and knew she didn't betray her distress. "I just realized I need to fix my dress before I'm ready for the day."

Vivian turned and walked back to the ladder. She heard little feet coming down the loft ladder, but she didn't turn to say good morning. The usual pleasantries would have to wait. She turned to rummage through her trunk and hid her face as the first tear fell. Her dreams were foolish, she realized. She might think she was coming to love Craig, but, in truth, she didn't know him. She thought he was a hero who'd saved her from the mischief of that night, and instead he was part of the rioting.

She mumbled something to Becky about being tired still and climbed back up to the empty loft. Breakfast went on without her. She could hear the sleepy voices and Mrs. Hunt complaining that they had only oatmeal for the meal. She didn't like the coffee, either. Instead, she apparently walked back to her bedroom and came back to offer the children tea biscuits from a Huntley & Palmers tin she explained she'd bought at the general store yesterday.

Vivian knew she had to go down and monitor the generosity of the older woman. She was quite sure neither the reverend nor Craig would approve of the children eating something sweet instead of their oatmeal for breakfast. A healthy life, she told herself, involved tough choices.

"Good morning," Vivian said brightly as she stepped down off the ladder. All of the heads swiveled to her, and she saw relief on all of them, which surprised her when it came to Mrs. Hunt.

"Tell them—" the older woman said with a gesture to the other adults "—that there's nothing wrong with eating a digestive biscuit in the morning. I often have one with my cup of hot chocolate, and I've lived to a—well—a comfortable age and with no ill effects."

Dry Gulch patted the older woman on the arm. "You're a woman in her prime."

Mrs. Hunt turned to glare at him.

"I do think the judge would want the children to continue on with their meals in the way they have been," Vivian said only to see Katy frown.

"No burnt porridge," she whispered to Vivian as she walked by.

"That's understood," Vivian agreed and was happy to see the frown leave the little girl's face. "The meals will be properly prepared. I'm sorry I was not able to do so this morning."

"The p-porridge is good today," Robbie assured her. "I f-finished mine. Could I b-be excused to go to the b-barn to see the dog? Uncle Finn said the dog was scared last night."

Vivian saw Craig and Robert look at each other.

"The dog is doing fine," Craig reassured the boy.

"He's out there taking a nap," Robert added sourly. "Which is more than I can say for any of us who didn't sleep well."

By then, Vivian was standing at the table and looking at the remains of the meal. Toast crumbs showed that Robbie had been busy. The pot of porridge was sitting beside Finn, so he must have served it up. That suspicion was verified when he looked at Vivian.

"I saved you some," Finn said to her. "It's no trouble to put it on to heat it a little."

"I'm sure she would prefer to have a biscuit from the tin," Mrs. Hunt said as she held out the ornate square box. The woman was right that some of them were digestive biscuits. Some were clearly sweets, though.

Vivian suddenly remembered the judge saying she was to be impartial. "I'll take a small bowl of oatmeal and one digestive biscuit."

"And you'll want coffee," Craig suggested from where he sat at the head of the table.

"And coffee," she agreed. Whether he knew it or not, she had offered him an olive branch. She would not marry him now, whether or not that had been what was on his mind last night. But she had a job to do for the courts, and she would be pleasant to both sides. She ate her breakfast and set to work on the rest of the day.

The reverend and his wife left after breakfast with heartfelt assurances that they would see everyone soon. Vivian, after a quick exchange with Craig, invited the couple to their Epiphany party to be held on January 6, eight days in the future. They accepted and said they hoped everyone would make it to the church service this coming Sunday.

The busyness of the day kept the sorrow from Vivian's mind. It wasn't the first time her heart had been broken, although she admitted the hurt had gone deeper than ever before. Still, the dishes had to be done and food needed to be prepared for the day. She could not shut herself in the now-empty bedroom and grieve.

It was almost noon, though, before she realized she wasn't the only one having a difficult day. Katy was sitting on the bench by the fireplace, looking miserable. She had her new doll on one side of her and her kitty on the other.

"What's wrong, sweetheart?" Vivian asked as she knelt down in front of her.

"Robbie and Becky went out to the barn," the girl said, her voice rising in self-pity.

"And you wanted to go with them?" Vivian guessed. She was sure the other two children had asked her to accompany them. The three had seemed inseparable only yesterday.

"I can't go," Katy was in a full wailing voice now. "I can't carry both the doll and Kitty."

"Ah," Vivian said. She saw the problem now.

"Kitty doesn't like to walk in the snow." Katy calmed down enough to confide in her. "It makes his feet cold. And the doll can't walk at all. I'd have to carry them both."

Vivian considered the problem. "Who do you think would enjoy going to the barn the most?"

"Kitty," the girl said without hesitation. "We were going to visit the chickens. Kitty likes to growl at them and make them run away. He'd never hurt any of them, though. He's a good kitty."

Vivian smiled for the first time that day. Katy saw the best in people—and animals.

"The doll will be mad if I don't take her," Katy confided. "I think she might be a little like Ga'ma."

"Oh." Vivian was trying to keep up. "Why is that?"

"Because the doll's perfect," Katy said innocently as she eyed the toy that was almost the same size as she was. "It has the princess hair. She's always smiling. Her dress would never get dirty. Her hair is always combed. And she just sits there."

"My," Vivian said.

"I never had a doll before," Katy added fretfully and then added with a smile, "But I have my kitty."

"I see," Vivian nodded. She wasn't sure, but she figured the problem Katy was facing was that she wasn't familiar with the world her grandmother wanted her to enter. It wasn't only life-sized dolls that would be there. It was sweets for breakfast. And not having rules. If Craig hadn't insisted last night, Mrs. Hunt would have demanded the children stay up until midnight admiring their gifts and chatting.

"I think the doll might like to take a nap," Vivian said. "You can lay her down in the small bedroom I am using." Mrs. Hunt had insisted on moving to the larger one. "Then we'll get all bundled up, and I'll take you out to the barn to see those chickens."

"Can we go now?" Katy asked as she stood up from the bench. "I haven't seen Gracie today."

"We'll go as soon as we get ready," Vivian said.

Katy hurriedly took the doll to the bedroom and laid her down on the bed.

Vivian had beans with bacon cooking on the back of the stove and potatoes ready to put in the small oven. She would open a jar of the canned green beans and take time to make a vanilla pudding. But she had time to check on the chickens Katy loved.

The sun shining on the snow cheered Vivian up as she and Katy walked to the barn. They didn't need the chore rope because there was no storm today, but they walked close to it because those who had gone ahead of them had broken up the drifts enough to make their footsteps easier.

Vivian wondered, as they made their way, if she wasn't as confused about life as Katy was. She had left her old life, and she didn't regret it, but she wasn't sure about anything in this new life she faced. All she could do was trust that God was guiding her. She should be grateful that He had shown her the kind of man Craig was. It was time, she decided, to unwrap the red cords keeping her grandfather's old Bible closed. The fact that her family had used that particular Bible for years to seek God's will would be comforting to her. She might even find some guidance on how to forget her feelings for Craig.

Chapter Eight

Three more cold, snowy days passed—it was now Saturday, January 1—and Craig had no more sense of what his life was going to be like than he had on that drive back from Cheyenne. The judge was scheduled to make his first visit later this afternoon, and everyone in the house was on edge in anticipation of it. No one mentioned anything in front of the children, not even Mrs. Hunt, but even they clearly knew something important was happening. It was the only thing that explained why they were no longer smiling.

This morning, Katy had sat in her old brown dress and glared at that big doll Mrs. Hunt had given her, from time to time muttering something about it being a bad princess. Craig had suggested Katy wear the new blue dress she'd gotten from Becky, but Katy refused. She said she was saving the dress for the Epiphany party, but there was no excitement in her when she mentioned it. In addition, the doll's dress had a tear in the hem, and Katy didn't seem worried about it. Normally, she'd be asking Craig to fix it. It was like she'd given up on that doll, though. He only hoped she hadn't given up on her life with him.

Craig had always wanted to buy Katy one of the dolls in the general store. He'd even saved some money for one last year. He'd never figured on giving her one as big as this, but he was surprised she wasn't delighted with what she had. He wondered if Katy was upset because Robbie wasn't spending much time with her. The two children had been inseparable until that dog had come home with Robert.

Now, the boy followed that dog everywhere, even though he hadn't completely adopted the dog yet. Robert had said Robbie could name the dog, but the boy refused to do that. Craig suspected Robbie knew what it would mean to name that dog—it would be agreeing that Robert was his father and was entitled to give him the animal. It might also mean he'd be going back to New York City with the dog.

Craig had used his rifle to kill a coyote in the middle of the night that was trying to get a chicken from the shed off the barn. The chickens were no doubt relieved, but Mrs. Hunt was in full battle array. Her grandchildren, she informed Craig, had no business living with guns. He tried explaining to her that rifles were necessary in the territory and for more than the sake of the chickens. She flatly disagreed, declaring that, when she was their guardian, they would not have guns anywhere near them.

"They would be protected properly," Mrs. Hunt had said. Craig had no idea what she meant.

Of all the people, Vivian was the most perplexing one, though. She would not meet his eyes. She had started wearing that net again, but this time, he believed she was hiding behind it. She spent her days hand-stitching white muslin. The fabric billowed out around her lap as she sat by the fireplace. Worst of all, though, she avoided him whenever he tried to talk to her. Finally, he had said plainly that he needed to explain about that fire, and she'd burst into tears and run into the bedroom. When he'd knocked on the door and asked what was wrong, she'd told him to go away.

The only one in the house who was happy this morning was Mrs. Hunt, and that seemed to be because she had been regaling Vivian with suggestions for all kinds of lavish entertainments that Vivian could enjoy if she would only return to New York City with her. Mrs. Hunt never said how Vivian was to manage the trip and what it would mean for Becky, but Craig finally decided that the older woman wanted Vivian to move back to the city with her and Robert so that Katy and Robbie would choose to go there, too.

Craig was afraid it might work. The children were very attached to Vivian. Craig didn't even ask himself how he would feel if she were gone. His day was gloomy enough without that.

It was early afternoon before the judge pulled his wagon up to the house. There was a scattering of snow, but most of the ground was bare. Craig had gone outside to walk up to the rise to see if a wagon was coming and so spied the judge's wagon before it came close.

Craig waited for the judge to pull his team to a halt and then patted the standing horses. He had one question as he looked up at the judge, and he needed to know. "Who is going to make the decision on the children? Is it you or someone else?"

The judge slowly climbed down from his wagon before he faced Craig. There was nothing but kindness in his face. "I'm going to do the best I can for all of you. That means you, too, Craig."

"I'm not so worried about me," Craig said. "I am afraid for the children. I don't think they can make a choice about their future—not a big one like this."

"I won't ask it of them," the judge replied. "I'll talk to them about how they are feeling about things and what they want to happen, but I will make it clear that the decision is mine. Children of that age want to please everyone, and it is impossible. That's why we have judges."

"Good," Craig said with a nod as he led the judge to the house.

Inside, the greetings for the judge were subdued. "Everyone's nervous," Craig said as he took the judge's coat and hung it on a peg by the door.

"How are plans for the party coming along?" the judge asked heartily.

Katy looked up from her position on the bench and said, "My doll doesn't want to go."

Robbie looked down from the loft and added,

"That d-dog would like to c-come, but he's n-not invited. Ga'ma said so. He's t-too dirty."

"We're saving back enough eggs to make a big king cake," Vivian offered from where she stood in front of the stove. She was wearing an apron and stirring a pot of soup. Craig was impressed that she was able to make eye contact with the judge while, at the same time, never turning in Craig's direction, even though he was standing right behind the judge.

"We don't have a baby to put in the cake," Mrs. Hunt said.

Katy gasped. "You bake a baby in the cake?"

Craig grinned. Something had finally gotten through to his youngest child. "It's not a real baby. We don't have a figurine like they use in the southern states. But we can use a bean."

Katy frowned. "A bean is not a baby."

"The person who gets the bean is supposed to have a very good year," Vivian added. "It's a game."

"Daddy should win, then," Katy said emphatically.

Craig was startled. He was not surprised Katy was that generous. But he was unsettled that she thought he needed encouragement.

The judge talked with both of the children separately, taking each of them for a short walk to the barn. After he did that, he sat with Vivian in her bedroom for a half hour. Everyone could hear the murmur of their voices, but they could not hear what words were spoken. When the judge had done all that, he ate a bowl of soup with everyone and enjoyed several biscuits with honey. They all chatted and tried to pretend they did not want to know what he was thinking.

The judge left after a couple of hours, and Craig felt like he had wrestled a dozen young bulls to the ground. Some hours later, Vivian prepared fried ham slices and baked potatoes for the evening meal. By that time, night had fallen.

It had been cold all day, and Mrs. Hunt went to bed early, claiming it was the only way for her to get warm. Finn and Robert left for the barn to do the evening chores. The children climbed up to the loft and decided to shake the wrinkles out of their quilts.

Craig was too tired to fuss at the children, and he was happy to hear them laughing. Mrs. Hunt came out of her bedroom in a pink velvet robe and shouted up for the children to be silent before stomping back and slamming her door. By then, Craig had finished washing the last dish. He was turning to leave the stove when Vivian, who must have put aside her sewing, was standing beside him.

She whispered, "I pray every night that the judge will leave the children with you. You're their father. No one can replace you."

Then she put her hand on his arm and he turned. The lantern was turned low; her face was in the shadows. He smiled because her hat was crooked. He could tell she'd been pushing that veil aside. He took his hand and covered hers.

"Thank you." He was finally at peace. Vivian was talking to him again. He couldn't stop himself. He made another attempt to tell her how he felt. "I don't want you to feel awkward, but I need for you to know how important you are to me—"

Vivian shook her head. "Not now. We can talk when the judge has made his decision. I'm trying to forgive, but I need more time."

Craig frowned. He wasn't sure what she was forgiving. She didn't know why he'd been at her house that night in New York City, but, even at that, he had done nothing wrong. Then it struck him. Her expression was so solemn, he wondered if she was worried that he would try to influence her in her report to the judge. He would never do that.

He stood there, holding his hand over hers and realizing how bereft he would be if she left him. He knew she had no plans to stay. He knew Mrs. Hunt was trying to tempt her to move back east. He had even heard the older woman muttering something about weddings. At the time, he had thought the children's grandmother meant a wedding between him and Vivian. He'd been surprised and delighted. There'd been no hint of that today, however. He suspected Mrs. Hunt was going to help Vivian find a rich husband in New York. He did not know how Vivian would be able to resist.

Dear Lord, he prayed silently, refusing to release Vivian's hand since she was making no move to step away. *Help me to accept Your will for Vivian. And Your will for me. You know how I feel about the children. Help me to trust You.*

With that, he turned to face Vivian fully and tenderly adjusted her veil. She was looking up at him sweetly.

Before he even thought of it, he leaned in and kissed her.

She looked stunned.

At the same time, they both heard the sound of feet descending the loft ladder.

"Daddy, daddy," Katy wailed as she hurried climbed down as fast as she could. Her face was red. "Robbie took my quilt."

She ran to hug Craig's legs.

"I'm sorry, I—" Craig said to Vivian before he let his hand rest on Katy's head.

"It's mine," Robbie answered from the loft. "You have the blue one."

"Kitty doesn't like that one no more," Katy declared.

"Later," Craig said softly to Vivian.

She nodded and turned her head so the veil effectively covered her entire face. Then she walked away.

Lord, what am I to do? Craig prayed silently as he watched her open the door to the bedroom she was using. He sensed that Vivian was not ready to hear the words he had to say, but he was fairly bursting to declare his love for her. Even if she left, he wanted her to know how he felt.

Vivian noticed there was no letup in the cold over the next two days. The wood piles for the house and the barn dwindled. Ice covered the outside of the house. Worse than that, she thought, was that the days were all overcast. What sun that did manage to break through was weak and strained. Nothing was cheerful, including that vacant-eyed doll that sat staring at the fireplace from her perch on the bench. Katy had all but abandoned the toy. It had seemed to make the girl angry more than happy.

Craig was more subdued as the days went on. Robbie had clearly been considering names for the dog. Craig managed to smile when the boy offered each of his suggestions, even though Vivian knew it was difficult for the man.

Of course, no one seemed content anymore. Vivian was in the bedroom brushing Becky's hair when she decided to bring up the decision she'd been weighing. "What say we move into Cheyenne after the Epiphany party?"

Vivian held her breath until Becky gave a slow nod of her head.

"If Katy and Robbie have to leave, I don't want to stay," the girl whispered. "It would be sad."

Vivian prayed that would not be the judge's answer, but she had reluctantly accepted her earlier decision. She cared deeply for Craig, but she was troubled that he wasn't an honorable man. She had always believed that, if she loved a man, he would be a bright and shiny hero. Craig likely had his reasons for rioting with his fellow longshoremen that night in New York City, but she didn't understand. She knew he wanted to explain, but she kept delaying that conversation because she didn't see how he could be blameless.

Vivian searched for a red ribbon. The dress the girl

had chosen to wear for Epiphany had red stars on it, and Becky wanted a hair tie to match.

"I thought we had one," Vivian said as she opened her valise and searched.

"Ah," Vivian said as she held up the old Bible she'd inherited from her grandfather. The red cords binding the book were the exact shade of red that they needed. "Just let me untie them and we can use one."

The knots in the cords were difficult to undo, but Vivian finally managed to loosen them. She slipped the red ties away from the Bible and the book fell open.

"Oh, my," Vivian exclaimed as she saw the ten-dollar bill tucked inside. She turned a page and saw another one. Another page revealed more.

Vivian looked up and saw Becky's wide eyes.

"Is that money for us?" the girl asked in awe.

Vivian blinked back tears as she flipped through the pages, taking out bills until she had them all. It was four hundred dollars. On the page that held the last bill, there was a note reading, "Thank you, my dears. You made my last years comfortable. May the peace of God be with you when I can't be. I love you both. Read the family page."

"Grandfather remembered us after all," Vivian said as the tears slid down her cheek. She had thought he cared about them, and now she was sure of it. He had hidden her inheritance where her brother and his wife would never look for it.

Vivian flipped back to the family page at the front of the Bible. She briefly looked through the records of her aunts and uncles and her cousins. Then her parents and her and—

Vivian gasped. There was Becky's name after an arrow coming from her brother's name. A question mark followed her name with the written notation saying, "Not proven, but almost certain." Her grandfather believed Vivian's brother was Becky's father.

"What's wrong?" Becky asked anxiously.

"Nothing, sweetheart," Vivian said as she closed the Bible. "Grandfather said something, and I need to pray about it before I know it's true."

That seemed to satisfy the girl. Vivian decided she would pray and consider the possibility before she told Becky. Her ward, maybe her niece, had known enough upheaval in her life. Vivian didn't want to add to it unless she was absolutely positive.

Becky's mother had never said anything about the man who had fathered her baby except for those words when she was dying—that Becky belonged with the Eastmans. At the time, Vivian had thought it simply meant that Becky was to go with her, but now she wondered if it was as close as Becky's mother could come to saying Vivian's brother was the baby's father.

Vivian's brother and Becky's mother were both a few years older than she was, and she supposed it was possible. Her brother had been rebellious then. Gambling. Going to wild clubs. Their grandfather had despaired of him settling down.

Vivian looked over at Becky, and she had a sudden insight as she studied the girl's eyes. They were the same color as her brother's. And, she had a thin nose like he had. Of course, Vivian realized then, that's why her sister-in-law, Edith, was so upset. The woman knew who Becky was. No wonder she wanted the girl out of her house. Becky was her husband's unclaimed daughter.

"Is the ribbon okay?" Becky asked as she shifted on her feet in front of Vivian. The girl had been anxious to go out and play with Katy and Robbie.

"It's fine," Vivian said as she forced herself to smile at the girl. "You look very pretty."

"Maybe I'll find the bean in my piece of cake," Becky said.

"Maybe," Vivian agreed as she gave the girl a nod, and Becky skipped toward the door. As she reached for the knob, though, Becky turned to ask, "Is the money a secret?"

Vivian nodded. "For now, it is. Let's wait until after the party to say anything. And, maybe we should wait a few days longer."

The judge was planning to announce his decision about Katy and Robbie this afternoon. That would be enough for everyone to handle. Besides, she didn't know Robert well enough to trust him with the knowledge that this much cash was in the house. She trusted Craig and Finn. And Mrs. Hunt and the judge, of course.

After Becky left the room, Vivian wrapped the Bible tightly in a wool scarf and placed it back where it had been. It nestled right down beside that Deringer her grandfather had given her. Now, the gun made more sense, too, Vivian thought wryly. Then, she pushed the valise under her bed.

It was time for her to finish up preparations for their noon meal. The round king cake was made and the dried black bean securely hidden in one of the twisted folds. Vivian knew that, to be a proper king cake, there should be purple icing for justice, gold for power and green for faith. She'd done the best she could with some dried blueberries cooked with sugar for the purple icing. The yellow came from several of Craig's lemon drops. The green had been a challenge, and she'd finally found an apple with light green skin and sprinkled tiny bits of the skin on a section of cake.

It was hot around the kitchen stove and Vivian had, early on, taken off her hat and veil. The men, along with Robbie, were all out in the barn, and the girls were in the loft giggling about something. Vivian set her hat and veil on the top of her bed, planning to rush in when everything was ready and put them back on before everyone came inside.

She went back and set the cake in the middle of the table. Vivian had to admit it was a glorious cake even if the colors weren't exact. The children had been teasing all morning about who was going to get the bean that she'd hidden.

In addition to the cake, Vivian had baked a ham and a pan of sourdough rolls. She'd cooked some carrots, cabbage and potato chunks with the ham. Everyone was sniffing the air in appreciation, except for when they were nervously looking out the window.

Surprisingly, Mrs. Hunt was the one to look down

the road most often. Vivian figured the woman was tired of the isolation on the homestead. It sure was different here than it was in New York City. Vivian found it rested her, however. She felt like she belonged in the peace of the wilderness prairie.

"Are you sure you made enough for an extra person?" Mrs. Hunt asked as she turned from the window and stepped toward the table. "You'll need an extra setting, too."

"I counted the judge," Vivian said as she went about opening a jar of beet relish. That and a jar of pickles would add a festive touch to their meal, she thought.

"I mean in addition to the judge," Mrs. Hunt said.

"I figured on Dry Gulch, too." Vivian was surprised the other woman was so keen on making sure the miner was fed.

"No, not him," Mrs. Hunt persisted. "I am hoping we will have a surprise guest."

"Today?" Vivian was appalled. "Are you sure that's wise? This is a stressful day for everyone. I'm not sure a stranger will be comfortable."

"He's not a stranger," Mrs. Hunt said smugly. "And, once he says his piece, I think you'll be very pleased he came."

Vivian stopped, a plate still in her hand. "Who?"

"You'll have to wait and see," the older woman said as she turned and walked over to stand in front of the fireplace.

Vivian shook her head as she went about preparing the table for the meal. She figured Mrs. Hunt had asked Mrs. Drummond to come. Who else could it be? Not that it mattered. She'd prepared plenty of food. She wanted to have leftover ham and bread for Craig, Finn and the children in case Mrs. Hunt's group left and Vivian and Becky did, too. Vivian refused to believe the judge would suggest that Robbie and Katy go back to New York City. She was sure both children had told the judge they wanted to stay here with Craig.

The door opened and Vivian turned to see Robbie come inside, leading the dog by a short rope.

"Cold outside?" Vivian asked with a smile as she walked over to the boy.

Robbie nodded. "Me and B-Big don't mind."

"You named the dog," Vivian said in surprise.

Robbie shook his head. "It's n-not a name. F-Finn and Daddy both s-said it can b-be a s-short name, n-not the real name."

"Ah," Vivian said with a smile.

"Like D-Daddy," Robbie continued. "It's n-not his r-real name. I j-just call him that."

"I understand," Vivian said, hoping that Robert wouldn't use this to pressure Robbie to go with him. Of course, regardless of the naming, it would be hard for Robbie to say goodbye to that dog.

"We can't s-stay," Robbie said turning back to the door. "I j-just wanted to tell y-you about Big."

"Thank you," Vivian whispered before he opened the door and left with his dog. She had to be careful, she decided, or she would be a puddle of tears by the end of the day. She was going to have a hard time saying goodbye to this family.

The door to the large bedroom opened and Mrs. Hunt stepped out. "Who was that?"

"Robbie," Vivian said as she turned back to the table.

"That boy should know better than to go around bothering people," Mrs. Hunt said with a frown on her face.

"This is his home," Vivian said, her voice no doubt irritated.

"He could still stand to get a good dose of discipline," Mrs. Hunt muttered as she went to the window again and looked out.

"He's coming!" Mrs. Hunt exclaimed as she turned away from the window and lifted her hands to her cheeks. "I'd better get ready. He'll be here any minute." She looked across at Vivian and frowned. "You could do with a look in the mirror, too. You'll want to look your best."

With that, Mrs. Hunt scampered into her bedroom, moving faster than Vivian had ever seen her move.

Curious, Vivian went to the window herself. The judge was coming in a wagon and a strange man sat beside him on the seat. It certainly wasn't Mrs. Drummond. Not that the other woman would have caused Mrs. Hunt's reaction. Vivian decided she wouldn't be able to place the mystery guest, but she was sure the man had nothing to do with her. And she had a holiday meal to get on the table. She'd let Mrs. Hunt worry about looking pretty.

The men had clearly heard the judge's wagon drive up by the house because there was soon a chorus of greetings and welcomes. Vivian was going to go to her small bedroom and put on her hat and veil, but the ham needed taking out of the oven and then she saw that the rolls were getting too brown.

By the time she had everything on the stove under control, the front door was opening, and she decided she would stay quietly in the kitchen until the men were all inside, and then she would slip into her bedroom. Her plan seemed like it would work. The judge came inside, and Craig took his coat to hang on the peg by the door. Finn led the judge to the bench and offered to find him a quilt to warm up more quickly.

The last man to come in the house, though, was the passenger on the judge's wagon. He didn't worry about his coat or a quilt. He came inside the house and immediately began searching the shadows.

"Vivian!" the man exclaimed and started walking toward her.

She was stunned. It couldn't be. No, it really couldn't be. "Ethan?"

And then he was there, smiling right down at her. "It's me, all right. Surprised?"

Vivian could only nod. She was still staring up at Mrs. Hunt's son when Craig came over.

"You know each other?" Craig asked, clearly puzzled.

Ethan turned and held out his hand. "I'm Mrs. Hunt's son."

"Oh." Craig seemed taken back. "I suppose you came to escort your mother back to New York?"

Ethan laughed, a slow, deep sound that Vivian remembered all too well. She used to love Ethan's laugh. She used to love Ethan.

"My mother doesn't need an escort," Ethan said. "No, I came to ask Vivian if she'd do me the honor of being my wife."

"What?" Vivian squeaked.

"I know it seems like I'm rushing things," Ethan said smoothly as he took Vivian's hand. "But we don't have much time, and it's not like we don't know each other from before."

"That's been six years ago," Vivian retorted. She finally felt like some blood was traveling to her brain. "You can't just come in here and—" Vivian stopped to gesture with her hands. She included the whole of the room and the many faces that were now turned their way. She even glanced up and saw the girls peering down from the loft.

"Mother finally approves," Ethan leaned down and whispered in Vivian's ear. "I wanted to propose six years ago, but—"

"I know," Vivian said. "The fire. The scars. The—"

"Oh, that wasn't it," Ethan said easily. "Even my mother didn't stop me. It was your sister-in-law. She told everyone you didn't want to have company. That you had asked to be left alone for a while. Everyone decided to step back. We thought you'd come around and let us know when you wanted to take up with us again. We never heard anything more."

Edith had been jealous of her even back then, Vivian thought.

"You're sure you want to marry me?" Vivian asked to be positive she understood.

"I very much want to marry you as soon as possible," Ethan affirmed.

She only needed to look in his eyes to see that he was sincere. The Ethan she had known was easily persuaded to things, but he didn't lie.

Vivian feared she was getting too much blood to her brain. Why was this happening now? She couldn't think.

Vivian suddenly realized she was holding Craig's hand. She couldn't remember if she had reached for his hand or if he had captured hers. But she did know that it felt like an anchor to her. Somehow, she knew, he would help her figure all of this out. The only thing she understood is that Ethan was saying she could have her old life back. She could go to New York and be accepted in the same social circles that she had known. She could raise Becky there. If she was married to Ethan, everyone would accept them.

Then she looked down at her hand, now solidly gripped by Craig. Did she even want her old life back? Then again, did she have the choice of a new one here?

Chapter Nine

Craig finally found enough of his voice to ask everyone to sit down to eat. Finn offered to set all of the food on the table. Then Craig sat Vivian down beside him without even asking her where she'd like to sit. She still had her hand in his, and he wanted to keep it that way. He knew Mrs. Hunt's son had just offered her more than he ever could if one was tallying up clothes and jewelry and opera tickets. But he would have never let her suffer in her isolation because of what someone else had said. He would have found a way to talk to her and help her if she needed to adjust to the scars.

No, Craig thought as he passed the ham, Vivian didn't belong with the Hunts. Ethan had not spoken up six years ago when she'd been hurt. What did that say about his care for her? Vivian needed someone who loved her.

Craig almost dropped the platter. He'd never used that word before regarding Vivian, not even in his own mind. He'd known he cared for her. He would have said they were friends. He believed she'd be a good wife to him. And he a good husband to her. But the truth had snuck up on him this past week, and here he was. He loved Vivian with his whole heart, and he had no presents to give her to make that fact plain.

The meal passed quickly. No one talked much, although Finn did make an effort to tease the children a little about the presents that were gathered under a sheet in the corner next to the loft ladder. The little ones tried to rally, but Craig could tell their hearts weren't in it. They were nervous and kept making quick glances at the judge as though they could read their fate on his face.

The judge looked thoughtful, but that was all Craig could tell about the man's decision. Other than that, Mrs. Hunt kept chirping about second chances in life. At first, Craig thought her comments were directed to Vivian but then the older woman flat-out said she regretted some decisions she'd made with her young daughter, Delores, and wanted a second chance to do things the right way. Craig asked her to be more specific, but she smiled and shook her head.

"Is it time for the king cake?" Katy asked quietly.

Craig noted that everyone had finished eating and laid their fork on their plate.

"A delicious meal," Robert said with a nod to Vivian.

"You cooked this?" Ethan turned to Vivian in surprise. "I didn't know you knew how to cook."

"I do," Vivian said, and Craig could tell she was proud. She sat up a little straighter on the bench.

"Well, you won't have to do any of that kind of work when you come back with me," Ethan said as though he didn't consider her efforts even proper. "We'll live in the Hunt manor, and there are enough servants, so you don't have to do much of anything but look pretty."

Craig saw the moment Ethan realized he'd said the wrong thing. "I mean—"

Vivian waved the man's words away. "I can always be half pretty. That will have to do."

There was an edge to Vivian's voice that Craig didn't understand. He was pleased that she didn't have her hat and veil on, but he had a hunch that she wished she'd taken the time to go into the bedroom and retrieve it before she'd sat down to eat. That would have meant convincing him to let go of her hand, though, and she hadn't even tried to do that.

"You don't have to answer right now," Ethan said. "I plan to stay for a few days after my mother leaves."

"Here's the cake," Katy exclaimed as Finn set the plate in front of Vivian.

"And a knife to cut it," Finn added as he placed the implement on the table, too.

"Remember, the twists in the dough are to show the many different paths the kings took on their trip to see Jesus," Vivian said to the children. "Maybe your father can read the story."

Craig had the verses marked in his Bible. He stood, took the book from the table by the door and opened it.

"Reading from the book of Matthew, chapter 2, verses 10 to 12," Craig said. "When they saw the star, they rejoiced with exceeding great joy. And when they were come into the house, they saw the young child with Mary his mother, and fell down, and worshipped him: and when they had opened their treasures, they presented unto him gifts; gold, and frankincense, and myrrh. And being warned of God in a dream that they should not return to Herod, they departed into their own country another way."

Everyone was silent for a moment after the words were spoken. Then Robbie asked, "Does God always protect people when they travel?"

"We can certainly pray for His protection wherever we are," Craig added. He could tell the boy was troubled.

"Does God know where New York City is?" Robbie asked.

"I never heard of such a thing—" Mrs. Hunt protested, clearly insulted. "Everyone knows where New York City is."

"God is with you wherever you are." Craig answered his son's question, and he saw the boy's shoulders relax. "You can pray to Him anywhere and He will hear you."

Robbie nodded but kept his chin tucked low.

Finn and Vivian passed the pieces of king cake around the table until everyone had one.

"We need to look for the bean," Katy said, her face determined as she poked at her cake.

It was some minutes before Craig realized the bean

was hiding in his cake, close to where his fork had slid. "I have it."

"That means you'll have a good year," Katy declared with a giggle.

"I'd rather you have a wonderful year," Craig said as he lifted the bean from his cake and placed it on top of the few bites left on Katy's plate.

"Can you do that?" she whispered in awe.

Craig nodded. "I sure can."

It didn't take long for everyone to finish their cake after that. The dishes were taken away, and Craig set them in the water that was heating on the stove. He knew the announcement everyone was waiting for, and he didn't want to delay it any longer.

"Have you made your decision, Judge Radcliff?" Craig asked.

Suddenly, the only sound in the house was the crackling of the two fires—the one in the stove and the other in the fireplace.

"I have," the judge said as he slid out from the bench and stood beside the table. "It wasn't easy, but I have followed the law as best as I know how." He waited for a minute, making eye contact with everyone at the table briefly.

Craig knew he wasn't going to like the judge's decision from the look of sympathy in the man's eyes.

"I've decided Katy will stay with her father, Craig Martin," the judge announced. "And that Robbie will go with his natural father, Robert Cassidy. I understand that Robert has a prison record, and so I am making his guardianship dependent on another law-abiding citizen of his choice helping him to raise the child. He has expressed the desire to have Mrs. Hunt, the boy's grandmother, parent with him, and that is acceptable to this court."

"No." Craig felt the whispered protest pulled from him. He couldn't lose either of his children. He loved them both.

"Well, I'd rather have the girl," Mrs. Hunt said with a sniff. "I'd be happy to trade Robbie for Katy."

Craig started at her in horror. "My children are not checker pieces to be moved around depending on your whims."

"Katy probably wants to go with me," Mrs. Hunt said with a sugary smile on her face as she looked at the girl. "You'd have lots of pretty dresses to wear, and there'd be lots of biscuits and servants. You'd be just like a princess."

Katy started to cry uncontrollably. "I—I don't want to be a princess."

Katy threw herself at Craig, and he opened his arms to hold her.

"I—I don't w-want to go, either," Robbie said as he started to step over to Craig.

Robert stopped the boy, though. "You're with us now. Where you belong. It's what your mother would have wanted."

"My mother was mean." Robbie burst forth with the accusations. "She didn't care if Katy cried. She didn't care if we were sad. She didn't like us. It's my daddy and Uncle Finn who love us."

Craig realized that was the first time in years that Robbie had spoken without stuttering.

Mrs. Hunt wasn't happy, though. Her face was purple, and she walked over to pull Robbie away from Craig and slap his face. "You're never to talk about your mother that way. She was a better mother than you deserved—that's for sure."

"That slap wasn't necessary," Robert protested to Mrs. Hunt. "The boy has a right to speak."

"Not like that, he doesn't," Mrs. Hunt said firmly and glared at Robert. "And I expect you to honor my decision on this. If he's going to live in my house, he will respect his elders. And obey them. I expect any child in my house to live up to the Hunt name."

"Wasn't that the mistake you made with Delores?" Ethan said mildly.

Mrs. Hunt didn't answer him, but she sent him a look that was sour enough to make a plant wither and die.

Both children were sobbing by then. Even the judge looked uncomfortable.

"May we have a ride back to Cheyenne with you?" Mrs. Hunt asked the judge. Then she offered up a brittle smile. "I want to get back east as soon as possible."

The judge nodded.

Mrs. Hunt turned to her son and Robert. "The two of you get Robbie ready to leave. We'll spend the night in Cheyenne and take the early train out of here."

"Can I take my dog, Big?" Robbie asked, his voice wavering.

"I did promise him the dog," Robert said quickly.

"Well, really, we have dogs in New York City," Mrs. Hunt said. "We'll get him a little white one when we get there. Something that doesn't look so very lower class. Common."

"Big can at least go to the train station with us," Robert said to Robbie soothingly. "He might like to stay around here anyway."

Robbie sniffed. "I want to stay, too."

Mrs. Hunt looked over everyone disapprovingly. "The sooner we leave here, the better."

Craig couldn't let go of Robbie. He decided to take Katy, Becky and Vivian to Cheyenne and spend the night in the hotel. Finn agreed to stay at the homestead tonight to take care of the animals; he'd ride one of the saddle horses into town tomorrow morning to say goodbye before the train came. That wouldn't be until midday tomorrow. They'd have that much more time with Robbie. Craig wondered how he could he squeeze a lifetime of hugs and words into less than a day.

"I insist you leave your guns here," Mrs. Hunt said as Craig reached for his rifle. "I won't have Robbie exposed to such things any longer."

"That's pure foolishness—" Craig began to explain.

Mrs. Hunt interrupted, "Judge, isn't it my right to decide if Robbie is allowed to be around weapons?"

The judge frowned. "Of course, but—"

"Then do it," Mrs. Hunt ordered. "Leave that rifle here."

Craig always carried his rifle on his trips to Cheyenne, and he didn't have time to convince the older
woman that it was necessary. She was already hus-
tling Robbie out to the wagon along with her son
and Robert.

Vivian had gone into her bedroom and come out
so quickly that she must have just grabbed her hat and
the valise she'd come with. Katy had thrown a few
quilts down from the loft. Becky had picked them up
and was waiting to go outside to the wagon.

They were ready to leave within five minutes. Finn
had harnessed the team and pulled the wagon around.
Katy lifted her kitty up into the wagon, and Vivian
hoisted her up as well. Craig saw to Becky.

"I can't afford a room at the Cheyenne Hotel—
which I'm sure is where Mrs. Hunt will stay," Craig
explained as he started his team forward. "But there
is a more modest hotel where we can stay."

He pulled the quilt up, enclosing Vivian and himself in their usual warmth. There was no snow falling, but the cold wind was blowing. There were some
gray clouds in the south, so they could come into a
storm later.

"I can pay for a room in the Cheyenne Hotel for
us," Vivian said as she patted her valise. She had refused to put it in the back of the wagon like before.
"For one night, it will be fine."

"I suppose you want to be near—" Craig choked
at the name of Mrs. Hunt's son.

"I want to be near Robbie," Vivian clarified. "He'll
be upset tonight. What if he has a bad dream? Maybe

Mrs. Hunt will let him spend the night in our room if we're on the same floor."

"Robbie doesn't like to be alone at night." Katy's thin voice came from behind them. She and Becky were wrapped up in quilts. Even the cat had a piece of Katy's quilt tucked around him.

"Those two have never been apart," Craig said, his voice low so only Vivian could hear him. "I don't know how they'll bear it."

Vivian patted his hand, and Craig's heart shattered. The next day would be the hardest one of his life—and that included the day he and Finn buried their *mam* beside their *daidí* in Ireland. At least they had known their parents were finally together again and at peace. He had no such assurances about Robbie—and he had no idea if Vivian would choose to go back east or not with Ethan Hunt. His heart might never be whole again.

Vivian's face was cold. The rest of her was wrapped up in the quilt. This was an awful, awful day. She understood the judge's reasoning, but she felt he had no compassion. She watched Craig as he kept his head pointed forward on this gray day. She could feel the tightly controlled grief in him. Not even the changing dips and rises in the ground seemed to interest him.

"It's not right," Vivian finally muttered. She knew it only added to Craig's burden to have others say such things. But it wasn't fair what was happening.

"Giddyup." Craig urged the horses up an incline.

He didn't answer her complaint. But then, what could he say?

Vivian noted that they were driving past a creek bed with assorted bushes nestled along it. The branches on the bushes were all bare, but there were many of them, and it was not possible to see through them. She saw a few spots of red and wondered if there were berries there.

She heard a low hissing sound coming from the back and wondered if Kitty sensed the painful emotions on their journey. Then she heard a dog bark in the wagon behind them. Robbie's Big might know something was wrong, too. Maybe even those chickens of Katy's would be raising a ruckus if they were coming along on this sorrowful ride.

Then Vivian heard a definite rustling from the bushes, and after turning her head, she saw that Robbie's dog, with a loud yip, had jumped over the edge of the wagon behind them. The dog was headed straight toward those bushes.

"Craig," Vivian said, putting her hand on his arm. Craig was looking ahead, and he wouldn't have seen the dog racing to the right of them.

They both turned around and were looking back just as Robbie vaulted over the edge of the other wagon and, dropping to the snowy ground, took off running toward his dog.

"Come back, Big," Robbie shouted as he went.

The dog didn't turn.

Vivian gasped. She saw why the dog wasn't retreating. "It's a wolf."

She'd only read about the beasts, but there was no mistaking the rangy strength of this gray predator. The dog was large enough but was still half the size of that animal.

"Robbie, come back," Craig yelled as he pulled his wagon to a stop. "Now."

"My dog," Robbie shouted back, still moving forward.

And then the boy stopped. Vivian could see why. Two more huge wolves had stepped out from the bushes.

"Foolish boy," Craig said and then began searching for something under the seat of the wagon. Then he sat up. "I forgot. I didn't bring the rifle after Mrs. Hunt made her request."

"Oh, dear," Vivian said as she, too, searched the bottom of their wagon. The floorboards were empty except for her valise and the snowy footprints they'd left when they'd climbed into the wagon back at the homestead.

"Robbie." The distressed cry came from the back of the wagon.

Vivian turned back in time to see a small figure launch herself off the end of the wagon. "Katy! Don't go out there!"

The girl turned. "But Robbie needs me."

With that, the little one was off and running.

"What in the blazes," Craig said as he stood up in the wagon and then swung himself off of the side.

"Come back here, both of you," Craig shouted as he started running after his children.

"Mama," Becky asked urgently. "Don't wolves eat little girls and boys?"

Vivian nodded. She had to do something. And then she remembered the two-shot Deringer her grandfather had given her. It was still in the valise at her feet.

"Don't you worry, now," Vivian said. "I'll be back."

And with that, Vivian put the Deringer in her pocket and climbed down out of the wagon as fast as she could before racing after Craig. The cold filled her lungs, and she had to blink back tears as she ran. She saw Katy had caught up with Robbie, and the two of them were huddled together. Vivian hadn't even noticed Kitty, but now she saw that the cat was in front of the two children, drawing the attention of the wolves.

The lead wolf came up to the cat, maybe in curiosity, and Kitty swiped at the animal's face so hard it yelped and ran back to where the other wolves were. The cat kept hissing and spitting loud enough that the dog finally came over and stood beside him.

By then, Craig was almost even with the children, and he shouted over to the other wagon. "Don't any of you have a rifle?"

Silence was the only answer.

"Wait," Vivian cried out as she came up behind Craig only to have him move forward.

Craig turned around, surprise and distress flooding his face. "What are you doing here? It's not safe."

"I wanted to give you this." Vivian took the Deringer out of her pocket. "It's not a big gun, but it works if you're close. It has two shots. And it's loaded."

"Bless you," Craig said. "Now start walking back to the wagon. If I don't kill these wolves, drive the children into Cheyenne. The judge can lead the way."

"You must come back," Vivian said. "I insist."

Craig looked up and smiled. "Don't try to rescue me if things don't work out. Just remember that I love you."

"You love me?" Vivian whispered, but he was already gone.

"Mama," Becky called from the wagon.

Vivian turned around and started to walk back. She had taken only a few steps when she heard the pop of the gun. She heard a wild yelp and then a whimper. She turned and saw that Craig had shot the lead wolf—the one that had come out to investigate Kitty and was met with the cat's claws. The other wolves had backed off a few yards, but the two left were looking at Craig warily. Vivian got the sense that they wouldn't stay back for long.

"Katy. Robbie," Vivian called. "Come back with me. Your father wants us to go back to the wagon."

"I'm afraid," Katy turned to whisper.

If the snow hadn't silenced all of their movements, Vivian wouldn't have been able to hear the girl.

"Come, meet me," Vivian said as she turned back to the children. "You, too, Robbie."

She walked closer to the children until she could hear the hungry growls of the wolves. She looked up and saw them snapping at Kitty. The cat kept them moving, but he was faster than they were and always managed to avoid their teeth. Vivian wanted to call the cat back, too, but she didn't want to turn those beasts loose against Craig.

Then she saw Craig take another step toward the wolves. Vivian wondered how she could have ever thought he was not a hero. He had not hesitated to step forward to save his children. Maybe she had misjudged him. She looked back at him. If she wasn't needed to coax the children back to safety, she would have stayed and stood by Craig.

She caught Craig glancing over his shoulder at the children. When Vivian had encouraged them far enough back to the wagon that they could make it in a good hard run, she heard the second pop of the gun. There was a thud and a low cry that went on for almost a minute.

She heard the rustle again of the branches of those bushes and worried that more wolves had come out to challenge Craig. That gun only had the two bullets, and they had both been used now. Vivian knew she should have bought more ammunition for that gun, but she'd long ago figured that she would never lose it. She wouldn't, she had reasoned, have the heart to kill another living being. She hadn't realized until now that she'd kill a whole army of criminals if they were attacking someone she loved.

They were almost back to the wagon before Vivian dared to turn around and see what had happened. Two dead wolves laid on the ground in front of those bare bushes. The third wolf was gone. Craig was starting to walk back.

Vivian lifted Robbie and Katy into the back of the wagon before she went to the side of the wagon and slowly climbed up into her seat.

"I was scared," Robbie said, and Vivian turned around. The boy was wrapped in a quilt.

"But you acted very brave," Vivian assured him.

Robbie nodded. "I did. Maybe I wasn't that scared, after all. I always worried I was not brave because I didn't go with my mother that time."

"You had to stay back with your baby sister," Vivian said, suddenly noticing that Robbie wasn't stuttering any more. "It was the best decision."

"It was, wasn't it?" Robbie said.

When Craig got to the wagon, he went to the back and opened his arms. Robbie rushed into them. Then Craig motioned for Katy and Becky to come, too, and they all stood, wrapped in his arms for several minutes.

Vivian was touched to see that Craig counted her Becky among his children. He had a big heart.

After the hug, Craig walked around and hoisted himself up onto the wagon seat. Vivian wrapped the quilt around both of their shoulders. Sitting as close as they were, she could feel the man trembling. He reached out and gripped her hand.

"I could have lost them," he whispered for her ears only.

She nodded. "But you didn't."

"Thanks be to God," Craig said fervently and then

turned to her. "And to you. I didn't know you had one of those little guns."

Vivian nodded. "My grandfather gave it to me after those riots in New York when—"

Vivian stopped. Now wasn't the time to ask.

"That night was just like this," Craig said. "I was scared spitless. I thought I'd lost Finn. He'd barely turned fourteen years old and he thought he was a man, but he had no more sense than a fresh-born pup. He was tagging along after this group of longshoremen that I worked with at the docks. They were a rough crowd; not men that a boy should be around."

Vivian watched his face and she knew he was telling the truth.

"When I came home and he wasn't there that night, Craig continued, "I knew he'd gone with them. I couldn't find him for so long that I was panicked, and then I saw him in the crowd by your house that night. He was standing there looking as troubled as I'd ever seen the lad. He had tried to talk the men out of setting that fire, but they laughed at him. After I got you on your way to the hospital, I had to hunt Finn down again. He was hiding behind a shed a few doors down, crying. He felt so bad, even though he'd done all he could."

"I didn't know," Vivian said softly. "I thought—"

"I can only imagine what you thought," Craig said. "But neither Finn nor I ever meant your family—or anyone else—harm that night."

They were sitting close with that quilt wrapped around them, and it was like they were in their own private world. Craig leaned forward and looked at her for a long minute before he kissed her. His lips were gentle at first, and then they grew more intense. Suddenly, the quilt felt too warm around them. That, and the sound of horses moving, made them draw apart.

"I'm glad you're the man I thought you were," Vivian whispered as she gazed up at his face. "You've always been my hero."

The jingle of the harness grew louder, and the judge drove his wagon up and parked it right beside them.

"Goodness," Mrs. Hunt shouted out from where she sat in the back of the wagon. "Whatever were you thinking?"

"Are you all right?" the judge leaned around the older woman and asked, concern in his voice.

Craig nodded. "That old tomcat did most of the work."

Vivian made a note to check the cat for scratches when they got into Cheyenne. Kitty had been quick, but those wolves had been deadly, and they hadn't liked his taking swipes at them.

"My dog, Big, did some, too," Robbie offered from the back of the wagon.

"He sure did," Craig said generously. Vivian was pleased that he didn't complain that the dog had been responsible for the children being in the predicament in the first place.

Vivian looked behind herself and saw that the three children had wrapped themselves in quilts. The dog and the tomcat were both sitting nearby and sharing some of the corners of the quilts. They looked tired.

"Robbie needs to ride in our wagon," Mrs. Hunt called out. "He's mine now."

"He's riding with us today," Craig said firmly. "After a scare like that, he needs his family around him."

No one said anything to that, but Vivian did notice Robert pursing his lips like he'd tasted something sour.

"There's room for you beside me now," Ethan called to Vivian from the back of the wagon.

"No, thank you," she said as politely as she would have if she'd been offered a cup of punch at some fancy New York City ball. "I'm settled here."

The truth of the matter was that she needed her family around her after that nerve-racking threat just as much as Robbie did.

"Allow me to buy everyone dinner when we arrive in Cheyenne," Robert added as Craig signaled his horses to continue. "There's a restaurant in the hotel."

"We'll be there," Craig said as he pulled farther away from the judge's wagon.

Vivian snuggled deeper into the quilt that was wrapped around her and Craig as they continued on their way. She knew nothing had been changed by that thwarted wolf attack, but it did remind her of how very young the children were. The wolves Robbie would face in New York City couldn't be shot with a Deringer. They would be people who wanted to take advantage of him. Maybe she should suggest to Craig that the boy learn to wrestle or box—or to at least speak up for himself.

But then, Craig wouldn't be the one giving any guidance to the young boy. Most of his daily care would fall to Mrs. Hunt, or perhaps a nurse or tutor. Robbie would be lonely, she thought. She was suddenly very hopeful he'd have Big with him.

For a second, she allowed herself to believe that Craig would just keep driving that wagon, past Cheyenne and on down to Denver. Mrs. Hunt wasn't likely to give chase. But Vivian knew Craig wouldn't. She'd finally realized he played by the rules. He would obey the judge's orders. He wouldn't like it, but he would do it. He was a good man, she told herself. She wasn't sure what their future held—or even if they had one together—but she was glad she'd come to know him better today.

Chapter Ten

The town of Cheyenne rose on the prairie, growing bigger as the wagons approached. Clouds had grown darker until they were now a deep gray. The wind had not let up, and the smoke of burning coal filled the air. Craig had to admit that, on an overcast winter day, the flat Wyoming land was a grim sight. A soft rumble of street noise increased as they drove closer. A lone shout was heard. The sun would set soon enough. Once the lanterns in town were lit, Craig figured everything would look livelier.

Craig was cold to the bone when he pulled his wagon up to the double oak door leading into the square-built plank building. The sign, with letters burnt into the wood, read The Cheyenne Hotel. Shining glass windows lined the front. The two-story structure was still new; the boards had not had time to turn gray. He'd never been inside the hotel, but he had to admit it looked impressive.

Craig only hoped it lived up to its reputation. It

was one of the first solid hotels the city had to offer. Before that, men would line up to share bunks in a tent. No one had slept well in those days.

He stopped the wagon as close to the front door as he could and carried each of the children inside. It wasn't totally necessary, but he enjoyed doing the small service for them. The lobby of the hotel was warm, and he could feel the children relax as he sat them, one after another, on a bench in the lobby.

The clerk, a dark-haired man with a mustache, had watched as he brought child after child inside. When he finally brought Vivian inside, the clerk smiled. Craig supposed that made them look like a regular family.

"There's room for the horses in that old livery in back," the clerk said. "Tell Gus you're staying at the hotel, and he'll arrange for your horses to have feed. Water's free, but grain is added to your bill."

"Any place for an old tomcat and a dog?" Craig asked as he walked over to the clerk's desk. "It's too cold out there for them, and they fought off a band of wolves earlier today, so I owe them a good night's sleep."

"Wolves?" the man asked, clearly skeptical as he looked over Kitty and Big.

Craig chuckled. "I'll admit they don't look the part, but they'd battle anything that wants to hurt my children."

Kitty limped over to Katy and curled up at the girl's feet. Big couldn't seem to decide where to settle. He still had some ribs showing, though, so he wouldn't win any prizes for beauty.

"I can put you in a suite," the clerk suggested as the door opened and Robert stepped inside, brushing snow off of his clothes. "They have a fireplace and a settee. I can set two rugs out so each animal will have its own place to sleep."

"I don't know about a suite," Craig said. He didn't want to borrow money for a room, and a suite would be more.

"Give them the suite," Robert said with a wave of his hand. "I'm paying. And give me another one right next to them."

Robert winked at Craig. "Mrs. Hunt gave me traveling money, and I have quite a bit left. Figure I should spend it."

"I'm obliged to you for covering the bill," Craig said. "But I'll pay you back when I can."

"You already have," Robert said.

"Huh?" Craig looked up in confusion.

"You saved my son's life this afternoon," Robert said, his eyes sincere. "I just sat there in the wagon, frozen in fear. Those wolves were fierce."

Craig nodded. "I'm glad it worked out as well as it did."

"Even that cat did a better job protecting my boy than I did," Robert said, clearly distressed.

Craig smiled gently. "Don't let the name Kitty fool you. That old tomcat has probably been up against other wolves or maybe even cougars in his life. He was a trapper's cat, and they roamed the mountains looking for all kinds of animals. The cat sure knew how to get his licks in with those wolves without getting touched himself."

Robert nodded and then they both looked over at the clerk's desk. Mrs. Hunt and Ethan were checking in, and the older woman was demanding the best room in the house. She didn't believe the clerk when he said she already had the best room, that the hotel didn't have a third floor.

Craig looked back into the lobby area and saw Vivian talking softly with the children as they all gathered around. Vivian had her valise. Robbie had a small trunk that Mrs. Hunt had produced from one of her larger trunks. Craig wasn't sure what the boy would have packed in the thing. He was wearing most of his clothes. He did have an extra pair of boots and the white shirt Vivian had made him as an Epiphany present. The reverend's wife had also made the boy a quilt last Christmas, and he would surely have that packed.

"We should have stopped at the reverend's place on our way into Cheyenne," Craig muttered to himself. The older couple had been unable to come to the Epiphany party and would want to say their goodbyes to Robbie and pray over the boy. And then there was Mrs. Drummond. She had difficulty relating to boys, but Craig knew she would want to sincerely tell Robbie she hoped all would go well.

"What's wrong?" Vivian asked when he arrived at the bench where they were all sitting.

Craig forced himself to smile. "I was just thinking how many friends Robbie has around here."

Vivian seemed to understand his concerns without him speaking them. "We'll have to go to the general store in the morning and buy Robbie some stationery. We'll help him write letters to everyone so he can say how much he's appreciated knowing them."

Craig nodded. "That would be good."

Robbie was frowning. "Will they know where to write me back?"

"I'm sure Mrs. Hunt will give us your address and we can give it to everyone else," Craig said and then was beset by worries. He looked over at where Mrs. Hunt stood, impatiently waiting for help. Would the older woman give him her address? Would she let Robbie correspond with anyone from Cheyenne, including him and Katy? He was suddenly very unsure. It would be needlessly cruel to Robbie if Mrs. Hunt insisted that he cut off all contact, but she might do it.

Craig watched as a young man came down the stairs and lifted Mrs. Hunt's trunk onto his shoulder.

"Suite five, at the top of the stairs," the clerk directed the young man.

Robert was standing in front of the tall desk, and once Mrs. Hunt had started up the stairs, the clerk turned to him and held out two keys. "You have suites eight and ten. They are side by side at the end of the hallway. A full-size bed and a smaller one in the bedroom and another child-size mattress tucked into a corner of the fireplace room, too."

"We'll meet in a half an hour in the dining room,"

Robert gestured to a door that clearly led to the eating establishment that was part of the hotel.

Craig had noticed the aromas coming out of that part of the hotel. It made him hungry. He expected the others were, too. Everyone had been nervous at noon when they'd eaten. By now, they'd want to eat whether they were upset or not.

Craig was halfway up the stairs when Ethan came rushing into the hotel.

"Wait," he said as he walked into the middle of the lobby. "Craig, I have something for you.

Ethan was carrying something in a canvas grain sack. Craig eyed it wearily until he could determine that the long object inside didn't move. He wasn't ready for another stray animal, although he'd consider a dog. He'd gotten used to having Big around in the morning when he walked out to the barn. Kitty was never awake that early, but the dog had been eager to make the trip with Craig.

"What is it?" Craig said as he walked down the stairs and came to the bottom.

Ethan drew the long rifle out of the bag.

"A Yellowboy!" Craig exclaimed. He could see the flash of the brass tacks on the handle of the lever-action rifle. "That Winchester has been sitting in the general store for months waiting for someone with the money to buy it."

"Well, it's all yours," Ethan said as he held the gun out to him.

"But I can't afford that," Craig said, reality settling in. It was the likes of General George Armstrong

Custer who owned a rifle like that. "And I have my Henry at home. That does well enough."

"My mother is buying it for you," Ethan said. "She was wrong to demand you leave your place without your guns and—truth be told—she should buy you a cannon instead. She needs to learn to stop telling people what to do. It can be dangerous. Like we all learned today."

Ethan kept his arm outstretched, offering the gun.

Craig wondered if he was being given something to stop him from complaining that they were taking Robbie away from him. He was going to refuse the gun, but then he told himself that Mrs. Hunt was taking Robbie no matter who took the gun.

Then he knew what to do. "Hold the rifle for Robbie. Tell him when he's old enough to come back to Cheyenne, he can bring it with him." He looked at Ethan square in the eyes. "You be sure to teach the boy how to shoot the thing. He might have to live in New York for a few years, but my boy will be coming back one day, and he'll need to know how to survive in the west."

Ethan nodded. "I'll see that he learns."

Craig held out his hand to the other man, and Ethan took it. "I know it's not your fault your mother is so set on having Robbie, but it will be hard on the boy. I trust you to look out for him."

Ethan nodded. "I'll do my best."

Craig was going to turn aside when he stopped. "I can't let you take Vivian, though."

Ethan grinned. "I figure she's already decided to

stay with you. I couldn't believe that she'd walk out there with those wolves just to hand you that little gun. What if it hadn't worked? She has some strong feelings for you and the boy."

Craig nodded. He'd have nightmares tonight about that. He didn't like to shoot a gun when he didn't even know for sure it was loaded. Vivian could have been mistaken when she said it was.

There was a noise, and he looked up to see Robert coming down the stairs.

"We're almost ready to go in to eat," the man said.

Craig wanted to wash his face before he sat down to a fancy dinner, so he nodded to the two men and made his way upstairs. He could have easily flown up to the second floor, his heart was that much lighter from Ethan's saying Vivian would be staying. Now, if he could only find some way to keep Robbie.

Lord, help me to accept Your will for Robbie, Craig prayed as he took the last step. He knew Mrs. Hunt could offer schools and career opportunities that Robbie would not have in Wyoming territory. Craig did not want to be selfish with Robbie's future. He just wished the boy had been older before he had to face a place like New York City.

Vivian led Becky and Katy down the stairs to the hotel lobby. They shared one of the suites. Robert was in the other one with Craig and Robbie. Both girls had a hand in one of Vivian's, and she knew they were slightly nervous. Neither of them had seen elegance like they were seeing tonight. The sun had set while they were upstairs, and the hotel lobby was lit with candles everywhere. The light reflected off brass-framed mirrors and the polished wood of the floor and counter.

"It's like the princess ball," Katy whispered as she looked around. "When she lost her shoe."

Vivian nodded. "It surely is."

Katy looked down. "I have both my shoes."

"Good girl," Vivian said with a smile.

"I guess I'm not a princess," Katy said, sounding discouraged. "Mama said I couldn't be a princess anyway since I don't have blond hair."

"I never heard anything like that," Vivian said indignant on Katy's behalf. "You can give me one of your shoes if you want. Then you can be a princess tonight."

Katy giggled, but she did sit down on the floor and take off her left shoe. Then she held it out to Vivian.

Vivian took the shoe. She felt like she wasn't dressed formally enough anyway, so it didn't matter. If she had known they were going to dine out like this, she would have taken the time to put on the hat and veil she had in her valise. As it was, she figured people would be so intent on studying the extra shoe in her hand that they wouldn't notice the scars on her face. She'd become totally relaxed about her veil. She wasn't sure it had ever hidden much anyway. Maybe she'd take the netting off of that hat and forget about her scars. Craig had encouraged her to do so, and she trusted his guidance.

There were people walking around the lobby.

Some of the men were in suits and a few of the women were wearing silk dresses. When they reached the end of the staircase, the clerk saw them and walked over. "This way to the restaurant."

The clerk opened the door to the restaurant and even Vivian gasped.

The gleam of the silverware and the ivory china plates all sitting on pure white tablecloths was exquisite. Each table had a candelabra with a dozen lit candles, and the light sparkled all over the large eating room.

Once they stepped into the restaurant, a waiter came and led them to a table. The men, including the judge, and Mrs. Hunt were already seated, and the men, except for Robbie, rose when Vivian and the girls came to the linen-covered table. Katy and Becky started to giggle and then stopped as the waiter seated them formally. Then, they were so impressed that they were speechless, it seemed.

The waiter informed the table that the special of the day was roast beef and corn pudding. Everyone ordered that, with roasted potatoes and rolls to go with it. Their crystal glasses were then filled with apple cider.

They received their food in good time, and for a while, no one spoke. Everyone was eating. Finally, Mrs. Hunt patted her lips with her cloth napkin and said, "The meal couldn't have been better if it came from Delmonico's."

Vivian had eaten at the famed restaurant in New York City and she agreed. She was surprised just how similar dining in this restaurant was to frequenting the establishment on the east coast. She would miss some of these niceties from the city if she were going to live here, but it appeared those luxury touches could be found in Cheyenne, too, so people here weren't missing anything.

She turned to Robert and said, "Thank you very much. This is a special meal."

That led to a chorus of grateful murmurs from the others.

Robert shook his head. "No thanks are necessary. I wanted to gather everyone together, along with our judge here, to announce that I have made a decision—which, according to the judge, is permitted. Instead of agreeing to have my son raised by Mrs. Hunt as we discussed earlier, I have decided to leave him in the care of Craig Martin, at least until Robbie reaches the age of fourteen. At that time, Mr. Martin, Mrs. Hunt and I shall discuss educational opportunities for the boy. To that end, the three of us will discuss the preparatory schooling Robbie will need beginning next year. A tutor might be sufficient. In fact, I am considering staying in Cheyenne, and I have a classical education that is not being used. I could easily spend time teaching Robbie—and Katy and Becky, if they so desire."

Vivian was stunned. She had to catch her breath. She looked across the table and saw that Craig had the same astonished look on his face.

"You're sure?" Craig managed to ask. "Tell me that you mean it. I can keep Robbie?"

"He can't do that," Mrs. Hunt exclaimed. She, too, had clearly been taken by surprise. "Robbie is mine. He's going back with me to New York City. It's been all settled."

The judge cleared his throat. "I'm afraid it is not settled. The guardianship is Robert's. He was going to transfer that to you, Mrs. Hunt, but he has decided to transfer it to Mr. Martin instead. I assure you that it is perfectly legal for him to do so."

"I'll—I'll file a—" Mrs. Hunt stammered.

"We'll accept the court's decision with good grace," Ethan interrupted and put his hand on her arm.

"But—" Mrs. Hunt began again until a look from Ethan stopped her. "Excuse me," Mrs. Hunt said as she rose from the table. "I'm not feeling well."

With that, the older woman left the room.

Vivian looked around the table. Katy was grinning and crying at the same time. Robbie was blinking back his tears, and Craig was hugging him like he would never let go of him again.

"Thank you," Vivian whispered to Robert.

The man looked down briefly. "I couldn't do anything else. Not when I saw Craig charging out after those wolves to protect his son with his bare hands. I might have done some foolish things in my life, but I couldn't take my boy away from a man like that."

Vivian saw Craig look at Robert and just nod his head.

"Besides," Robert continued after clearing his throat, "Cheyenne seems like a good place for an ex-convict to get a new start on a law-abiding life. If you'll have me as a tutor, I'll make a plan to teach Robbie and the girls—if the girls want, that is." Robert looked at where Becky and Katy were sitting, wide-eyed by now. "Would you like to learn math and reading? And some history? You know battles, kings, queens."

"Can you tell me about princesses?" Katy asked eagerly. "Did any of them have red hair?"

Robert grinned. "They must have, since there were lots of redheaded queens, especially in England."

"Queens?" Katy repeated, looking puzzled, and turned to Vivian. "Did they have the pretty dresses, too?"

"Oh, they had the most beautiful dresses," Vivian assured her. "They were mamas to the princesses, so they wore bigger crowns, too."

"Did queens wear both of their shoes?" Katy asked.

Vivian chuckled and nodded her head. "All of the time. I don't think they ever left their shoes off."

"Good," Katy said. "My toes are cold. It's winter."

Vivian leaned over and handed Katy her shoe. The girl eagerly slipped it back on her foot.

"It's hard being a princess," Katy said. "I'll be a queen instead, if that's okay."

"It's very okay," Vivian assured her.

Everyone shared a moment of grins and goodwill.

Then Craig said, "Robert, I want you to know that we'll be grateful for your teaching. We might even have a few neighbor children join us, and we can make a proper school."

"I always thought I'd make a good teacher," Robert said. "If people will have me, with my past."

"We'll start out with the three children we have and let the other families make their decisions," Craig said. "I think most families would like to see their children educated, so we'll see."

Robert nodded. "Thank you."

"And," Craig continued, "I've no objection to Robbie having two fathers. A growing boy can use all the love he can get. All I ask is that you include the girls, too."

"Remember they all have an uncle, too," Ethan said.

Vivian felt there was a rosy glow around the whole table, and then Ethan took a grain sack out from under the table and handed it to Craig. "I'm guessing you'll want to keep this for the boy. Break it in for him in the meantime. According to the owner of the general store, the rifle will shoot straight."

Vivian loved watching Craig. His face grew happier and happier, which made her heart feel warm. She noticed his eyes kept coming back to her until finally they locked on her and neither one of them looked away.

She heard rather than saw the two men take the children away. Finally, it was only her and Craig sitting at the table. The candles were burning down. The waiter had removed the plates. The buzz of fellow diners grew quieter. And then Craig smiled.

"I need to ask." He leaned across the table and took her hands into his. "Will you marry me? Not because the bridal agency sent you. Not because I need you for the children. Will you be the wife of my heart? I love you, Vivian Eastman, and I always will. Please say you'll marry me."

Vivian studied his eyes. He seemed sincere, but how could she know?

Then he stood up and his hands went to his neck. He pulled out the cord that held the thin gold wedding band. "Will you wear my *mam*'s wedding ring?"

She knew what that ring meant to him. Her lips parted and grew into a big smile. "I will be honored to marry you. I love you. I trust you. I want to live my life with you. And I'd love to wear your mother's ring."

"This ring means family to me," Craig said simply. "My *mam* would be happy to see me marry for love. Not that—" he hesitated "—I mean, I am determined to give you the best life I can. I don't want you to regret marrying for love. I'll work hard to give you those extra luxuries that women enjoy."

Vivian winced and stood up, too. "About that— we won't suffer. As it happens, my grandfather left money for me in his old Bible. Four hundred dollars' worth."

"What?" Craig asked in astonishment.

"We'll be able to buy a few extra things," Vivian said as she stepped around the table so she was standing next to him. "New clothes for the children. Maybe a few pounds of smoked salmon here and there. A tin of oysters at Christmas. A new leash for Kitty."

Craig laughed as he took her in his arms. "No one is going to tie that cat up to anything. He deserves to walk free."

With that, Craig kissed her. If she didn't know the candlelight was glittering in the room, she would have thought she was outside under the stars. Everything sparkled. She felt his kiss down to her toes.

"We need to walk free, too," Craig whispered. "Free but together."

"Always together," Vivian agreed, and they walked arm in arm out of the restaurant.

Epilogue

Wyoming Territory—over four months later

Vivian Eastman Martin was back waiting at the train station in Cheyenne. Winter was finally over, and the sunshine was warm and bright. Wagons rolled by on the dirt street behind her; only a few people waited on the railroad platform to greet travelers.

Vivian had been gloriously happy since she'd married Craig on January 9 of this year, the first Sunday after he'd proposed. The dear Reverend Thompson had gladly performed the ceremony following the usual service in the small Crow Creek church. Finn, sporting a new white vest, had stood up as Craig's best man. The day before, Vivian had flustered Mrs. Drummond by asking her to be her matron of honor. The older woman had stood proudly at Vivian's side. The children—Becky, Robbie and Katy—had lined up in their new clothes and clapped as Vivian walked down the aisle.

After the ceremony, Mrs. Drummond had told everyone who would listen that she knew Craig would be marrying his mail-order bride the minute the woman stepped inside his house. It was a perfect match, she'd said. No one corrected her, but a few of them did smile knowingly.

Vivian never tired of remembering her wedding day, but she had other business right now. She looked to her right and saw her husband standing up straight beside her, counting the minutes as well. He knew she was worried and had offered to go alone to meet her brother, Joseph, thus saving her the trip. But she realized she would only be nervous longer if she had to put off seeing him.

She had written her brother a short letter after her marriage, assuring him that she and Becky were well. She had told him where they were and had given him Craig's name. She had not expected to receive a letter in reply. Therefore, she'd been shocked when he'd said he wanted to come and see her.

"I wonder if Joseph will recognize me without my veil," Vivian fretted as she twisted her hands. She hadn't worn a veil since she'd married Craig. She did have on a new pair of gray gloves, though, and a new hat, also in a dove gray. She wasn't sure whether she should mention to Joseph the money their grandfather left in that old Bible. She'd deposited most of it in the bank, but she had kept enough out to make sure everyone had a proper outfit to wear to the wedding and to church.

"He'll recognize you," Craig said patiently. "He's your brother. And he saw you less than a year ago."

"He only saw me from a distance." Vivian wasn't sure if she was ready to forgive her brother for abandoning her and Becky. She was half prepared for him not to come or for some other disaster to happen.

"I hope he doesn't bring Edith at the last minute." Vivian couldn't seem to stop fretting. She wondered if her brother had changed. Was it even possible that he had? Of course, she believed anyone could change with God's help, but she'd never seen any indication that Joseph was interested in knowing God.

"Joseph will have to take us as we are, and we'll take him as he is," Craig said as he captured her hand in his. Even through her glove, she could feel his finger rub the ring on her finger. He did that now and again. Those were times when she knew he was remembering how important family was to him. Maybe today he was also considering the imperfections possible in a family. The disappointments that could happen and the forgiveness that was needed.

Vivian nodded and then turned to look the other way because she heard the sound of the train coming. Finally, the engine stopped, and the passenger car was right next to the platform. The doors opened and people started spilling out.

"Joseph!" Vivian called. She saw her brother the minute he stepped through the door. He turned to look and she waved so he could see her. He lifted his hand in greeting and headed toward her.

As she watched him come, the love she had for him, which she had thought was dead, was once again a living feeling in her heart.

"Joseph," she said again when he was close enough to hear her voice.

"Vivian," he said and embraced her in a tight hug. They stood that way for a few minutes and then he pulled himself back. "I am so sorry. So very sorry. I didn't know what to do when you and Becky came to our house."

The words poured out then. "I was afraid Edith would hurt Becky if I said anything to either of you. She is fiercely jealous. I can't stay long, but I wanted to explain in person. And to meet Becky. Edith thinks I'm on a business trip."

"Oh, Joseph." Vivian couldn't help but feel the pain in her brother's voice.

Joseph cupped her cheeks then and kissed her on the forehead. "I'm so glad to see you are well and happy."

With that, Joseph turned his face slightly and held out his hand. "You must be the Craig my sister wrote about."

"I am," Craig said and shook his hand.

"I wasn't sure you knew about Becky," Vivian said then.

Joseph nodded. "I didn't know for sure until Grandfather told me before he died. I wish Becky could live with us, but I fear what Edith would do to her. I had intended to send you some money to cover her care, but Edith keeps track of every penny spent. I was glad Grandfather had put money in that old Bible of his. Does Becky know about me?"

So, her brother had known about the money, Vivian thought to herself. She realized he could have taken it and she'd never have known.

"I told Becky who you were when I knew you were coming," Vivian confessed. "She's asked about her father so many times, I thought she should know. But she knows how to keep a secret, so you don't have to worry about her telling anyone. She won't even mention it to you if you don't want her to."

"I don't want her to have to keep it a secret from anyone," Joseph said. "Edith is a world away from here. Plus, she already knows. She overheard Grandfather telling me. Edith doesn't want to deal with it, but she knows."

While they had been speaking, the train porters had unloaded an assortment of leather bags. Joseph walked over to claim one of them.

"Let's go home," Craig said as he indicated the direction to the wagon.

Vivian had placed enough quilts in the back of the wagon to cushion a dozen passengers. So, she settled in nicely. She was pleased to have Joseph on the seat with Craig so the two of them could visit. She studied her brother as he talked. She could forgive him, she decided. He was a weak man, but he hadn't taken the money from the Bible. Family members were not always perfect.

Some hours later, Becky was standing out in front of the house, wearing her new pink dress with the white collar, when Craig pulled the horses to a halt.

Joseph climbed down from the wagon, and Craig went around to the back of the wagon to lift Vivian down. Of course, as was his habit, he didn't just swing her down—he had to kiss her as well. Vivian never got tired of his kisses, and she knew she never would. She did hope though that, eventually, her cheeks would stop blushing every time their lips met.

After a second kiss, Vivian stepped back and straightened her hat.

Then she looked over and saw Becky beaming as Joseph talked to her. Finally, the girl opened the door to the house.

"Come meet my other daddy," Becky called out. That started a rush as Robbie, Katy and Finn all filed out.

Vivian smiled and turned to Craig. "We've gotten quite used to other daddies around here."

Robbie still called Craig *daddy*, but Robert was earning a place in the boy's heart, too.

"The more love, the better," Craig said as he put his arms around her and snuggled her close. "I don't think I've told you yet today that I love you."

"I never get tired of hearing it," Vivian said. "I love you, too. With all my heart."

"Well," Craig said. "That's all I ask."

Then he kissed her again. This time, Vivian didn't even care if she blushed. She'd never been happier. Her family weren't perfect, but they were together, and that was enough for her.

* * * * *

WE HOPE YOU ENJOYED
THIS BOOK FROM
⟨H⟩ HARLEQUIN

PRESENTS

Escape to exotic locations where passion knows no bounds.

Welcome to the glamorous lives of royals and billionaires, where passion knows no bounds. Be swept into a world of luxury, wealth and exotic locations.

8 NEW BOOKS AVAILABLE EVERY MONTH!

Get 4 FREE REWARDS!

We'll send you 2 FREE Books plus 2 FREE Mystery Gifts.

FREE
Value Over
$20

Both the **Love Inspired®** and **Love Inspired®** Suspense series feature compelling novels filled with inspirational romance, faith, forgiveness and hope.

YES! Please send me 2 FREE novels from the Love Inspired or Love Inspired Suspense series and my 2 FREE gifts (gifts are worth about $10 retail). After receiving them, if I don't wish to receive any more books, I can return the shipping statement marked "cancel." If I don't cancel, I will receive 6 brand-new Love Inspired Larger-Print books or Love Inspired Suspense Larger-Print books every month and be billed just $6.49 each in the U.S. or $6.74 each in Canada. That is a savings of at least 16% off the cover price. It's quite a bargain! Shipping and handling is just 50¢ per book in the U.S. and $1.25 per book in Canada.* I understand that accepting the 2 free books and gifts places me under no obligation to buy anything. I can always return a shipment and cancel at any time by calling the number below. The free books and gifts are mine to keep no matter what I decide.

Choose one: ☐ **Love Inspired**
Larger-Print
(122/322 IDN GRHK)

☐ **Love Inspired Suspense**
Larger-Print
(107/307 IDN GRHK)

Name (please print)

Address _____ Apt. #

City _____ State/Province _____ Zip/Postal Code

Email: Please check this box ☐ if you would like to receive newsletters and promotional emails from Harlequin Enterprises ULC and its affiliates. You can unsubscribe anytime.

Mail to the Harlequin Reader Service:
IN U.S.A.: P.O. Box 1341, Buffalo, NY 14240-8531
IN CANADA: P.O. Box 603, Fort Erie, Ontario L2A 5X3

Want to try 2 free books from another series? Call 1-800-873-8635 or visit www.ReaderService.com.

Get 4 FREE REWARDS!

We'll send you 2 FREE Books plus 2 FREE Mystery Gifts.

FREE Value Over **$20**

Both the **Harlequin® Historical** and **Harlequin® Romance** series feature compelling novels filled with emotion and simmering romance.

YES! Please send me 2 FREE novels from the Harlequin Historical or Harlequin Romance series and my 2 FREE gifts (gifts are worth about $10 retail). After receiving them, if I don't wish to receive any more books, I can return the shipping statement marked "cancel." If I don't cancel, I will receive 6 brand-new Harlequin Historical books every month and be billed just $6.19 each in the U.S. or $6.74 each in Canada, a savings of at least 11% off the cover price, or 4 brand-new Harlequin Romance Larger-Print books every month and be billed just $6.09 each in the U.S. or $6.24 each in Canada, a savings of at least 13% off the cover price. It's quite a bargain! Shipping and handling is just 50¢ per book in the U.S. and $1.25 per book in Canada.* I understand that accepting the 2 free books and gifts places me under no obligation to buy anything. I can always return a shipment and cancel at any time by calling the number below. The free books and gifts are mine to keep no matter what I decide.

Choose one: ☐ **Harlequin Historical**
(246/349 HDN GRH7)

☐ **Harlequin Romance Larger-Print**
(119/319 HDN GRH7)

Name (please print)

Address   Apt. #

City   State/Province   Zip/Postal Code

Email: Please check this box ☐ if you would like to receive newsletters and promotional emails from Harlequin Enterprises ULC and its affiliates. You can unsubscribe anytime.

Mail to the Harlequin Reader Service:
IN U.S.A.: P.O. Box 1341, Buffalo, NY 14240-8531
IN CANADA: P.O. Box 603, Fort Erie, Ontario L2A 5X3

Want to try 2 free books from another series! Call 1-800-873-8635 or visit www.ReaderService.com.

*Terms and prices subject to change without notice. Prices do not include sales taxes, which will be charged (if applicable) based on your state or country of residence. Canadian residents will be charged applicable taxes. Offer not valid in Quebec. This offer is limited to one order per household. Books received may not be as shown. Not valid for current subscribers to the Harlequin Historical or Harlequin Romance series. All orders subject to approval. Credit or debit balances in a customer's account(s) may be offset by any other outstanding balance owed by or to the customer. Please allow 4 to 6 weeks for delivery. Offer available while quantities last.

Your Privacy—Your information is being collected by Harlequin Enterprises ULC, operating as Harlequin Reader Service. For a complete summary of the information we collect, how we use this information and to whom it is disclosed, please visit our privacy notice located at corporate.harlequin.com/privacy-notice. From time to time we may also exchange your personal information with reputable third parties. If you wish to opt out of this sharing of your personal information, please visit readerservice.com/consumerschoice or call 1-800-873-8635. **Notice to California Residents**—Under California law, you have specific rights to control and access your data. For more information on these rights and how to exercise them, visit corporate.harlequin.com/california-privacy.

HHHRLP22R3

HARLEQUIN
PLUS

Try the best multimedia subscription service for romance readers like you!

Read, Watch and Play.

Experience the easiest way to get the romance content you crave.

Start your **FREE TRIAL** at
<u>www.harlequinplus.com/freetrial</u>.